CHASING SHADOWS AT DUSK

AN AGENTS OF HIS NOVEL

Sheila Kell

Cunningham Publishing

USA

Titles by Sheila Kell

HIS Series

His Desire
His Choice
His Return
His Chance
His Destiny
His Family
His Heart
His Fantasy
A Hamilton Christmas

Agents of HIS Series

Evening Shadows
Midnight Escape
Afternoon Delight
Bayou Sunset
Chasing Shadows at Dusk

Coastal Investigation Series

Deadly Betrayal
Read Between the Lines
Fractured Trust

CHAPTER ONE

"DO YOU WANT to know?" Ash "Casper" McNabb asked his teammate Romeo after sliding onto a barstool beside him.

For the last five weeks, Casper had fervently searched for a ghost of his own. Romeo's significant other, Daisy Mae, mysteriously vanished without a trace. She disappeared without a word to anyone, including her closest friends and family, leaving them all in the dark about her whereabouts.

While Romeo recuperated from his injuries on a treasure hunt, Casper took a personal leave of absence from his position at Hamilton Investigation and Security to track down the elusive Daisy Mae. Locating her had required all of his investigative skills and perseverance.

The air in the bar crackled with tension as Romeo turned to his friend, concern etched on his face. "I no want to know. I *need* to know."

"What are you gonna do if she isn't ready?" Casper's voice was laced with doubt, reflecting the uncertainty that loomed over Daisy Mae's readiness for a new relationship, given her history of running away.

Romeo's confidence wavered momentarily before he responded, "She be ready. Besides, I thought ya would have my six on dis."

Casper met the Cajun's gaze with a reassuring smile and a nod of understanding. He caught the bartender's eye and silently signaled for a beer, affirming his unwavering support. "You know I do," he said quietly, his words carrying the weight of their unspoken bond between HIS teammates.

After Casper revealed Daisy Mae's whereabouts, he had to physically restrain Romeo to prevent him from bolting from his barstool and pursuing the woman. "Dude, it's midnight. You can't do anything now. Let's plan and figure out how you'll do things right this time."

During the next hour, under the dim glow of the bar lights, the two friends engaged in a spirited discussion as they delved into Romeo's intricate strategy to win back the heart of Daisy Mae. Together, they painted a vivid picture of Daisy Mae relocating to Maryland with Romeo, envisioning a life intertwined with possibility and love. However, despite the allure of this future, Casper, with a steadfast commitment to their team, expressed his reluctance about Romeo leaving and following Daisy Mae wherever she would establish her charter business.

"How are you, really?" Casper asked.

Romeo, having recently been shot twice, nodded. "I be fine."

Casper hesitated to trust the Cajun fully but ultimately let it slide. Keeping an HIS agent subdued for an extended period was a constant challenge. The agency's men and women were relentless in their pursuit of mission success, a goal that Casper had also made his own. He refused to label it a triumph until Daisy Mae relocated to Maryland.

"I no can thank ya enough for dis," Romeo said. "She be my everything."

Casper nodded thoughtfully as he remembered when Romeo had been hospitalized, Daisy Mae fled, and Casper had been there for her. She had been distraught, feeling unwanted by Romeo, who had not shown his love for their commitment to a future together.

With an unexpected move, she managed to slip away from him, becoming the first person ever to evade his grasp. As a former Green Beret and Delta and now serving as an HIS agent, he took her escape as a direct challenge to his exceptional skills. Throughout his career, he had never failed to track a target or protect someone under his care. In this instance, he was responsible for her while his teammate was incapacitated, making her successful evasion a personal affront.

"Why ya do dis?" Romeo asked after requesting another brew from the bartender.

For the exact reasons he'd been thinking. Because he'd failed at his mission, and he'd had to make it right.

Casper took a leisurely sip of his beer, savoring the taste as he drained the last drops from his glass. Placing the empty mug on the polished bar, he paused before responding, "Because you couldn't."

He rose from his seat, gave Romeo a reassuring pat on the shoulder, and exited the dimly lit bar. Stepping into the quiet parking lot, he sighed heavily, contemplating the task ahead. His commitment to supporting Romeo in winning back Daisy Mae was unwavering. Casper was genuinely fond of her, recognizing her ability to bring out the best in his friend. Despite referring to Romeo as a friend, he couldn't ignore the professional nature of their relationship as fellow agents. However, the bond they formed during their last mission to protect Daisy Mae had undeniably deepened their connection.

As he settled into the driver's seat of his rugged Jeep, he couldn't help but feel a sense of reluctance about the impending journey from the remote wilderness of Louisiana to the bustling city of Baltimore. With the hour growing late, he resigned himself to the prospect of seeking accommodation at the nearby bed-and-breakfast, hoping for a vacancy. Failing that, he knew he would have no choice but to venture to the next town in pursuit of a suitable hotel for the night.

As the engine hummed to life, he shifted the Jeep into gear and exited the parking lot onto the familiar backroad he had traversed countless times during their last operation. Glancing at the pier, he nodded, acknowledging the extensive repair work to mend the damage. The memory of the day when the explosion had rocked the area, causing significant destruction to the small pier, flashed through his mind.

He consciously tried to avoid dwelling on the past, instead focusing on his upcoming return to HIS and a genuine operation. He needed to visit the shooting range and discharge a few rounds to reacquaint himself with his skills. Four weeks of relentless tracking had mentally drained him. Daisy Mae had proven to be quite cunning.

As he drove through the night, he cranked up the radio to stave off drowsiness, yearning for the freedom of wind rushing through the open top of his Jeep. It felt like an eternity since he had truly savored his journeys. Maybe it was time to plan a proper getaway and escape to the beach. He struggled to recall the last time he had surfed the waves with his trusty board.

His idyllic upbringing by the water had been everything to him. However, Biloxi, Mississippi, didn't offer the kind of waves suitable for surfing. He only acquired that skill after leaving home at eighteen to enlist in the Army. The decision went against his mother's wishes, as it reminded her of his father, who had served in the Air Force and had deeply hurt her.

Hell, it had broken her. Yet, while he loved her as his mother, Casper couldn't like the woman she'd become after the divorce when he'd been a budding teenager.

He shook his head and cleared his mind of the negative thoughts. His goal was to find a quiet room to meditate, which would allow him to regain focus on the present moment.

Arriving at the quaint bed-and-breakfast, he couldn't help but feel a twinge of anxiety about rapping on the door well past midnight. Would the owners welcome him with open arms or shoo him away for disturbing their peace? Regardless, he desperately needed rest before embarking on the arduous journey home.

When Casper's phone vibrated, he knew it couldn't be good. The late-night call signaled urgency, and he hesitated momentarily before reluctantly retrieving his phone from his pocket. As he glanced at the screen, his heart skipped a beat.

"Mom? Everything okay?"

"Ash," his mother said, her voice wavering, "I need you. Your brother has done it this time. He's in jail. It's— It's not good. They're talking real jail time."

Mixed emotions filled Casper as he contemplated the latest turn of events. On the one hand, he didn't want his brother behind bars. However, Aaron had a habit of finding himself in trouble.

"What happened?"

"They're saying DUI, but I know my son; he wasn't drunk."

Inwardly, Casper sighed. His mother always defended his baby brother, no matter what he'd done, sometimes refusing to believe the truth.

"It's just like last time. The policeman set him up. They even said he was driving without a valid license. How else was he supposed to get around? If they hadn't illegally taken it the first time—"

Casper drowned out the sound of his mother's angry tirade as she made excuses for Aaron. The memory of his brother's previous DUI and the resulting probation and loss of his license flooded Casper's mind. He pinched the bridge of his nose and closed his eyes, hoping for peace and rest, but it seemed out of reach.

"I'll be there in a few hours." He'd have to stop and grab a caffeinated drink to help keep him awake. Although, thinking of all the times he'd bailed James out of trouble should do the trick.

"Hurry. They are arraigning him in the morning and are talking no bail. I need your help to straighten this mess out."

As he watched the prospect of a peaceful rest and a return to normalcy slip away, he shifted the Jeep into reverse and drove out of the bed-and-breakfast parking lot. He couldn't fathom why he always ended up having to fix things.

"Oh, Ash," his mother said, drawing his attention to where the call had automatically connected to the Jeep's Bluetooth speaker. "You must call your father."

"Sure, Mom." The call ended. He dreaded seeing his father and mother in the same space. Their inability to coexist had deeply impacted his teenage years. As he contemplated the situation, he couldn't help but wonder about its potential effects on him now.

HIS eagerly anticipated his return, but deep down, he had a sinking feeling that his brother's DUI might create a rift within the family that he would have to navigate and address.

He was aware of the time and understood the tasks at hand. With that knowledge, he pressed the button on his steering wheel to connect the call. "Call Jesse Hamilton."

A groggy Jesse answered the call on the third ring. "What's up, Casper?"

"I hate to ask, but I need more time. Something has come up at home."

Casper was struck by the profound silence that followed his question. It made him wonder whether Jesse would deny his request for time off. After all, Casper had just taken five weeks off to pursue Daisy Mae. It occurred to him that his boss might be within his rights to refuse his request. If that were to happen, Casper wondered what his next action would be. Would he consider quitting for his family?

"Take as long as you need. Can we help in any way?"

"Yeah, you can knock some sense into my brother," he said jokingly.

"If only it were that easy. I've navigated the twins growing up, so call me if you need anything."

"Thanks." He ended the call.

A minute later, he pulled to the side of the roadway and stopped. "That's it. The top comes off."

Casper labored to detach the soft top from the Jeep, carefully folding and stowing it. As the wind tousled his hair, he embarked on a journey fraught with the risk of losing his family. This time, he was stubborn and unyielding. His brother's wayward ways demanded correction, and his mother's overprotective nature required an end. He was prepared to sever ties with them if they did not mend their paths.

Lost in contemplation about the familiar comforts of home and the uncertainties ahead, Casper drove away, oblivious to the solitary figure standing in the middle of the road, urgently signaling for his attention. When he finally noticed, he slammed on the brakes, the force of the sudden stop pushing the seat belt to cut into his shoulder. The tires emitted a loud, high-pitched squeal.

"Oh shit!"

CHAPTER TWO

ANNETTE "NETTIE" BROUSSARD stood frozen, her feet firmly planted in the center of the road as a speeding vehicle hurtled toward her. A surge of fear sent a shockwave through her body, momentarily jolting her from the haze of intoxication.

When the Jeep skidded to a stop mere inches from where she stood, terror overwhelmed her so intensely that she feared she might lose consciousness. Despite this, she remained wholly paralyzed, small tremors rippling through her.

A towering figure—everyone seemed towering from her five feet and one inch vantage point—sprang out of the vehicle and charged toward her. "What in the hell is the matter with you?" he bellowed.

Standing there, she had meant to wave down a car to help her and her friends with a tire change. Despite her buzzed brain, it seemed like the right thing to do. Buzzed brain? Hell, she'd been almost three sheets to the wind, which was probably why she stood in the street and not on the shoulder like a sane person.

Softer, the giant asked, "Are you all right? Are you hurt?"

As Nettie gazed upward into his mesmerizing sea-blue eyes, she could not respond. The intensity of his concern held her captive, or at least what she interpreted as concern, amidst the shifting shadows cast by his headlights.

"I—"

"Aw fuck. You smell like a brewery," he said, cutting her off. "I hope you aren't driving."

As a wave of anger surged within her at the very thought of the reckless act of driving under the influence, she swiftly gestured toward the car parked on the shoulder of the road. "Lily drove."

In the stillness of her thoughts, she became acutely aware of the slurred quality of her speech, a stark contrast to the clarity she sought while trying to regain her composure. It was as if the weight of her emotions had seeped into her words, transforming them into a muddled distortion that betrayed her inner turmoil, even as her mind began to sober from the haze of distress.

After narrowing his eyes at her, he turned to the car. "Who is Lily?"

"Hey, handsome," Nettie's friend Penelope slurred, her words slightly jumbled from the effects of too much tequila. With an unsteady gait, she wobbled over, her long, sequined blouse shimmering under the Jeep lights. Surprised, the stranger raised an eyebrow as she sidled up to him, a mischievous grin spreading across her flushed cheeks.

"Um, I'm Lily," her friend, who somehow managed to retain a sober demeanor amidst the chaos, said. She raised her hand as if in a classroom, seeking the teacher's attention. "I'm sorry about both of them," she added with genuine concern as she glanced toward the two individuals, their expressions clouded by awe at the stranger. It was a moment filled with unspoken tension, as if the air was thick with an unacknowledged weight, and Lily's honesty cut through it like a faint ray of hope.

"Please tell me you haven't been drinking," he said.

Lily shook her head. "Nope. I'm the designated driver."

He turned his gaze back to the two women before him. Nettie stood directly in front of him, completely still, as if time had momentarily paused around her. Meanwhile, Penelope gazed at him with wide, flirtatious eyes. Her playful demeanor contrasted with her companion's rigidity.

As if snapped out of a trance, Nettie grabbed Penelope's arm. "Leave him alone. He's going to change our tire for us."

The stranger raised an eyebrow at Nettie and cocked his head to the side. "I am, am I?"

Her scrambled mind couldn't handle word games, so she answered her question. "Of course you are. This is the South, and Southern men always help distressed women."

That generated a grin from him. "Is that so?"

"Of course you are." Nettie's eyes sparkled with leftover anger as she pointed her finger at him. She teetered on the edge of falling into his chest as if the movement had almost toppled her over. "You're a good Southern man, aren't you?"

He crossed his arms over his chest. "I hate to break it to you, sweetheart, but I live in Maryland."

Nettie felt irritated whenever a man addressed her as "Sweetheart." To her, it was more than a term of endearment; it felt condescending, reducing her identity to a mere label. She remembered moments from her past when she had worked hard to establish herself in a male-dominated world, and such terms undermined her efforts, reminding her of unwanted attention and assumptions about her role. Each utterance of that word seemed to twist the knife of gender stereotypes deeper into her experience, leaving her longing for respect and recognition as an individual rather than a romanticized notion. She would brush off her annoyance in those moments, but the feeling lingered, a reminder of the societal expectations she constantly battled against.

Amidst the darkness, he gestured urgently. "Let's move off the roadway, and I'll take care of your flat tire." With determined strides, he returned to his Jeep. Engaging the reverse gear, he skillfully maneuvered behind Lily's car, casting a beam of light from his headlights to dispel the enveloping darkness.

"Come on, Nettie," Penelope said. "Let's go watch Mr. Hunk change the tire. I bet his muscles ripple under that shirt." She tottered off toward his vehicle. "You who, handsome, are you single?"

Nettie observed the stranger tense up. Then it hit her. He was a total stranger, and they'd allowed him to stop and help them. She wouldn't worry about a Southern boy, but he said he was from the North. Didn't they have rapists and murderers there? Granted, they had them in the South also, but….

She stiffened her shoulders and walked to the car. "What's your name?" she demanded in her brisk work tone.

From the open trunk, he looked around at her and hesitated. "My friends call me Casper."

"What kind of name is Casper? Are you a ghost? You don't look like a ghost, does he, ladies?" She was on a roll and continued. "No, what's your name?"

He leaned in toward her and said, "What's yours, sweetheart?"

Once again, she was confronted by that same old "sweetheart" label. It was a term often tossed around with casual affection, but this gentleman was about to discover just how deceptive that label truly was. Beneath her charming exterior lay a complexity he could hardly imagine, and it wouldn't be long before he realized just how little of a sweet heart she truly possessed.

As her gaze swept over him, she couldn't help but notice the undeniable age gap that separated them. He appeared to be at least a decade older than her, his face marked by subtle lines of experience and wisdom. His demeanor exuded the confidence that often came with age, and the stories in his eyes hinted at a life lived fully, contrasting with her youthful exuberance.

As Penelope had pegged, he was undeniably handsome. His tousled blond hair looked like a result of the Jeep's absent top. Despite his appearance, which might have led one to underestimate him, he embodied the all-too-common stereotype of a northerner. This type of individual often flung around labels with reckless abandon, attaching them to people and circumstances without fully understanding their implications or the complexities involved.

However, this was not the appropriate moment for a heated discussion or disagreement. They were in a bind and required his assistance to change the flat tire. Once that task was complete, he would be free to depart. Nettie had reached her limit with his indifferent attitude and dismissive demeanor. Frustrated yet determined to move forward, she took a deep breath and finally introduced herself. "I'm Nettie."

"Nettie sounds like an odd name to me. So, just call me Casper." Turning away from her, he lifted the spare tire Lily had loosened but couldn't lift. Then, he loosened the nuts on the flat tire, ignoring them.

Or, so she thought.

"What are you ladies doing out here this time of morning? This is not a much-used route."

As the fog of intoxication gradually lifted, Nettie finally grasped the latter half of his statement. A wave of deep curiosity washed over her, mingled with a subtle but unmistakable tinge of fear, intertwining her emotions. She felt an unshakable urge to understand the implications of his words, even as the darker edges of anxiety crept into her thoughts, urging her to tread carefully in this newfound clarity. "Then, how did you know it was here?"

He didn't look up from his task but shrugged. "GPS took me this way."

She doubted it but left it since Lily piped up with, "We were at a party, celebrating—"

Nettie nudged Lily in the ribs a bit more forcefully than intended. "He doesn't need to be privy to our activities," she said with an edge in her voice. For a reason she couldn't understand, Nettie was adamant about keeping the fact that it was her twenty-fifth birthday a secret from this unfamiliar—yet striking—individual.

With her lack of filter or awareness of Nettie's thoughts, Penelope said, "It's Nettie's twenty-fifth birthday!"

"Penelope!" Nettie reprimanded. "He doesn't need to know that."

Casper looked back at her, giving her an up-and-down perusal that left her feeling vulnerable yet heated. "That's almost young enough to be my daughter."

"Oh," Nettie said, trying not to feel offended by the comment, "you have a daughter?"

He shook his head. "No, but if I did, she could be about eighteen now."

"Well, I'll have you know, there's a big difference between eighteen and twenty-five."

Lily—the peacekeeper—stepped forward. "Children, let's play nice."

Casper stood and put the flat tire in the car's rear, locked it down, and closed the trunk. "Done. Now, you'll want to go slow on this tire. I'll follow you until— How far are you going?"

"Don't tell him," Nettie said, her back still bowed for no reason whatsoever.

"Nettie, it's okay," Lily said. "We're headed back to Biloxi."

Casper smiled. "How ironic, so am I."

"That's what a mass murderer would say," Nettie spat out without thinking. She needed to work on her brain-mouth filter when she drank.

"They would." He turned back to his Jeep, turned it on, and honked at them. "Let's get going, ladies. I don't have all night."

The three piled into Lily's car with Nettie in the passenger seat. Penelope passed out almost the moment she sat in the back. "Are you sure you should let him follow us?" Nettie asked.

"Chill, Nettie. He seems fine. He did change the tire after all."

As she reflected on the encounter, she couldn't shake the feeling that there was something off about the man. Perhaps it was the lingering effects of the tequila coursing through her system or the realization that she was unexpectedly drawn to an older gentleman. Either way, she tried to brush it off. After tonight, she likely wouldn't see him again. Biloxi was large enough that they wouldn't happen to run into each other at the market.

"You liked him," Lily said teasingly.

"What? No, I didn't." Although she had no affection for him, she couldn't help but admire his striking appearance, especially for someone his age. His well-defined features and confident demeanor exuded a certain charm that was hard to overlook, making her appreciate the allure he possessed despite her personal feelings toward him.

"Oh yes, you did, and it scared you. Otherwise, you wouldn't have pulled your prosecutor hat on him."

Recalling her role as a prosecutor, she realized that she had an upcoming court session in the morning. She was scheduled to handle another round of arraignments for individuals charged with driving under the influence. She had vigorously fought to keep these cases in jail, believing that releasing them would only lead to repeated offenses.

The tragic loss of her parents, caused by a driver under the influence, fueled her determination to prevent other families from enduring the same heart-wrenching nightmare.

As she slowly drifted off into a peaceful slumber, her mind was preoccupied with the impending day at court. She couldn't help but wonder how many offenders she would encounter in the morning. She stood in the courtroom with Casper on the docket in her vivid dreams. This scenario presented her with her first moral dilemma as an assistant district attorney.

She awakened before determining the amount of bail to ask for or whether to release him. "You're home, Nettie," Lily said.

Nettie stretched and noticed the headlights behind them. Great, now the northerner knew where she lived.

CHAPTER THREE

CASPER DESPISED THE prison system with a deep-seated passion. After enduring a harrowing experience as a captive for an agonizingly brief period, he resented the claustrophobic confinement that stripped away his sense of freedom and autonomy. His captivity, imposed by a ruthless group of terrorists, was mercifully short-lived; it was only through the relentless efforts of another brave Delta team that he and his comrades were ultimately rescued. The experience left indelible scars on his psyche, shaping his views on imprisonment and heroism forever.

After safely escorting the ladies to their homes, he finally went to his mother's residence in the early morning when the world was dark. With the sun yet to rise, it was far too late for him to attempt any rest. Instead, he stepped into the shower, letting the warm water wash away the night's fatigue. Once refreshed, he mentally prepared himself for the painstaking task ahead: navigating the complexities of the legal system to secure his brother's release from jail, a process that promised to be both challenging and emotionally draining.

Years had passed since he moved away from town, and as a result, he was out of touch with the key players in the area. Recognizing his need for assistance, he contacted JD Walker at Coastal Investigation. He'd met JD during a previous job and hoped that JD's familiarity with the local legal scene could help him navigate this situation. He aimed to find a capable attorney for Aaron since his bond hearing was this morning. After a brief conversation, JD mentioned Bryce Jacobs as a potential candidate to take on Aaron's case. However, JD's tone suggested he wasn't enthusiastic about Bryce, leaving the impression that there might be underlying concerns about the attorney's friendship with JD.

Despite any reservations, Casper decided they would seize the opportunity if JD recommended him. With that thought in mind, Casper contacted Bryce, waking him and eager to determine if he was available to take on the case. Time was of the essence, as the man was expected to arrive in just a few minutes. Once he was there, they would discuss the particulars with Aaron, who was waiting for them to arrive. This meeting could change everything for his brother's current situation.

Casper's mother had been unusually persistent in her pleading that morning as the sun poured through the kitchen window, filling the room with a warm glow. Her voice, filled with desperation and hope, grated on his nerves, and it felt like a constant echo in his mind. Frustrated, he left the house earlier than necessary, the late morning air feeling cool against his flushed skin.

In her eyes, Aaron was still the innocent boy she remembered, who could do no wrong. But Casper knew the truth all too well—his brother was a bad seed, continuously embroiled in trouble that seemed to follow him like a shadow. Each time he landed in a difficult situation, she reacted the same way: crafting elaborate excuses for him, puffing out her chest defensively as if taking on the world for his sake. She rarely acknowledged the reality. Instead, she pointed an accusatory finger at the system, blaming it for his brother's failures and struggles, refusing to see the man he had become or the choices that led him to this point.

As the door swung open, a tall man in a tailored suit purposefully strode in, clearing a path through the crowd. His shoes clicked against the polished floor, drawing attention as he approached. Sensing the man's authoritative presence, Casper instinctively rose from his seat. "Mr. Jacobs?" he inquired with a mixture of curiosity and respect.

With a warm and confident smile, Bryce Jacobs extended his hand, the gesture inviting and friendly. "Bryce, please. You must be Ash," he said, making eye contact that conveyed familiarity and friendliness, amplifying the connection they were about to forge in this meeting. "Let's go see our boy. Shall we?"

Casper nodded, the attorney's measured voice pulling him into the moment's gravity. As they walked side by side through the sterile, fluorescent-lit corridors of the building, the faint echo of their footsteps reminded him of the seriousness of the situation. Casper felt his heart race slightly as the attorney paused in front of a small, nondescript room.

Upon entering, a wave of discomfort washed over Casper; the cramped space, with its cold institutional furniture and stark white walls, made his skin crawl. The air was heavy with an unsettling stillness, broken only by the distant sounds of muffled voices.

Thankfully, just moments later, a corrections officer entered the room, guiding Aaron through the heavy steel door. Aaron's expression brightened as he stepped inside, lighting up his face with an unmistakable charm. He flashed a sly smile at his brother, one that seemed to say, "I'm an innocent kid in every possible way," exuding an air of mischief mixed with naive confidence. It was as if, despite the bleak surroundings, he could still convey a sense of playfulness and hope, assuring his brother that everything would turn out all right.

Only Casper wasn't so confident.

The brothers nodded at each other in greeting.

"Mr. McNabb, I'm Bryce Jacobs, your attorney," Bryce said, extending his hand in a firm but friendly gesture.

Aaron glanced between Casper, who had been his rock during tumultuous times, and Bryce, who exuded a calm confidence. After a moment of uncertainty, he accepted the attorney's handshake but didn't speak.

"Let's sit," Bryce directed, motioning toward the chairs in the small, sparsely furnished meeting room, where the air felt heavy with tension and unexpressed thoughts.

"I understand that you are fairly familiar with the system as a result of this being your second driving under the influence charge," Bryce stated, his tone steady and professional.

Aaron nodded, his expression revealing defiance. "Yeah," he replied tersely, avoiding eye contact.

A surge of frustration hit Casper at his brother's dismissive attitude. He wanted to kick Aaron for being so curt with Bryce, who was genuinely trying to assist him in navigating the legal ramifications of his situation. Instead of appreciating the help offered, Aaron responded with an attitude that could only complicate matters further.

"Well," Bryce continued, adjusting his glasses as he glanced at the documents across the table, "today marks an important point in your case—your arraignment hearing. We'll advocate for your release on your recognizance, which means you won't have to pay to be released while awaiting your trial. It's a significant step, showing trust in your commitment to appear in court."

Bryce shuffled some papers, his brow slightly furrowed in concentration. "However, if they decide to request bail during the proceedings, I need to know—are you in a position to pay that amount, or should I start looking for a bail bondsman to assist in your release?" His tone was steady, conveying professionalism and a hint of concern for his client's situation.

Amid a precarious situation, Aaron instinctively resorted to his usual course of action—he turned his gaze toward Casper, hoping for a reprieve. Their unspoken bond was palpable, and Aaron silently pleaded for Casper to rescue him again.

Casper was acutely aware that his mother was struggling financially, her pockets nearly empty, burdened by the pressures of life. His mind wandered to Aaron, who had likely squandered the meager resources they had left in a haze of reckless behavior. With a slow, deliberate nod, Casper resolved to act.

He was determined to do whatever it took to ease his mother's worries, even if that meant putting aside his doubts about Aaron's readiness to re-enter the world. Helping Aaron secure his release from jail felt right, yet Casper couldn't shake the nagging thought that perhaps a few more days behind bars would benefit his brother. It might give Aaron the time he needed to confront his addiction and fully realize the damaging grip it had on his life. Casper's emotions were in turmoil—love for his brother and a profound concern for his well-being. He was caught between family loyalty and the harsh reality of Aaron's issues, aware that his decision could have lasting repercussions for all of them.

"We do," Casper affirmed with steady yet filled with a quiet determination. He had resolved to put up any amount of money—so long as it was within reason—to fix this pressing issue that weighed heavily on the family. Like many challenges before, this one brought a flicker of worry to his heart, yet he felt compelled to act. With unwavering loyalty, he would stand by his brother one last time.

Finally, Casper reached a breaking point as the family's perpetual rescuer. No longer could he bear the weight of their expectations and dependency. With a heavy heart but newfound resolve, he would gather them for a meaningful conversation and would clarify that he would no longer be their financial support—no longer their cash cow, tirelessly providing with no gratitude in return. He was stepping away from the burden of their problems, asserting his right to prioritize his own life and well-being. They would have to learn to navigate their challenges and find solutions without relying on him as their knight in shining armor.

"Great," Bryce said, a hint of satisfaction in his voice as he meticulously stacked the scattered papers. He carefully slid them into his briefcase, the sound of the zipper punctuating his decision. "You might want to take this into account. Miss Broussard, the Assistant District Attorney handling the case, is known for her unwavering determination and assertiveness. She is particularly relentless when it comes to preventing drunk drivers from being allowed back onto the streets. Her commitment to public safety often leads her to challenge leniency in sentencing, ensuring that those who endanger others face appropriate consequences."

Casper stood at the edge of uncertainty. On the one hand, he felt a spark of hope that the government had appointed a formidable prosecutor to his brother's case; perhaps this was the turning point they desperately needed. After all, the weight of addiction had been a relentless burden on his family for years.

On the other hand, worry gnawed at him like an uninvited guest. Would this attorney have the power to effect real change? Would she have the foresight to recognize his brother's dire need for rehabilitation? The prospect of a plea deal that included access to treatment rather than punishment stirred a fragile optimism in his heart. Maybe, just maybe, things could be different this time, and his brother might finally get the help he desperately needed.

"We'll meet you in the courtroom," Bryce said. As he stood tall, Casper mirrored him, both men poised and ready to leave the office behind.

"Hey, Ash," Aaron interjected, his tone more serious, "would you stay a minute?" Aaron's eyes held a request, drawing Ash's attention back to him.

Casper shot a knowing look at the attorney, acknowledging the unspoken camaraderie. "I'll meet you in court," he assured Bryce, who nodded briefly.

With that, Bryce turned and exited the room, his footsteps echoing in the corridor.

Aaron stood there, his posture tense as he gazed up at his older brother, frustration evident on his face. "You know this is bullshit, don't you?" he challenged, cutting through the silence between them.

Casper raised a brow, an expression of astonishing disbelief playing on his features. Somehow, he had anticipated that his younger brother would resort to confrontation, unwilling to overlook the situation. It was typical of Aaron, deflecting blame and refusing to acknowledge his part in the unfolding drama. As the tension grew, the bond between the brothers felt strained and unbreakable, with each stuck in their stubbornness.

"Yeah," Aaron continued. "The cop who pulled me over claimed I was above the legal limit for alcohol in my system, but that's just not true. I know I was under the limit."

Despite his insistence on his innocence, his admission of drinking and driving hung heavily in the air.

Casper's heart sank at the thought. He despised anyone engaged in reckless behavior. He had never personally experienced the devastation of losing someone to a drunk driver. Still, he was painfully aware of the countless lives forever altered by the careless choices of others. The weight of these tragedies loomed large in his mind as he grappled with the consequences of Aaron's actions and the potential harm they could inflict.

"Aaron—" Casper began, his voice tinged with frustration as he tried to maintain control of the situation.

"Don't Aaron me," his brother shot back defiantly, his eyes wide with anger. "I'm innocent."

A familiar surge of irritation hit, but Casper forced himself to close his eyes, taking measured breaths as he counted to ten, trying desperately to hold onto his calm. Each number was a reminder to breathe, to leave his anger behind. When he finally opened his eyes, he was met not with resolution but uncertainty.

"Let's just see how this goes," he said, his tone more resigned than anything else. With those words hanging in the air, Casper turned sharply on his heel, his footsteps echoing as he walked out the door, leaving Aaron in a swirl of unresolved tension.

As Casper settled into the courtroom atmosphere, a wave of relaxation washed over him, prompting a deep, heartfelt sigh of relief. Bryce Jacobs exuded confidence and capability, embodying all the qualities JD had promised would aid in this critical moment. Casper couldn't help but admire his composure and his air of professionalism. Now, all that remained was the hope that this skilled attorney would perform brilliantly at the arraignment hearing, ultimately securing his brother's release on his own recognizance and ensuring he would not have to spend another moment in confinement.

As he glanced around the bustling gallery, his eyes landed on a familiar face—Nettie, animatedly chatting with a visitor. The air was filled with the soft hum of conversations, but she stood out amidst the crowd. Determined, he weaved his way toward her under the bright lighting.

When she finally turned toward him, her expression shifted from friendliness to surprise. He couldn't help but offer a warm smile, hoping to ease the unexpected tension. "Hello, Nettie," he greeted warmly.

However, to his dismay, she stiffened at the sound of his voice. The ease of their previous encounter had seemingly transformed into a palpable discomfort.

As she parted her lips to reply, her body trembled with emotion. But before she could utter a word, a deafening barrage of gunshots sounded, shattering the tense silence around them and echoing around the courtroom.

Without hesitation, Casper sprang into action, instinctively resorting to his primary role—protection. With a surge of adrenaline coursing through him, he dove toward Nettie, wrapping his arms around her just as the chaos unfolded around them. They landed on the courtroom floor with a thud, Casper's body shielding hers. In that split second of uncertainty, he felt an unmistakable sting as a bullet grazed against him, the sharp impact striking his backside. He could sense the urgency in the air, the tension rising as the danger loomed ever closer.

CHAPTER FOUR

NETTIE'S HEART RACED in her chest as the stranger who had called himself Casper appeared and lunged toward her unexpectedly. Before she could process what was happening, he grabbed her by the waist and pulled her down to the ground, pinning her with an urgency that sent a shiver down her spine. The world around them blurred, and Nettie could only focus on the stranger's grip, bewildered and frightened, wondering what danger was lurking beyond her view, as the sudden sound cut through the tension.

Could it have been gunshots she had just heard? The echo of the sound reverberated in her mind, sending a jolt of anxiety coursing through her. Memories flooded back, vivid and unsettling, of the tense atmosphere that had permeated the air before the arraignment hearings. The room had been thick with unspoken words, heavy with anticipation and fear, as she observed the anxious faces of the others, all anticipating what may come next. The sharp crack of the shots sliced through her recollections, blending the past and present into a singular moment of dread.

The stranger, brow furrowed in agony, let out a low grunt that echoed the pain etched across his features. Had he been shot while valiantly protecting her? The thought made her heart heavy with guilt and concern. Desperate to understand the scene unfolding around her, she squirmed slightly, straining to glimpse what was happening beyond their immediate surroundings.

"Stay still," he growled, his breath warm against her ear, a mix of urgency and protectiveness that sent a shiver down her spine.

While her instincts screamed for her to move, she sensed the gravity of his command, the strength in it urging her to remain immobile amidst the chaos.

Next, she heard Paul—the courtroom bailiff—shouting urgently for someone to "Put your weapon down!" The tension in the air was palpable as her protector lifted his head, cautiously assessing the scene unfolding around them. He turned his gaze to her, his expression firm but reassuring, instructing her to "Remain down until told otherwise." In a swift motion, he got to his knees. Then he was gone.

Nettie's curiosity surged forward. She lifted her head slightly, desperate to glimpse the turmoil that had erupted. Though she promised to stay down, she rationalized that a small peek couldn't hurt. It was a flimsy excuse, but risking her safety for clarity felt justifiable.

The sight of Casper stealthily maneuvering behind the shooter, who was locked in a hair-raising standoff with Paul, caught her attention. Frozen in place, her heart raced as she witnessed the unfolding drama. The stakes were high, and every moment counted as the tension escalated before her eyes.

It wasn't long before Casper lunged toward the man, swiftly grabbing the assault rifle from the startled assailant's hands. Meanwhile, Paul quickly approached, expertly cuffing the man to prevent further resistance. With a sense of relief, Paul called out an authoritative "All clear," signaling the success of their operation. He then shook Casper's hand firmly, a gesture of camaraderie and mutual respect.

Nettie grumbled while slowly pushing herself to her feet, her frustration simmering just beneath the surface. As she shifted her weight, there was the unmistakable tug of fabric giving way. Her heart sank as she noticed the rip tearing through the elegant fabric of her expensive skirt—a spur-of-the-moment purchase to commemorate her twenty-fifth birthday in a moment of indulgence and self-celebration. Now, as she inspected the tear, doubt crept in. Could this beautiful piece indeed be repaired?

Considering that she hadn't been shot, the skirt issue should have seemed trivial at first glance. Yet, it loomed large in her mind, for it was the only aspect of her situation she felt she had any control over. This feeling intensified as she noticed Casper walking back toward her, his footsteps steady and purposeful.

"Are you all right?" he asked, a hint of concern in his bright eyes.

Nettie squinted at him, her expression sharply disapproving. "Was it absolutely necessary to tackle me? You could've hurt me. Couldn't you have just told me to 'get down?'" Her words hung in the air, tinged with frustration. The encounter had rattled her to the core, unable to shake the remnants of shock as she faced him, grappling with his actions' physical and emotional implications.

Casper—*what a ridiculous name,* she thought—raised his eyebrows, a mixture of curiosity and challenge etched across his face. "So, that means you are okay with that sharp tongue intact. Pity the shooter missed it."

Her body reacted with a jolt of shock at his audacious words. "What did you just say?" she inquired, fully aware of the precise nature of his comment but wanting to verify his intentions.

Casper took a step closer, his gaze piercing as he narrowed his eyes, making it clear he was undeterred. "You heard me loud and clear. You have quite a sharp tongue. A simple thank you is usually the customary response when someone goes out of their way to save another's life."

Paul rushed up to them, his brow furrowed with genuine concern. "Miss Broussard, are you okay?" he asked, as he assessed her condition.

She observed Casper flinch at the question, an unexpected reaction that piqued her curiosity. Why did he seem so shaken? She brushed off her skirt with a delicate hand, relieved that the tear caused by her earlier mishap wasn't conspicuous. "I'm fine, Paul. Thank you for checking on me," she replied, attempting to sound more composed than she felt.

"Miss Broussard?" Casper interjected with a hint of disbelief in his tone. "As in ADA Broussard?"

Nettie nodded slowly. "Yes," she confirmed, her heart racing slightly.

"Son of a bitch," Casper exclaimed, before abruptly turning on his heel and striding away, leaving Nettie and Paul momentarily stunned in silence. The intensity of his reaction left a lingering tension between them, and a question formed in Nettie's mind about why her identity affected him so profoundly.

As she stood there, her gaze shifted toward the approaching figure of Bryce Jacobs, the attorney representing the defendant in her first arraignment. It struck her suddenly—no wonder Casper seemed upset that he had inadvertently rescued the opposing party from a complicated legal tangle. His relationship with the defendant was shrouded in shadows, leaving her to wonder just how intertwined their fates were and what personal stakes he might have had in this new legal battle.

Paul caught her attention with a serious expression on his face. "Court is suspended for this morning. The deputies will be conducting interviews with everyone present to ascertain what exactly happened."

"What did happen, Paul? I heard shots fired, but do we have any information about who the shooter might be and what prompted the incident?" Nettie's voice trembled slightly, betraying her concern.

The bailiff shook his head solemnly, his brow furrowed. "It's still too early to determine all the details. The shooter didn't look familiar to me."

Paul started to walk away but paused and turned back, his tone shifting to something more personal. "Are you still receiving those anonymous threats that were troubling you?"

Nettie rolled her eyes in exasperation. It wasn't that she was entirely without fear; instead, she found the threats childish and unoriginal. "Not lately," she replied, steadier now. But in her mind, "lately" meant this week, which had only begun today, adding further tension to her already fraught feelings.

"Inform the deputies about the potential threats, Nettie," Paul urged. The weight of his words finally sank in, and she instinctively placed a hand on her throat, feeling a fresh wave of fear wash over her.

"You don't think—" she began, her voice trembling, unsure of what conclusion her mind was racing toward.

Paul shook his head firmly. "I don't know for certain, but it's always better to be cautious than to take unnecessary risks." With that, he turned and made his way to the closest deputy.

Sheriff Beau Necaise approached Nettie with a concerned expression. "Are you all right, Nettie?" His words carried an undercurrent of sincerity and care, a rare quality given their tumultuous love-hate relationship with the sheriff's department.

"I'm fine," she replied, trying to convey strength while putting on her brave front. In truth, her emotions were a jumble, and she felt a creeping uncertainty. The unsettling thought that the shooter might have been targeting her lingered ominously in her mind, casting a shadow over her composure.

"Good. I'll take your statement when you're ready. The deputies will get the rest of the courtroom," Beau assured her, his calm demeanor contrasting with the chaos surrounding them.

Nettie realized with a hint of irony that her position as an employee of the county afforded her some unusual privileges. Being the highest-ranking official present, especially in the judge's absence, meant she avoided the usual procedural crowd. "I'm ready," she stated earnestly, wanting to move past the incident surfacing. She was anxious to resume her responsibilities, as postponing her cases would only pile onto her overwhelming workload.

"Let's go down to my office," he suggested, gesturing toward the sheriff's department on the main floor of the government building. The atmosphere was tense, but Nettie felt a flicker of resolve as they prepared to confront the aftermath of the day's events together.

Unable to resist the powerful urge to look back, Nettie found herself ensnared by the intensity of Casper's gaze. He and Bryce leaned in close, their heads bent together as they engaged in murmured conversation, likely attempting to hear each other over the raucous clamor of the crowded room. Yet, despite the surrounding noise, the weight of Casper's stare penetrated her as if it was burning through her very soul with an unsettling sense of guilt. It struck her that she had not thanked him; perhaps that was the source of this discomfort.

Drawing in a steadying breath, Nettie steeled herself. "Hold on a second, Beau," she announced, firmly yet anxiously, before pivoting sharply on her heel and striding purposefully toward Casper and Bryce.

"Mr. Casper," she began, her heart racing as embarrassment washed over her for addressing him as such. "Thank you for protecting me during the shooting." The words tumbled out into the chaotic atmosphere of the room, and as they lingered in the air, she felt a strange mix of courage and vulnerability. She had expressed her gratitude, yet strangely, the anticipated relief remained elusive, leaving her wondering why her heart still felt heavy.

Bryce extended his hand with a warm smile. "Hello, Miss Broussard. It's always good to see you," he said, his voice full of genuine affection.

Nettie shook her head slightly, a playful smile tugging at her lips. "I bet, counselor," she teased, arching a brow.

Bryce chuckled, the sound rich and hearty. "Well, it's certainly a relief that you weren't injured in the chaos."

Her mind drifting, Nettie recalled the harrowing moment when Casper had valiantly thrown himself over her, an anguished look etched on his face as he shielded her from harm. "Mr. Casper, are you injured?" she asked, concern lacing her tone.

"That's none of your concern," he replied sharply and tinged with an acrid bitterness that hung between them, a stark contrast to the warmth of the previous exchange.

Put in her place, Nettie stiffened. "Okay. It was good seeing you, Bryce." Knowing nothing else needed to be said, she walked away but heard Bryce say, "Why didn't you tell her you'd been shot?"

CHAPTER FIVE

CASPER WATCHED AS Nettie walked away, her silhouette gradually fading into the distance. A complex blend of relief and lingering unhappiness churned within him after her departure. It struck him with startling clarity that she was no longer an ally but a formidable adversary. Nettie held the title of Assistant District Attorney, the very person responsible for prosecuting his brother's case. She was the tenacious prosecutor that Bryce had often spoken of, the one who relentlessly pursued those charged with driving under the influence. Her unwavering resolve in the courtroom represented a professional duty and a personal vendetta that now felt like a tangible threat to Casper and his family's peace.

"It's no big deal," Casper reassured Bryce with a wave, the corners of his mouth lifting to mask the discomfort. "It's just a graze."

Bryce's expression darkened, and he grimaced, his eyes narrowing as he pointedly replied, "On your ass."

Casper shifted slightly, wincing as he realized the bullet had indeed grazed his rear end. It stung, a sharp reminder that he'd feel the consequences for some time, especially when sitting down. Worry flickered through him—how easily things could have turned out far worse. With a deep breath, he tried to embrace gratitude for his relatively minor injury, counting the blessings he still had.

That brief relief was shattered when a sheriff's deputy arrived. Much to Casper's disbelief, the young man overreacted and immediately sent for a medic.

"This is the last thing I need," Casper lamented, his frustration palpable as a medic gestured for him to follow to a more secluded area. There, under the harsh fluorescent lights, he would have to drop his pants so the medic could assess the gory details of his wound.

"Go with them," Bryce instructed. "I need to consult with Aaron and brief him on everything that's unfolded. Once I have more information, I'll inform you about the rescheduling of the arraignment. They're likely to fit it in tomorrow."

With a sense of resignation and nowhere else to turn, Casper complied and followed the medic down the stark corridor. They found a small interrogation room where Casper reluctantly exposed his injury. The medic assessed the damage carefully and then advised, "I recommend using a blow-up donut for a few days to alleviate any pressure on the area during recovery."

Casper nodded thoughtfully, a mix of discomfort and contemplation in his expression, as he replied, "I'll consider that." The thought of sitting on a padded ring was strange, but anything for relief seemed worth it.

As Casper was led into the sheriff's office, a mix of anticipation and anxiety churned in his stomach. Though he had expected to meet with a deputy, the sight of the sheriff himself brought an unexpected weight to the encounter. The room was alive with activity; several deputies were clustered together, engrossed in taking statements from various witnesses. Their voices were a low hum punctuated by the occasional sharp question.

The office door swung open, revealing Nettie, who emerged startled and seemed to freeze briefly as their eyes met. "Oh, you," she gasped, an unmistakable shock clear on her face.

Casper lifted his brows in surprise, a faint smirk tugging at the corners of his lips. "Yeah, me," he replied, his tone teasing yet curious, wondering what had caused her sudden discomfort.

Nettie glanced momentarily into his eyes but quickly looked away. With a quick, flustered movement, she ducked her head, then maneuvered around him. The tension between them hung thick in the air.

As he stood there watching Nettie walk away, Casper's brow creased in deep thought, a storm of conflicting emotions swirling within him. He couldn't quite pinpoint why he felt such uncertainty toward the prosecutor. Rumors had been circulating, and if they proved true, she was poised to argue for no bail for his brother, a prospect that filled him with dread. The thought of his brother remaining behind bars was unbearable. He could already imagine the fallout—his mother's reaction would be explosive. She had always been fiercely protective and emotionally driven; if she discovered the truth, she'd erupt with worry and frustration, and Casper knew he'd have to endure her endless lamentations. It would be a relentless cycle of anxiety and disappointment, and he could not bear the thought of facing that alone.

"Mr. McNabb," a deep, resonant voice intoned from behind him, momentarily pulling Casper's attention away from Nettie's slowly disappearing silhouette. He turned to find a tall, robust man with broad shoulders and an authoritative presence. The man extended his hand, which spoke of both formality and warmth. "I'm Sheriff Beau Necaise," he introduced himself with a hint of pride.

Before Casper could express his thanks, the deputy accompanying him vanished, leaving Casper alone. He grasped the sheriff's hand, feeling the strength in the sheriff's grip. "Nice to meet you. Call me Casper," he replied.

A faint smile broke across the sheriff's face, his eyes glinting with amusement and familiarity. "She mentioned that you'd want to be called that," he said, his lips curving slightly as if he held a shared joke with someone they both knew.

Curiosity piqued, Casper wondered about this mysterious "she." He had only one person in mind, and that had to be Nettie. "Well, she was right," he acknowledged, a smile creeping onto his face as he felt the connection solidify between them. The warmth of their exchange hinted at the beginnings of mutual respect and understanding.

As Casper stepped into the office, he noticed the desk was immaculate, devoid of clutter, and adorned with photographs showcasing the sheriff alongside notable figures and celebrities. The walls told stories of achievements and alliances, creating an atmosphere of authority and respect. He sat across from Sheriff Necaise, who observed him with appreciation and skepticism.

Casper's wound burned, but he refused to squirm in front of the man. Instead, he slightly lifted his right buttcheek to alleviate some of the pressure on the wound. It wasn't perfect, but he'd survived worse.

"I hear thanks are in order," the sheriff began with a hint of caution. "While I will protest any civilian interference, I appreciate your efforts. However, son, did you stop to consider the ramifications of your actions before jumping into the fray? It's a dangerous game."

Casper met his gaze and nodded thoughtfully. "Of course, Sheriff. I fully understood the potential consequences. I wouldn't have intervened if I believed the bailiff controlled the situation, if the deputies had arrived earlier, or if I thought I'd fail."

The statement struck a nerve with the sheriff, a subtle jab that Casper hadn't intended. The atmosphere shifted slightly as the sheriff's brow furrowed, perhaps stung by the implication that his team had been lacking in their duties.

The sheriff leaned back in his black executive chair, spinning a silver pen between his fingers. His brow furrowed slightly as he scrutinized the young man across from him. "It appears you've had some formal training. Can you tell me about your background?"

Casper despised discussing his past accomplishments, which felt more like bragging than sharing. However, he understood that the sheriff would likely criticize him for his supposed "interference" during the recent incident if he didn't provide some insight into his qualifications. Taking a deep breath, he squared his shoulders and replied, "I've been a paramedic, an Army Ranger, and have spent time in Delta Force. Currently, I'm an agent with Hamilton Investigation and Security in Baltimore."

The sheriff's eyes narrowed with interest. "Hamilton Investigation and Security," he echoed, a note of curiosity in his tone. "Weren't they who assisted JD and Cassie up in Oxford to retrieve his boy?"

Casper nodded, his expression steady. "Yes, we were part of that operation." Given the region's interconnected nature of law enforcement and private investigative work, it didn't surprise him that word of their work had traveled from Gulf Island to Biloxi. He reflected on how their overlapping jurisdictions often led to shared stories and collaborative efforts in times of need.

Beau leaned forward in his chair, an unmistakable sense of satisfaction lighting up his face as he dropped the pen onto the desk with a soft clatter. A playful grin spread across his lips. "Well, hell, boy, we are genuinely happy to be able to thank you for your assistance. Not being in the loop on that one really chapped my ass, but I understood the situation since they only passed through my jurisdiction without a heads-up." The nuance in his tone suggested a layered frustration, not just about the oversight but also the implications it carried for his authority.

Casper merely nodded, uncertain if a verbal acknowledgment would be appropriate or if silence was his best route in this intricate dance with the sheriff.

"Still," Beau continued, leaning back slightly with his arms crossed, his gaze sharpening, "you need to be careful. Will you be carrying in my neighborhood?"

Casper nodded in response, realizing he hadn't intended to ask permission for his concealed carry, but it seemed prudent given the sheriff's tone. "I'd sure like to keep my ankle piece if that's okay. I don't see a need for my sidearm on this trip," he replied, trying to sound as cooperative as possible while gauging Beau's reaction.

"I don't see it either," Beau replied dismissively, signaling that Casper's assessment was accepted. "The ankle piece is fine. Just keep it hidden away." His expression softened slightly as if offering a moment of camaraderie. "We have lots of open carries here, but remember, the less visible, the better. It helps avoid unnecessary attention."

The gravity of the conversation hung between them, an unspoken understanding forming as they navigated the complexities of local law, trust, and safety in their shared environment.

"So, tell me, what brings you to Biloxi and the courthouse?" the sheriff inquired, his eyes narrowing with curiosity as he sized up the newcomer.

"My brother," Casper replied, his tone steady yet hinting at the weight of his concern.

Before Casper could elaborate further, Sheriff Necaise's expression darkened—his brow furrowed. "You mean Aaron McNabb? That boy has been the bane of my existence since I took office as sheriff," he lamented, a note of exasperation creeping into his voice.

Unfortunately, Casper didn't find it hard to believe. Just recently, during a tense phone call with his mother, she had painted a troubling picture of Aaron's spiraling life—one consumed by an insatiable appetite for alcohol and high-stakes gambling. The images of reckless nights and shattered trust flickered in his mind, but he needed to know more. "And now?" he pressed, his concern palpable.

The sheriff paused momentarily, drawing out the suspense like a thick fog descending on the scene. "Well," he began, his tone grave, "this is the second DUI we've pulled him in for. But to be honest, I'm certain it's not the only time he's gotten behind the wheel after drinking."

A troubled silence enveloped them, heavy with the weight of familial bonds and the consequences of choices made in darkness.

"We're thrilled to have ADA Broussard on the case," the sheriff said. "She's one tough cookie when dealing with drunk drivers. You can count on her not to pull any punches during the trial. In fact, she's never lost one of those cases."

Great, Casper thought, feeling a flicker of hope amidst his worries. Yet, there was always the possibility of that first time. Once more, the little devil inside him whispered that incarceration might be the best option for his brother's burgeoning problems. But Casper couldn't bring himself to consider such a fate for anyone, especially not for family. No, rehab—that's what he'd push Bryce to advocate for. Maybe that was the solution that could address the issues his brother faced, something no one else had been able to manage effectively.

"So, she's that good?" Casper inquired, wanting to know more about this formidable attorney who was now against his brother.

"Yeah, absolutely! And I truly can't thank you enough for looking out for our little prodigy," the sheriff replied proudly.

"Prodigy?" Casper echoed, a puzzled look crossing his face as he recalled that she had only just turned twenty-five.

"Oh," the sheriff replied, rocking slightly in his chair as if conveying a secret. "You haven't heard about her past, have you? Boy, how long have you been away?"

"Too long," was Casper's honest, if somewhat vague, reply, though he hadn't meant he'd been away from his family for an extended time. Yet, the thought crossed his mind that maybe if he had been present, he could have intervened and helped his brother before things escalated to this level.

"Let me tell you," the sheriff continued, leaning forward, engaging Casper's curiosity. "She graduated from college at just nineteen and finished law school by age twenty-one. The girl is truly as sharp as a whip."

Although attempting to mask his emotions, Casper was impressed and leaned forward, his curiosity piqued. "Does she opt for rehab, probation, or prison time?" he inquired, his tone steady yet introspective.

The sheriff took a moment, furrowing his brow as he weighed the options. "She chooses rehab, but only while serving their prison sentence. She firmly believes that probation offers no real chance for recovery, as it places alcohol too readily within reach."

Casper paused, contemplating the implications of this. Yet, he thought, there's always a first time for everything. While probation seemed acceptable in theory, the reality of prison time felt far too harsh. If she wouldn't advocate fiercely for rehab, he'd take matters into his own hands—he would personally see to it that his brother was placed in a rehabilitation facility.

"Given that this is Aaron's second DUI, it's likely she'll fight for the maximum sentence," the sheriff added.

Casper's expression hardened at this news, a fierce resolve settling within him; over his dead body would he let that happen. Determined not to let this slide, he resolved to find a way to assist Bryce in winning the case. Or perhaps he'd persuade Nettie to adopt a different strategy for the trial altogether. He couldn't afford to remain a passive observer any longer when his brother's future hung in the balance. He would dive headfirst into the battle, ready to do whatever it took to secure his family before he turned his back again.

CHAPTER SIX

AS NETTIE STEPPED into the bustling lobby of her office suite, heads turned, and whispers broke out among her colleagues. Each pair of eyes followed her, intrigued by her confident presence. With a radiant and bold smile, she made a point to greet everyone she passed, her warm and lively demeanor brightening the atmosphere.

She finally reached her office door and pushed it open, stepping inside the familiar space she had made her own. Without hesitation, she dropped her new leather briefcase onto her cluttered desk, the thud marking her arrival with authority. Next, she slid open the bottom desk drawer, neatly placing her purse inside, ensuring that her belongings were tucked away and out of sight.

With a soft sigh, she sank into her chair, the cushion enveloping her as she tried to settle into what was left of the day. But within moments, the world's weight felt heavy on her shoulders. She leaned forward, her head resting in her hands, both elbows pressing down onto the polished surface of her desk, surrounded by scattered papers and a dark computer screen. The silence of her office contrasted sharply with the lively lobby, leaving her alone with her thoughts, battling the challenges that awaited her.

She couldn't believe the events of her day. Earlier, they had been caught in a terrifying situation when gunfire erupted around them, sending everyone into a panic. Thankfully, despite the chaos and fear, no one was seriously injured. However, two individuals sustained injuries that were severe enough to necessitate medical attention, and they were promptly taken to the hospital for evaluation and treatment. The sheer shock left her shaken as she grappled with the reality of what had just occurred.

Could it have been her fault that this nightmare had unfolded? They had yet to extract any information from the gunman, who had firmly clammed up after his arrest, invoking his right to remain silent and asking for an attorney. The unsettling thought crept into her mind—could he have been lurking nearby intending to harm her, just as the series of threatening notes had ominously suggested? Every detail replayed in her mind, amplifying her anxiety and confusion about his motives and the events that had led to this moment.

Then, Casper seemed to materialize out of thin air, capturing her attention entirely. Embarrassed by how she had behaved the night before, she felt an overwhelming urge to appear poised and unruffled in his presence. But, oh, how handsome he looked, with his effortlessly charming demeanor and striking features that made her heart race. When she noticed who he chatted with, she realized Casper was there for the defendant. The very defendant she had been strategizing about, intending to plead with the judge to impose no bail and subsequently advocate for the harshest sentence permissible under the law. Suddenly, her internal conflict deepened, sculpting a delicate interplay of attraction and professional duty that left her flustered and determined.

And, in that crucial moment, he had saved her life, risking his own without a second thought. But it left her grappling why did he feel the need to go and perform such a courageous act? It was infuriating. How was she supposed to solidify her determination and harden her resolve if he continued to act with such unwavering heroism instead of challenging her and giving her the grief she felt she deserved? His selflessness seemed to undermine her attempts at courage, complicating her inner struggle even further.

A sharp knock reverberated against the door, pulling Nettie's gaze from her scattered thoughts. Quickly, she tucked stray strands of hair behind her ear, an unconscious gesture of composure. "Come in," she called, her voice steady despite the unease swirling within her.

The door opened, and Joann Sullivan, her ever-busy paralegal, rushed in. "I heard what happened. Are you all right? If I hadn't been held up in traffic, I would have been there with you. The thought of it all scares the hell out of me. I can't even fathom experiencing that kind of horror firsthand."

Nettie couldn't help but roll her eyes inwardly at Joann's ability to pivot every conversation back to herself. No matter the gravity of the situation, she had a knack for linking it back to her own experiences or feelings, as if the world revolved solely around her. It truly boggled Nettie's mind how this woman had navigated life to reach the age of fifty without losing sight of her knack for self-centeredness. Yet, recalling the countless times Joann had delivered insightful assistance in their legal battles, Nettie did recognize a strange form of resilience in her paralegal.

Nettie took a deep breath, grounding herself in the moment, pushing away the chaotic noise of her thoughts. She was ready to address Joann's concerns while carefully guarding her own vulnerability.

"I'm fine. Thanks for asking," Nettie said with a faint smile, gesturing for Joann to sit across from her. The room felt heavy with unspoken words. "It was horrible, but I don't want to speak of it right now. I need to concentrate on my workload." Her tone was firm, a clear boundary set.

Joann nodded, her shoulders slumped slightly in disappointment. Nettie could see the glimmer of curiosity in her paralegal's eyes. Joann thrived on juicy gossip to share around the office, but Nettie wasn't about to give in. "They're reopening court after lunch," Joann said, redirecting the conversation. "I can get the caseload and review everything thoroughly to ensure you have everything you need for your preparations."

Nettie nodded, determined to shift the focus back to their work. She knew Joann would have to wait for the details she craved. With a warm smile, Nettie felt a profound sense of reassurance, knowing she could always rely on Joann to help her stay grounded amidst the chaos. "Have you heard any updates regarding the arraignments that were on the docket this morning?" she asked, her curiosity piqued by concern for those involved.

Joann nodded thoughtfully, her expression serious yet determined. "Yes. They're planning to process the arraignments over the next few days, so you'll need to act quickly to ensure they're moved through the arraignment hearings efficiently."

"What about McNabb?" Nettie blurted out. She wasn't entirely sure why that specific name had come to her mind, other than it brought her back to one person: Casper. "What is his brother's name?"

Joann looked momentarily taken aback, her brow furrowing as she processed the question. After a beat, she lightly tapped her finger on her chin, a thoughtful gesture as she attempted to summon the details from her expansive memory. "Let me think," she murmured, closing her eyes for a moment as if searching through a mental archive.

What Nettie appreciated most about Joann was her exceptional ability to recall even the tiniest details from their case files. This skill had proven invaluable to Nettie multiple times, often shedding light on the intricate nuances others might overlook. Joann's memory was a treasure trove of information, and Nettie felt grateful for having her as a colleague.

"Ash," Joann remarked, shaking her head in disbelief. "I have no idea what was going through their mother's mind when she named him."

Nettie was lost in thought as she grabbed her pen, twirling it between her fingers absentmindedly. Ash McNabb—that was his full name. Yet, she couldn't help but ponder the origins of his nickname, Casper. Why Casper? The question nagged at her curiosity, but she hesitated; asking Joann might feel like imposing a personal favor, and she wasn't sure if Joann would appreciate that kind of intrusion into her paralegal's private life. After a long moment of contemplation, she set the pen down decisively. "Yeah, weird," Nettie finally replied, trying to shake off her thoughts about names. Shifting her focus, she continued, "Okay, let me know what they decide. I'll be ready for court after lunch."

As Joann departed, the intercom on Nettie's desk phone rang, piercing through the quiet hum of the office. With a slight frown that quickly morphed into curiosity, she picked up the receiver, cradling it gently against her ear. "Yes?" she inquired.

Laylianna, the ever-cheerful receptionist, responded with a hint of mischief in her tone, "Sheriff Necaise is on line one for you. He's insistent that you aren't too busy to take his call. And if you don't pick up, he'll barge over here and stride into your office."

Nettie couldn't help but smile, affection blooming in her chest. Despite the significant age difference, she adored the sheriff. He was like a father figure, always treating her with gentle mentorship and playful banter. Memories flooded back—she recalled the fateful day when he drove to see her at the University of Southern Mississippi, his face a mix of concern and sorrow, to deliver the heart-wrenching news of her parents' untimely demise in a tragic car accident. She remembered collapsing into his embrace, her sobs echoing off the walls of her dorm room as she mourned the loss of the only family she had known. It felt like an eternity, drowning in despair at sixteen years old. She was starting college, loaded with ambition but utterly lost in her personal life, navigating the storm of grief with no guardians to guide her.

In the wake of her tragedy, they sought to place her in the system, a notion that ignited a firestorm of anxiety within her. But then, Beau, a steadfast ally, stepped in, determined to help her petition the court for emancipation. He fought for her freedom with unwavering determination, advocating against the tide of bureaucracy. She emerged victorious as the court acknowledged her unique circumstances—her parents had left her a modest inheritance, including the cherished home where she had grown up. The label of "child prodigy" granted by the court, often seen as a blessing, became her armor, shielding her in a tumultuous world where grief and resilience intertwined.

She clicked on line one. The familiar flicker of playfulness danced across her mind, but he cut her off with an unexpected declaration just as she opened her mouth with "Hello."

"I'm placing you in protective custody," he stated firmly. His tone was serious, betraying the underlying urgency of the situation. She paused, momentarily taken aback, the weight of his words settling heavily on her shoulders, igniting a spark of curiosity and fear all at once.

"What?" she asked. "You heard me. Two deputies are on their way to you now. You *will* leave with them," he replied, his tone leaving no room for argument.

The air thickened with tension as she processed his statement. What kind of danger loomed over her that the sheriff deemed it necessary to send deputies for her protection? Beyond the immediate concern for her safety, her mind raced with thoughts about her formidable caseload. Who would take over her responsibilities?

They had only one other Assistant District Attorney in their small office and another unfilled position. David, the only other ADA, was already burdened with his cases and had a court hearing scheduled shortly. His plate was complete, leaving no one available to manage her arraignments or the critical cases that needed immediate attention.

"Can we make a deal?" she ventured.

"What kind of deal?" he pressed.

"Well…" Caught between the fear of the unknown and the pressing demands of her job, she hesitated, searching for a way to navigate through the chaos threatening to engulf her.

CHAPTER SEVEN

"I WANT TO help as much as I can," Casper said earnestly, as he spoke to Bryce over the phone. "I need to be involved in this process." Although he felt a deep conflict about what his brother truly deserved as punishment, Casper was acutely aware that sending his brother to rehab was the most viable solution to help him achieve sobriety. The thought of Nettie advocating for the maximum sentence filled him with dread. He couldn't let that happen. Casper believed his brother needed a chance to heal and was determined to intervene before it was too late.

Furthermore, the maximum sentence that could be handed down would plunge his mother into a state of emotional turmoil that he felt utterly ill-equipped to manage, mainly while he lived in Baltimore. The weight of the situation would create a significant burden on her, as she would have to navigate through her distress alone, leaving him feeling helpless and deeply concerned for her well-being.

Casper let out a deep, almost invisible sigh as frustration washed over him.

"I think it might be wise to include JD and Cassie in this," Bryce proposed. "We'll need investigators along the way, so let's start with them immediately."

This suggestion resonated with Casper. He felt a sense of relief at the prospect of involving JD and his fiancée, Cassie, in the unfolding situation. The more hands they had on deck, the better equipped they would be to tackle the challenges ahead. It was true that JD and Cassie were not legal experts, but Casper believed their unique perspectives and skills could contribute to gathering vital intelligence that would aid their investigation. Despite the uncertainty of what information they might uncover, he felt it was a risk worth taking. Deep down, Casper knew that when it came to matters like these, he couldn't afford to dismiss any potential allies, mainly when Bryce agreed on this approach.

Together, they would forge ahead, each bringing their strengths to the table, united in pursuing what was best for his brother.

"I agree," Casper responded thoughtfully, nodding slightly as he spoke. "Can they meet today? I want to tackle this before we get a new arraignment date for Aaron. Time is of the essence, and I want us to be ahead of the game."

"Let me get back to you," Bryce replied, his tone steady and professional. "I'll contact JD and let you know when."

Casper felt a tug at his instinct to step in and contact JD himself. However, he reminded himself that this was Bryce's responsibility and needed to respect the chain of command. He took a deep breath, acknowledging the tension in his chest, but ultimately decided it was best to let Bryce handle the reins for now, at least until the urgency required a different course of action.

When Bryce contacted him, JD proposed they meet aboard his sailboat. The thought of being back on the water, with the boat's gentle rocking and the soothing, rhythmic sound of the waves lapping against the hull, conjured images of a tranquil oasis amidst the impending storm for their discussion. The mixture of the idyllic setting, with the scent of salt in the air and the distant cries of seabirds, contrasted with the severe nature of their gathering, creating a vivid juxtaposition that intrigued Casper deeply as he anticipated the day ahead.

He imagined the sun setting on the horizon, casting golden hues across the water. He wondered if such beauty could soften the weight of their conversation or merely heighten the gravity of their deliberations. This encounter promised to be unlike any other, stirring excitement and apprehension in him as he prepared for the complexities that awaited them.

As they glided through the calm waters, the sea's serene beauty enveloped them, providing a stunning backdrop while they prepared to navigate the intricate details of the case. Casper closed his eyes, surrendering to the soothing embrace of the ocean breeze that gently caressed his skin. The salty air filled his lungs, bringing back a wave of nostalgia. It had been far too long since he'd felt the thrill of being out on a boat in the vast expanse of the Gulf of Mexico, with its shimmering waves and endless horizon.

Growing up on the sun-drenched coast, he'd spent most of his carefree days on the golden sandy beach, swimming in the ocean's refreshing embrace or riding the waves behind a speedboat. Those days felt like a blissful eternity, filled with laughter and the salty breeze. However, his circle of friends gradually dispersed. They had all enlisted in the military straight after high school. He often pondered about their lives, where they might be stationed, and how far apart they had drifted, significantly since their once-tight bond faded after the first few years of separation.

Yet, amidst these profound reflections on life and the choices that led him here, he continuously reminded himself of the importance of living in the present moment. While he longed for happiness, he understood that this personal joy must be temporarily set aside. His primary objective was to liberate Aaron from the burdens of his creation, a complex web of challenges and entanglements. This realization drove him to prioritize Aaron's freedom, knowing that only by helping his brother untangle himself from this self-imposed coil could he hope to find peace and fulfillment in his life and with his family.

Casper took a turn diligently assisting JD in managing the sails of their boat. The sun glinted off the water, casting a shimmer that added a sense of magic to the moment. As they worked together, the sturdy fabric of the sails billowed in the breeze, filling the air with a sense of adventure. Casper had found solace in handling the sails himself. The ropes' rhythmic pull and the boat's gentle sway helped clear his mind, allowing him to reflect on what truly mattered.

Family. No matter the complexities of his relationships with them—joy or frustration—one truth remained unwavering: he loved them deeply because they were bound by blood, shared history, and a lifetime of memories. Each interaction, whether tender or tumultuous, strengthened that unbreakable bond, reminding him that at the core of it all was love, pure and simple.

As he took a break, Cassie approached him. "I heard you drew Nettie instead of David for Aaron's case," she said. "That's going to be challenging. Nettie has an impressive track record that sets a high bar for anyone she faces. It'll be particularly tough for Bryce to contend with her."

"JD recommended him for the case. Do you think he isn't strong enough to handle it?" Casper asked, raising an eyebrow, intrigued by her apprehension.

"You're misunderstanding the situation," she replied, carefully plucking hair from her face as the sharp gusts of wind whipped it back. "It's not just about strength or skill. Anyone stepping into that ring with Nettie will face a monumental challenge. She's relentless and has built a reputation for never losing her cases."

"Not yet," Casper interjected, a hint of optimism in his voice.

Cassie's expression softened as she smiled, her earlier seriousness momentarily lifting. "You're right. Not yet."

JD expertly dropped the anchor, causing the boat to sway gently, its hull creaking slightly as it settled amidst the vibrant waves.

Bryce waved his arm to beckon Casper to where he stood amid leather-clad benches at the stern of the boat.

"I guess it's time to find out if this will be her first loss," Casper called out. Excitedly, he gently guided Cassie to where Bryce and JD waited.

Seated, Casper observed Bryce extract a legal pad and a sleek pen from his well-worn leather briefcase, his movements deliberate and methodical.

The attorney looked around the group purposefully before announcing, "Let's get started." Then he turned to Casper with a severe expression, his brow slightly furrowed. "I have both good news and bad news for you. Which would you like to hear first?"

Casper's stomach twisted at the question, a familiar irritation bubbling up within him. It was a cliché that he had grown to despise, yet he knew the importance of managing expectations, especially given what lay ahead. After a moment of contemplation, he looked back at Bryce, his eyes brimming with apprehension and anticipation. "Let's start with the good news first. That way, we can face the bad news with a more positive mindset," he replied, his tone resolute despite the nervous flutter in his chest.

Bryce nodded, his expression a mix of relief and concern. "The good news is that the couple whose car Aaron collided with is being released from the hospital today. Thankfully, their injuries are relatively minor."

Casper, however, struggled to categorize a broken arm and a concussion as minor injuries. He nodded, compelled to keep the conversation flowing despite his reservations. "Is that all the good news?" he asked, his tone filled with a hint of apprehension.

"Unfortunately, yes," Bryce replied.

Casper took a deep breath, feeling the air fill his lungs before slowly exhaling. He needed to center himself…clear his mind of distractions…and prepare for the inevitable waves of bad news he sensed were about to crash over him. A nagging feeling dictated Bryce's upcoming reveal would not be pleasant, but he was determined to stay mentally present for whatever lay ahead.

Bryce cleared his throat as he leaned forward intently, resting his elbows on his knees. "Your brother's insurance was canceled a year ago," he explained, his tone serious. "He never acquired new coverage for his car. Since the vehicle wasn't financed, he was only required to keep basic coverage, but he failed to do that."

Confusion washed over Casper's face as he processed this alarming news. He scrunched his brow, trying to make sense of the situation. "Why was the insurance canceled?" he pressed, his mind racing with thoughts. If his brother had squandered his insurance money on gambling instead of paying the bills, there would certainly be a heated conversation ahead. Then, like a sudden flash of clarity, it dawned on him, connecting the dots. "Was it suspended due to the DUI arrest? I thought all he got from that was probation."

Bryce nodded, his eyes dropping to his notes. "That's correct. Although he received probation for the DUI, his license was also suspended. He's been driving around without a valid license or insurance coverage."

Casper grappled with the implications of his brother's reckless choices. He hadn't been in the country when his brother had experienced his first DUI. He had been deployed on a military operation overseas. Although his mother had kept him updated on family matters, the details surrounding the incident were still somewhat unclear, leaving a lingering confusion and concern.

Frustration bubbled up inside him. Why, of all things, would his brother jeopardize his life and future in such a reckless manner?

Casper couldn't shake the thought that Aaron had been incredibly fortunate that the couple he had struck in the accident hadn't suffered fatal injuries or been left with life-altering trauma. The injuries they sustained, which Bryce described as "minor," were enough to instill fear in Casper's heart. He feared the impending repercussions, as it seemed almost inevitable that the couple would pursue legal action against Aaron, potentially draining their family's finances and peace of mind. This reckless act could spiral into a disaster that would affect them all, and the weight of that possibility pressed heavily on Casper's shoulders.

Bryce continued. "We'll ignore the couple's legal action for now. The arraignment is impending and must be our primary focus."

"Do you think you'll get him out?" Casper inquired, desperation creeping into his tone.

Bryce looked thoughtful, furrowing his brow. "I'm not entirely sure. There are a lot of obstacles stacked against Aaron. He's already facing the consequences from his first DUI, has previous speeding tickets on his record, and now this latest incident involves another DUI —plus the fact that he's driving without a license and insurance.…"

Understanding dawned on Casper like a heavy weight settling in his chest. Bryce was preparing him for the grim possibility of a loss, an outcome that felt unacceptable to him. "Find a way. If it weren't my baby brother caught in this mess, I'd say let him deal with the consequences because he dug his grave. But this is my brother, and my mom is counting on me to take care of this and set him free."

He felt a brief relief, knowing that he would free Aaron for now, at least until Casper intervened and got him into rehab. However, he was acutely aware that this reprieve was only temporary. The real battle awaited him —the inevitable confrontation with his mother, a struggle he intentionally postponed until he deemed it necessary. It was a delicate situation, fraught with the emotional weight of past grievances and unspoken concerns, demanding careful consideration before directly engaging her about his addiction and the need for recovery.

"Oh, I'm going to dedicate everything I have to this case," Bryce assured him firmly. "I just wanted to prepare you for the possibility that things may not go as we hope. Miss Broussard is notoriously tough on DUI cases. She lost her parents to a drunk driver and has made it her life's mission to ensure that all drunk drivers face serious repercussions for their actions."

Before Casper could process Nettie's loss, JD cleared his throat, a subtle act that signaled the gravity of what he was about to say. "Speaking of Nettie," he began, his voice steady, "I received a call before we left that Sheriff Necaise was putting her into protective custody."

Casper felt his heart lurch violently at the mention of protective custody. His mind raced as he processed the implications. Protective custody. What. The. Fuck? "Was the shooter after *her*?" he asked, desperation creeping into his voice. That had to be the reason for such drastic measures. Yet, a nagging thought lingered in his mind— there could undoubtedly be more he wasn't privy to, details that could paint a clearer picture.

"Yeah," JD confirmed with a grave nod, his expression betraying the weight of the situation. "She's been receiving threatening notes for weeks now, and they can't ascertain if the shooter was acting alone or if this is part of something larger."

The air felt heavy with unsaid words, and Casper's mind spun with the potential dangers looming over Nettie, helpless in this chaotic moment.

Cassie bit her lip, her brow furrowing with concern. "Do you think they'll transfer her cases or just put them on hold?"

Casper was lost in thought. He wondered what that would mean for his brother's ongoing case, feeling a knot tighten in his stomach as the situation's implications settled in.

"I was hoping to speak with her later today about Aaron," Bryce said, mentioning his brother's name like a lifeline. "If I could just get a moment to chat with her, maybe we could reach some sort of agreement." His gaze darted over to Casper.

Casper finally lifted his gaze from the endless expanse of the ocean, recognizing the depth of their dilemma. "I'll do it," he declared firmly, determination etched across his features.

"But you aren't an attorney. You can't just get an agreement from her," Bryce interjected.

Standing tall and adjusting his stance to counterbalance the boat swaying with the rhythmic waves, Casper met their gazes with unwavering resolve. "I'll do it," he insisted, the weight of the world on his shoulders but still willing to take on the challenge. His determination burned bright amid the uncertainty surrounding them.

No one uttered a word as he gracefully moved to the side of the boat, taking a deep breath before diving into the water with a fluid motion that seemed almost artistic. Beneath the surface, as the saltwater burned his wound, he thought of Nettie and the urgent conversation that awaited them. He needed to convince her to consider Aaron's situation more empathetically and urge her to show leniency, which might allow Casper a shot at rehabilitation for Aaron. He felt a flicker of hope, believing she might agree to an arrangement that would benefit them all.

As he swam back to the boat, a troubling thought crept into his mind: would the sheriff permit him to visit

Nettie if she were placed in protective custody? The likelihood seemed grim, casting a shadow over his plans.

Reaching the boat, he effortlessly hoisted himself back on board, his heart racing with determination. "We need to head back now so I can catch her before they take her away," he said urgently, glancing at JD, who nodded.

JD stood and retrieved the anchor—urgency palpable as the sailboat shifted with the movement of the water.

In the depths of his mind, he steeled himself—*Hello, Miss Nettie. I'm not going away without a fight, not when it's for my brother's sake. So watch out because the battle lines have been drawn, and I'm ready to face whatever comes next.*

CHAPTER EIGHT

AS CASPER WADED back onto the familiar shore, the harsh waves receding like a reluctant tide, he sought refuge from his mother's relentless tirade. Her voice, a symphony of frustration and fervor, was drowned out by his thoughts, primarily focused on her claims that "the system was fundamentally against Aaron." After swiftly slipping away from the escalating drama, he retreated to the cleansing solace of his shower, letting the warm water wash away the day's burdens.

Once invigorated, he dressed carefully, sliding into tailored slacks that felt smart and practical. He paired them with a crisp button-down shirt, the fabric cool against his skin, rolling the sleeves up to his elbows to embrace a more casual demeanor. Although he begrudgingly donned what he often referred to as his "monkey-suit clothes," a lighthearted jab at the formalities he associated with such attire, he consciously decided to keep his combat boots—recognizing that sandals would stand out too starkly in a setting that expected a hint of sophistication. With this subtle yet significant wardrobe change, he aimed to balance his desire for comfort with the need to fit into the expected social norms of the day.

As he slid into the driver's seat, the sound of his phone ringing pierced through the warm air. Glancing at the screen, he recognized the caller's name immediately.

"Hey, Jesse," he greeted, his words mingling with the engine's growl as he started the Jeep. He felt the smooth rumble beneath him.

With a quick flick of his wrist, he adjusted the air conditioning, grateful for the cool rush of air that now circulated. The sun hung high in the sky, casting a golden hue over the coastline, and the heat of September clung relentlessly to the air. Wearing full-length slacks and a long-sleeved cotton shirt, he felt like he had stepped into a sauna, the fabric sticking to his skin despite the cuffs being rolled up to his elbows. Sweat beaded on his brow, but he brushed it away, determined to achieve his goal for the day.

"I wanted to see how things were progressing," Jesse said.

Casper shifted in the Jeep's driver's seat, wishing he'd taken the EMT's advice and acquired a donut for his wound. The seats had heated under the relentless sun, and he was careful not to burn his fingers on the steering wheel. Dust particles floated in the late afternoon light, creating a hazy atmosphere inside the vehicle.

"Thanks for reminding me that JD lived down here. He hooked me up with an attorney specializing in cases like ours, and he has committed his investigative support should we need it," Casper replied, relief washing over him.

"Good. I also wanted to let you know that Romeo got the girl," Jesse added, a hint of excitement in his tone.

Casper's lips curled into a smile, his heart warming at the news. He hated missing that reunion, but he felt good knowing he had played a part in bringing them back together. "I'm glad to hear it."

"I'll let him elaborate further on the situation, but she's relocating to Baltimore."

He persistently feared Romeo might abandon his promising career and move closer to Daisy Mae, a relocation that seemed unthinkable. He couldn't grasp why HIS men would choose to leave such a remarkable profession for a woman. The career was thrilling, filled with opportunities and achievements, and he couldn't envision ever walking away from it, regardless of temptation.

"JD is exceptional at investigative work, showcasing a keen eye for detail and an impressive ability to connect the dots that others might overlook. However, don't hesitate to ask if you require additional resources on the ground. With three teams at our disposal, one is particularly eager and ready to jump into action, just waiting for a task to tackle."

Nettie's security quickly flashed through his mind, but he instantly dismissed it. He reassured himself that the sheriff would adequately handle her safety concerns. This was not his responsibility, and he intended to keep it that way.

"Thanks, Jesse," Casper said, slightly hesitant but resolved. As he ended the call, an odd weight settled on his shoulders. He shifted the vehicle into gear. Outside, he could see his mother sitting on the front porch, her expression pinched into a sour frown, eyes narrowed.

The thought lingered in his mind: why had he even considered protecting Nettie? She was the enemy in every way that mattered—a formidable opponent in his brother's conflict. Yet, he couldn't deny that he had no personal animosity toward her. He found himself secretly admiring her accomplishments. Her striking appearance often caught him off guard, an unexpected twist that made him uneasy.

But her involvement in her brother's case set off alarm bells in his mind, making her irrevocably unacceptable. The conflict was apparent: his growing admiration tangled uncomfortably with his fierce loyalty to his side. This loyalty demanded that he see her as nothing more than a rival, one to defeat or dismiss.

As Casper pulled into the parking lot of the county courthouse, a looming structure that housed the sheriff's office and various county officials, apprehension mixed with determination coursed through him. He parked his Jeep, taking a deep breath to steady his nerves as he mentally prepared himself for the impending confrontation.

His thoughts raced with the memories of past conversations, strategies, and approaches, all leading to this moment. He desperately wanted her to see things from his perspective, to join him in his quest for resolution. He needed to bring forth his best skills as a mediator, even though he knew deep down that his abilities paled compared to those of Nettie, the experienced arbitrator who had successfully navigated many conflicts. Still, he had to give it his all. This encounter could mean everything. He couldn't afford to back down now.

As he stepped through the large, heavy doors of the building, a sheriff's deputy approached him with a metal detector wand in hand, signaling an official search for any concealed weapons. The air was thick with tension, and Casper felt relieved that he had been smart enough not to bring a firearm, especially after the chaotic events that had unfolded earlier that day. His mind raced with thoughts of his brother, who might very well be out on bond if the sheriff's department had conducted this precautionary search hours ago. Aaron could have been in a conference room, strategizing a defense with his attorney, instead of locked away in the unsettling confines of jail.

The realization gnawed at him; if only the deputies had been more vigilant, there could have been one less act of violence. It struck him as bizarre that the courthouse, which was supposed to uphold law and order, didn't utilize the simplest security measures. Why was there no metal detector at the entrance? Given the potential risks associated with such a public space, it felt like an essential oversight that should have been addressed years ago.

As he continued to scan the elegant marble corridors, his eyes landed on a patch of the tile floor that had been cut. The edges were rough, and it was evident that a machine had once occupied that space, designed for security and protection—but it was now absent. The thought sent another wave of frustration through him.

The deputy seemed to read his mind as he contemplated the lack of security measures. With a slight nod toward the ground, he said, "Our machine is being replaced, but unfortunately, the old one broke down before the new one could be installed." There was a hint of regret in his voice, but Casper couldn't help but feel that a mere apology wouldn't undo the consequences of their oversight.

"Where are you headed?" the deputy inquired, raising an eyebrow as he cleared Casper to pass through the courthouse entrance.

Casper hesitated, his hands sliding into his pockets as he nervously fiddled with the cold metal of his keys. "To ADA Broussard's office," he finally replied.

The deputy blocked his way, holding up a hand. "Hold on a sec. What's your name?"

Casper could sense the scrutiny in the officer's gaze. He knew the name he had in mind wouldn't suffice to gain entry. With a resigned sigh, he replied, "Ash McNabb."

The deputy quickly scanned a clipboard, finger skimming down a printed list Casper couldn't make out from his angle. After a moment, he looked up, skepticism etched on his face. "You don't have an appointment."

Casper's stomach dropped. He hadn't anticipated that she would secure a meeting beforehand. "No, but I'm sure she'll see me," he asserted, though uncertainty gnawed at him. "I'm here to discuss a case."

The deputy cocked his head, eyes narrowing suspiciously. "Are you an attorney? I don't remember seeing you around the courthouse."

It figured he'd encounter a Barnie Fife wannabe today—an overzealous officer eager to flex his authority.

"No, I'm not an attorney," Casper admitted, trying to maintain composure. "I'm a family member and here on behalf of counsel."

With narrowed eyes, the deputy stated, "Let me check." He picked up his radio, his voice authoritative as he called in for verification, the static crackling as he waited for a response.

Casper stood there, anxiety swirling within him. He expected Nettie to refuse his visit, so he'd gamed the system with a surprise attempt. Just as he was about to turn and leave in defeat, he caught the words filtering through the radio speaker: "Send him up."

Relief washed over him, mingling with anticipation as he braced himself for what lay ahead.

CHAPTER NINE

NETTIE SAT AT her desk, staring at the stack of papers representing her current caseload, but her mind raced. She couldn't believe that she had offered to meet with Ash McNabb. This was unexpected and yet oddly compelling. After all, he didn't belong here. The attorney representing his brother should be the one handling such matters.

Her thoughts spiraled back to the implications of this meeting. Why would Ash even consider jeopardizing his brother's case by personally discussing things with her? It was a gamble that made little sense in her mind, yet it piqued her curiosity.

Nettie glanced at the clock, reminding herself that this meeting needed efficiency. At least it happened in her office, where she felt a sense of control. She resolved to keep it brief and strictly professional, but the undercurrent of personal stake was impossible to ignore. She contemplated having Joann sit in on the meeting to ensure she maintained professionalism. Joann's reassuring presence might help keep the conversation on track and minimize further emotional undertones that could complicate matters.

With a deep breath, Nettie prepared herself for the complex dynamics of this unexpected encounter with Ash McNabb, an encounter that—something told her—could change everything.

Nettie startled as the sharp knock on the door pierced the quiet of her office. She took a deep breath, steadied herself, and replied with an outward calm that belied her internal turmoil. "Yes," she said, her voice measured and professional, masking the frantic thoughts swirling in her mind.

A sheriff's deputy casually pushed his head through the doorway, his presence commanding yet familiar. "Ash McNabb, Miss Broussard," he stated.

Nettie recalled the strenuous negotiations she had had with Sheriff Necaise. They agreed she could continue her work, but only with a dedicated personnel protection detail. This measure now felt painfully necessary after the recent attack on her.

"Let him in," she instructed, as her hands fumbled with the papers across her desk, a futile attempt to convey busyness as a means of deflection.

She didn't look up immediately, but her senses prickled with awareness as his quiet presence filled the room. The air felt different, charged with unspoken energy. When she finally caught a glimpse of him—solid, slacks-clad thighs moving confidently toward her desk— she looked up, and her breath caught in her throat. Her mind raced, confronting a flurry of emotions. Why did he have to be so good-looking? It felt almost unfair.

"Miss Broussard," he said in a professional and coolly detached tone as if they were strangers—not the kind of tension that had crackled between them before.

She gestured for him to sit across from her, her thoughts a tangled web of strategies to involve her paralegal in the upcoming discussion. "Let me call in my paralegal, Mr. McNabb."

He sat fluidly, crossing one sculpted leg over the other as if the motion was as natural as breathing, yet she noticed the slight wince when he did so. "Casper, please," he said smoothly. "And there's no need for a paralegal." His words lingered in the air, resonating with a confidence that intrigued and unsettled her.

It suddenly became clear that the stakes of their conversation had just changed in ways she hadn't anticipated.

Hesitant about whether to meet him alone or include Joann, she took a moment to reflect, feeling a mix of anxiety and determination swirl within her. After a brief pause, she resolved to proceed with the meeting. Still, she kept the option of calling Joann open should she feel the need for professional support or her sense of security in the delicate situation.

Rearranging herself in the chair, she consciously mirrored his relaxed shoulder posture, attempting to create a sense of calm and professionalism. "What can I do for you, Mr. McNabb?" she asked. Although she was aware that he preferred to be called Casper, she felt it imperative to maintain the formal tone required by the circumstances of their meeting.

Casper narrowed his eyes at her in a way that made her stomach churn slightly, but she pushed aside the discomfort it invoked. This was a professional setting, and she wouldn't let her personal feelings cloud her judgment.

"I want to discuss my brother's case," he stated, low and urgent, as though the matter were paramount.

She shook her head firmly, her expression resolute. "This is highly unethical, Mr. McNabb. I should be meeting with Mr. Jacobs, not the defendant's brother. This conversation crosses a line that cannot be ignored."

Casper wiped a hand across his face. He deliberately uncrossed his leg, leaned forward, and placed his elbows on his thighs, drawing her attention completely. "Okay, let's discuss when we first met," he proposed.

Taken aback by his sudden shift in focus, she shook her head with a hint of disbelief. "I'm sorry, but my personal life is not up for discussion," she retorted, her tone firm, hoping to draw a line.

He quirked an eyebrow, tilting his head slightly as if considering her response carefully. "So, no business and no personal. Why did you agree to see me then?" His question hung in the air, a weave of curiosity intertwined with an unmistakable challenge.

That was an excellent question that had been lingering unaddressed. "Well," she replied, picking up a sleek pen from her desk, letting its weight rest in her palm as she twirled it nervously. "I guess because your actions earlier today could have saved my life." The admission slipped out with unexpected honesty.

His grin widened, transforming his previously severe features into something softer, almost boyish. Seeing it sent an involuntary flutter through her stomach, catching her off guard. "Well then," he said in a slight Southern drawl, his voice low and playful. "I'm glad to be of service. Sounds like you owe me."

Her mind raced at the implications of his words. "What do you mean?" she stumbled out, her grip tightening around the pen, which had come to a standstill, mirroring the sudden tension in her chest.

"I saved your life, so you owe me a favor, and I'm calling it in." His eyes gleamed with mischief, leaving her both intrigued and apprehensive about what he might ask of her next.

"I'm not discussing your brother's case," she reiterated, a hint of frustration lacing her tone, hoping desperately that she had understood his question correctly.

"Hear me out," he insisted.

"Go ahead," she said, bracing herself, fully aware she would regret this momentary lapse in judgment within a few seconds. Yet, she acknowledged that she had to listen. It was the right thing to do.

"I know my brother's case doesn't look good on the surface, but if you could work with us on finding a way for him to get rehabilitation instead of prison time, I'd sincerely appreciate it. Consider it a gesture of goodwill, a returned favor for your saved life." His eyes searched hers, revealing the weight of his plea, the desperation echoing in his voice.

She lifted her hand slowly, signaling for silence. "That's enough, Mr. McNabb. I can't discuss this further," she asserted.

He settled back in his chair, his gaze fixed intently on her. The way he watched her made her skin prickle, as though she were exposed, laid bare before him. An electrifying sensation sent a jolt through her, making her acutely aware of every detail—his piercing eyes, the slight smirk at the corner of his mouth. She felt overwhelmed, unable to process her thoughts, pushing them aside for the moment.

"Well, what can we discuss then?" he queried, his brow arching playfully, curiosity dancing in his expression.

Nettie swallowed hard, clearing her throat as she regained her composure. She tried to shake off the butterflies that fluttered chaotically in her stomach at the sight of him, particularly the tousled blond hair that tempted her to reach out and straighten. "There's really nothing except," she began, her voice momentarily wavering, "my gratitude. Thank you again for saving my life."

Her words hung between them, heavy with meaning yet filled with an unexpressed tension hinting at uncharted emotions lingering beneath the surface.

He resumed discussing the case as if she hadn't uttered a word. "My brother isn't the best of people. I get that," he admitted, a hint of resignation in his voice. "And I understand that what he did warrants some justice. But I genuinely believe that what he needs most is rehabilitation. No one should have to be confined in a cell just for indulging in reckless behavior and acting foolishly."

The thought nagged at her mind, memories flooding back of how her parents' murderer had managed to escape proper accountability by merely attending a rehabilitation program. She straightened her back, determination brewing within her. "Is that genuinely how you see the situation?" she confronted him.

Casper shrugged, a flicker of vulnerability in his eyes. "It's my brother, after all. It's how I must cope with this reality."

Nettie sat quietly in her office, contemplating the weight of the familial stigma surrounding criminal behavior. She understood the emotional turmoil family members might endure, knowing that their loved one could be perceived as a felon. Her thoughts fixed on Aaron—though he had not yet faced trial—she couldn't shake the possibility that he could have been responsible for the tragic demise of the couple in the other car. As Casper had described them, his reckless behavior and foolish choices created an aura of danger that Nettie couldn't ignore.

With resolve, she rose from her chair, signaling the end of their meeting. "Mr. McNabb," she began, "I'm sorry, but I believe it's time for us to conclude our discussion. I have court in just a few minutes and must finalize my paperwork."

To her dismay, he remained seated, his expression unreadable. Just when the tension peaked, Nettie caught a break. Her paralegal knocked and poked her head through the door, her presence a much-needed interruption. "You're due in court in five, Miss Broussard," she informed, glancing at the man in the room.

Nettie nodded appreciatively at Joann. "Thank you. Mr. McNabb was just leaving."

However, the atmosphere shifted as Casper cocked his head, a stubborn glint in his eyes. "I can wait," he replied defiantly.

Joann sensed the underlying tension and leaned closer. "Should I send in a deputy?" she asked, concerned.

Nettie raised her hand to stop Joann. "That won't be necessary. Just give me a minute." Once Joann exited, leaving the door slightly ajar, Nettie directed her full attention back to Casper.

"Mr. McNabb," she reiterated, her tone sharpening, "as I mentioned earlier, your presence here is highly unethical. If you refuse to leave voluntarily, I'll have to instruct the deputies outside my office to escort you out of the building."

Casper held her gaze and then slowly stood, a grin creeping onto his face. "Then, let's have dinner to discuss the matter more thoroughly."

CHAPTER TEN

STUNNED AND MOMENTARILY disoriented, Nettie instinctively reached down to grasp the edge of the heavy wooden desk for stability. A whirlwind of emotions surged through her as her mind reeled. Had he genuinely just asked her out after she had explicitly told him this meeting was wholly inappropriate? After taking a deep, steadying breath to collect her scattered thoughts— because a small, rebellious part of her was tempted to accept his invitation—she firmly met his gaze. She decisively stated, "No, Mr. McNabb. Now, please leave."

"We *will* discuss this further, Nettie. Don't think for a moment that I'm giving up on this matter." With that resolve evident in his voice, he turned on his heel and strode out of her office, casting a quick nod at the deputies stationed at her door to ensure her security.

Nettie plopped heavily in her chair, feeling the world's weight on her shoulders. The meeting had spiraled out of control, crossing lines of ethical conduct that she thought were firmly in place. With a heavy heart, she could only hope that Casper would abandon his claims related to his brother's case and allow the attorney to handle it from there. Unless…. A sudden realization struck her like a bolt of lightning. She shot up from her desk, her heart racing. "He's trying to get me removed from the case and have the entire case thrown out of court, all under the guise of unethical behavior!" She couldn't believe his audacity. Son of a gun!

Determined not to let anything deter her from her goals, Nettie firmly resolved that she would not allow such obstacles to hinder her progress. As Joann reemerged at her office door, the lingering tension from her earlier encounter faded, replaced by a focused clarity.

"I'm coming," she called out, her tone firm yet brisk. With swift motions, she gathered her files—piling them into her briefcase, careful not to drop any crucial documents. In the flurry of her movements, she hurried out the door, following closely behind her paralegal, who was already navigating toward the bustling office.

As they exited, Nettie took a moment to speak with the deputies who had been assigned as her escort. "Max, please don't allow Mr. McNabb into my office anytime," she instructed with an air of authority and professionalism.

The deputy nodded in acknowledgment. "Sure thing, Miss Broussard. Are we headed to court now?" Max inquired.

Nettie, momentarily forgetting the two would escort her to court, said, "Yes. Come on," she replied, her focus shifting entirely to the day ahead. She felt the weight of the files in her briefcase and the responsibility of the cases awaiting her.

As she approached the entrance of their secondary courtroom—the very space where the tragic shooting had unfolded, now an area still being meticulously processed by law enforcement officials—she came to an abrupt halt. Her heart thundered in her chest, each beat resonating with the weight of the situation, while beads of sweat formed on her palms, betraying the rising tide of anxiety that surged through her. Though she understood it was rather far-fetched to entertain the possibility of another shooting, especially considering the extensive safeguards the sheriff's department had implemented to ensure the safety and security of all, a persistent thread of fear clung to her like a shadow, whispering unsettling doubts that refused to be silenced.

As Max opened a door further down, the din from the courtroom washed over her, pulling her from her tumultuous thoughts.

"Did you forget something?" he asked, cutting through the heavy silence.

Startled out of her reverie, she shook her head vigorously. "No, Max." Gathering her resolve, she straightened her spine, a signal of determination, and strode forward, embodying confidence with each purposeful step. She had cases to battle, fights that demanded her unwavering commitment, and justice that awaited her defense. These fleeting notions held no substance or validity, and she understood that allowing them to divert her attention would ultimately hinder her in her quest for the profound and significant sense of justice she was determined to pursue and uphold.

As she navigated her way to the prosecution table, Nettie observed Joann with a keen eye. Joann meticulously organized her extensive files and notes, each document carefully positioned to ensure a smooth presentation. Nettie, the youngest Assistant District Attorney in Biloxi's history, had been fortunate to have Joann by her side for every court appearance.

In stark contrast, Nettie's other colleagues were not afforded this luxury. Nettie reflected on this privilege, knowing that initially, it stemmed from the underlying fears of her peers regarding her ability to manage cases independently. Yet, after an impressive streak of never losing a case, Nettie had come to see their partnership as a model that the city should adopt. Together, they formed a formidable team, blending Joann's experience with Nettie's fresh perspective, proving that collaboration could yield exceptional results in the often intimidating courtroom arena.

Setting her files methodically on the polished wooden table, Nettie took a moment to scan the bustling courtroom, her keen eyes assessing the familiar surroundings. The air was thick with anxiety, punctuated by the hushed whispers of spectators awaiting the upcoming proceedings. She nodded at the bailiff, a gesture of gratitude for his earlier efforts to maintain order. Although Casper had stepped in to help, Nettie firmly believed that the bailiff, with his seasoned instincts and unwavering determination, could have subdued the shooter independently, without any assistance.

Turning to her left, Nettie watched as tall and solid Max and another deputy took their positions beside her desk, creating a protective barrier. "Is that absolutely necessary?" Nettie asked, a hint of exasperation in her voice. "Can't you sit behind me or something?"

Max flashed a reassuring grin, his eyes sparkling with determination. "No, ma'am. We need to be close to you. It's for your safety and our duty."

Nettie nodded, understanding the gravity of their roles, but she didn't fully agree with their decision. She preferred her space. However, as she returned her focus to preparing for the first fight of the afternoon, she felt the weight of the responsibilities on her shoulders. The case at hand involved another drunk driver, and the thought gnawed at her, a sharp pain in her heart. When would it ever end? This relentless cycle of recklessness and its devastating consequences seemed unyielding, and she could only hope for a glimmer of change in the future.

As the afternoon progressed, Nettie poured her heart and soul into her pursuit of justice. Each case brought new challenges, and she felt the weight of each decision as she navigated through a series of plea deals that filled the afternoon with intensity and urgency.

Her superior, a seasoned legal veteran, approached her with a proposal that weighed heavily on her mind. While he expressed unwavering confidence in her skills and belief that she could win each case, he was also acutely aware of the office's fiscal constraints. This dual focus on success and financial responsibility added a layer of complexity to her already challenging role.

Still, she fought fiercely to maintain the integrity of her pleas. She deemed it essential that the terms of the deals remained stringent. In her view, no one should escape the consequences of their actions. Justice was not merely a word for her—it was a commitment, a moral obligation to ensure that every crime was met with appropriate accountability. As she stood before the court, Nettie was resolute, channeling her passion and determination into every argument. She was driven by a profound duty to uphold the law and serve the community she loved.

As the judge pounded the gavel for the last time that day, a wave of relief washed over Nettie. The weight of the courtroom's tension began to lift. Her shoulders relaxed noticeably, as though a heavy burden had finally been set free.

Turning to Joann, who was already methodically gathering the extensive files they'd used, Nettie said, "I'll be right back. I need a moment."

Joann looked up from her work, her expression understanding as she nodded. "Go ahead. I'll take care of these for us," she assured warmly, her hands still busy sorting through the papers, but her full attention on her colleague's need for a brief respite.

Nettie felt reassured, knowing she could depend on her paralegal's meticulous attention to her files. Each document was organized to her specifications, ready to be seamlessly returned. With a steadying breath, she turned to approach the bailiff, her heart heavy yet filled with gratitude.

"Paul—" Her voice trembled, thick with emotion as she momentarily struggled to articulate the depths of her appreciation.

With a warm smile, he opened his arms wide. "Come here, young'un."

Despite the looming sense of professionalism, Nettie felt an overwhelming urge to embrace the older man who had become a steadfast figure in her life. She rushed into his embrace, feeling the weight of her struggles melt away in his presence.

"Thank you, Paul," she whispered. She felt the rush of gratitude that practically overwhelmed her.

He gently released her, allowing her to step back. She sniffled, composing herself.

"It's what I'm here for," he said with a kindness that offered solace. His words reaffirmed the bond they had formed through their shared experiences in the often harsh world of law.

She smiled softly, nodded in acknowledgment, and turned away, aware that her simple gestures conveyed a profound gratitude to the law enforcement officer. As she made her way toward her office—her ever-present escort by her side—her boss awaited her arrival.

Kevin King, the esteemed district attorney, had taken a chance on Nettie, a fresh graduate who had recently passed the bar exam without prior experience. Despite her youth at just twenty-one, he placed his unwavering trust in her abilities, and she worked tirelessly each day to prove herself worthy of his faith.

Kevin glanced at her with a knowing smile. "You've had some sort of day, haven't you, prod?" he inquired, gesturing toward her office to suggest they continue their conversation in the comfort of her workspace.

The term he used—"prod," a casual shorthand for "prodigy"—was the one quirk of his that irked Nettie. While it didn't truly hurt her feelings, it felt too informal for her taste and less professional than the relationship she had envisioned.

Once inside her office, after Max conducted his usual check for safety, Nettie sank heavily into her chair, feeling the day's weight settle on her shoulders. Across from her, Kevin settled comfortably into an armchair, his expression open and attentive.

"It has been challenging, to say the least," she confessed, ready to share the burdens of her day with the one person who truly understood the pressures she faced in her budding career.

"Well," Kevin said, his tone firm yet surprisingly gentle, "I'm ordering you to drop everything and go home for the day."

Shock swept over her as she processed his words. She couldn't remember the last time she had left the office before sunset. It was her second home, where she spent hours preparing meticulous notes and strategizing for the next morning's cases. "But I have so much to do," she protested, as she glanced at the desk overflowing with files clamoring for her attention.

"Then, come in early if it pleases you," he replied with a slight shrug, his eyes softening, "but you must go home now." He waved his hand dismissively, as if to brush aside her concerns. "Take a bubble bath, run on the beach, do something to unwind, and forget all about today."

The idea of sand between her toes began to entice her, offering a glimpse of peace amidst the chaotic whirlwind of her work life.

She would never forget this fateful day, regardless of her mundane activities. It lingered in her mind like a vivid photograph, a constant reminder of the unfolding tumultuous events. Deep down, she understood her role and the expectations placed upon her. When Kevin asserted his authority and firmly put his foot down, she knew obedience was no longer a choice but a necessity.

"Thank you," she replied. She was acutely aware that this was the response Kevin anticipated, one that would satisfy their unspoken agreement.

"Good," he replied, rising from his chair with an air of finality. He was in charge, his confident demeanor making her feel comforted and constrained. "As I understand it, Max and Ryan will be trailing behind you on your way home. However, they won't be the only ones looking out for you. In a couple of hours, they'll be relieved by another set of deputies."

He paused, shaking his head slightly as if the situation frustrated him. "I trust every one of them. They're dedicated, and their commitment will see you safe."

Nettie stood by her desk, her heart racing as her boss finally left the office. The quiet hum of fluorescent lights filled the space, amplifying the moment. She slowly pulled her purse from its designated resting place in the cluttered desk drawer, her mind momentarily drifting to thoughts of her paralegal. With a quick flick of her wrist, she picked up the receiver, her fingers hovering over the buttons as she dialed Joann's extension.

"Joann—" she started.

"I know," Joann interjected, her tone light but echoing a shared understanding. "He already told me to leave as well. I'm just waiting for you to wrap up your day."

A wave of gratitude washed over Nettie, making her feel a little lighter. "You didn't have to do that, but thank you. I'm on my way out now," she replied, a smile creeping onto her face despite the long day behind her.

"How early will you arrive tomorrow?" Joann asked.

With a heavy sigh, Nettie answered, "Early." The weight of her responsibilities settled on her shoulders once again.

"See you then."

The call ended with a soft click, leaving Nettie with her thoughts as she turned toward her office door. "Let's go, Max and Ryan," she said, her tone cheerful as she breezed past them, ready to escape the confines of her office into the evening air. The promise of tomorrow lingered in her mind, but the day was finally ending for now.

Only when she pulled into her driveway did the familiar sight of a Jeep come into view. Adrenaline surged through her, almost compelling her to slam on the brakes and retreat to her office. Why was Casper here, of all places? The memory struck her like a lightning bolt— she'd forgotten he'd followed them home, meaning he knew her address. Yet, she had never anticipated that he would arrive at her house, especially without warning.

With a deep breath, she parked her car beside the Jeep, every instinct on high alert as she caught sight of his unmistakable silhouette inside the vehicle. It was as if the universe had conspired to set this scene, turning her quiet evening into a tense moment. The sheriff's car was positioned behind them, effectively boxing them both in. As if to add to the mounting anxiety, one of the officers inside the vehicle suddenly flicked on the car's flashing lights, casting a surreal glow over the scene and illuminating her sense of dread.

CHAPTER ELEVEN

SHIFTING TO RELIEVE the pressure on his wound, Casper cursed softly under his breath as the sudden flash of blue lights illuminated the interior of his vehicle, cutting through the dim twilight. He knew that deputies would accompany her, but a flicker of hope had lingered that he might have a moment to persuade her to speak with him before they swooped in to intervene. With the situation's urgency, he realized he would have to quickly recalibrate his approach and adapt to whatever unfolded next.

The deputy he had encountered earlier that day—the one who had knocked on Nettie's door—approached his window, which Casper had already rolled down. As he prepared for the interaction, Casper's palms pressed firmly against the cool surface of the steering whccl, and tension coiled in his muscles, trying to gauge the tone of the confrontation.

"Mr. McNabb—" the deputy began, but he was quickly cut off.

"Just tell her I want to speak with her," Casper insisted calmly. "You can supervise if she feels threatened in any way," he added, the words tumbling out in a rush as his anxiety bubbled to the surface. He met the deputy's gaze, his eyes pleading for understanding. "Look, it's my brother we need to discuss. That's all." The gravity of his request hung in the air, almost palpable.

The deputy studied his face intently, glancing around the interior of his vehicle before he nodded slowly, his expression softening a bit. "Hang on," he said, turning to comply with the request.

As the deputy skirted around the Jeep, Casper steeled himself for what he anticipated would be a stern "No" from Nettie. His heart rate quickened, and uncertainty gnawed at him.

The deputy approached her, their silhouettes converging in the receding sunlight, yet the conversation remained out of his earshot. Both took turns stealing glances at him, their expressions unreadable. What exactly had the deputy conveyed to her?

Nettie gave a quick nod, and a wave of relief washed over him, albeit briefly, as he caught sight of the deputy approaching.

"She's going to speak with you on the front porch," the deputy stated firmly. "But," he interjected, his gaze unwavering, "I'll be close by."

Casper nodded in acknowledgment and gingerly stepped out of his vehicle, moving slowly to avoid an adverse reaction from the vigilant deputy. He extended a hand toward the officer, introducing himself. "Ash McNabb, but you may call me Casper."

The deputy raised an eyebrow at the introduction but said only, "Max Norton and my partner here is Ryan Watts."

Casper nodded as their hands clasped in a firm handshake. "Don't worry," he reassured Max, his tone steady, "I mean her no harm."

Max's grip tightened ever so slightly as if conveying an unspoken warning. "You'd best not," he replied, low and serious. "She's the best ADA we've ever had in these parts, and we aren't about to let anything happen to that little lady."

Though Casper wanted to roll his eyes at the patronizing term "little lady," he held his tongue, knowing that Nettie could more than fight her own battles.

"She gave you five minutes," Max stated bluntly as he stepped back, giving Casper a chance to prepare for the conversation ahead. "The clock is ticking."

Casper nodded in understanding and followed Nettie as she ascended the brick steps leading up to her inviting front porch. The porch, bathed in the warm glow of the front porchlight, featured a charming small white wicker loveseat adorned with vibrant, plush cushions in hues of sunflower yellow and sky blue, perfectly complemented by two matching wicker chairs positioned on either side. When Nettie gracefully lowered herself into one of the chairs, Casper paused to assess his predicament. He glanced at the seemingly delicate chairs, pondering the possibility: Would one of those dainty chairs be sturdy enough to support his tall, six-foot-two frame without collapsing beneath him?

As if intuitively grasping the conflict within him, Nettie let out a soft chuckle. "They're stronger than you'd expect," she remarked almost playfully, a glint in her gaze. "But why don't you take the loveseat? It's sturdier than it looks."

He released a soft, almost reluctant sigh that mingled resignation with contemplation and shrugged slightly, acknowledging the weight of his circumstances. He realized that standing defiantly would only force her into a defensive posture, which he wished to avoid at all costs. With an internal battle of reluctance, he cautiously lowered himself onto the loveseat—the furniture he had always regarded more as a decorative ornament than a genuine, functional choice for the numerous porches and patios he had frequented. To his surprise, as he sank into the cushions, he felt an unexpected plushness that enveloped him in comfort, starkly contrasting with his rigid perceptions about the purpose of such furnishings.

"Before you begin, Mr. McNabb—"

"Casper," he responded in a low, almost gravelly tone, frustration evident in his voice. He paused momentarily, aware that his terse reply wasn't the right approach. Taking a deep breath, he softened his expression and added, "I wish you'd just call me Casper. Mr. McNabb makes me feel older than I am, and I'd rather we keep things a bit more casual, don't you think?"

"Although I recognize that you *are* significantly older than I am, I feel compelled by customary formalities to maintain a formal tone in our communication. After all, we're engaged in a professional meeting rather than establishing a personal friendship. As I have previously stated, the current situation is unethical and unsustainable and cannot persist. I promised to allocate a few moments for this discussion, but let me clarify: this marks our final meeting, Mr. McNabb."

As she passionately argued her point, he couldn't help but notice her body's subtle yet captivating movements. With each gesture, her head gracefully turned, framing her face beautifully, while her hands danced in the air, emphasizing the weight of her words. He was entranced by how her expressive eyes sparkled with conviction, illuminating her entire presence. How had he overlooked her undeniable beauty all this time? Even clad in her formal, fitted blue suit that hinted at an uptight demeanor, with her hair tightly pulled back from her neck, she radiated a stunning aura that left him almost breathless.

"Mr. McNabb, did you hear me?"

Casper felt a sudden jolt, yanked from his unprofessional musings about Nettie, swirling in his mind like a whirlwind. He realized he needed to refocus, gather his thoughts, and regain his composure. This was not the time for distractions. He had to think clearly and strategically. "I wanted to know if you'll fight for no bail in my brother's arraignment?"

Nettie's gaze bore into him, her dark eyes searching his face. Just when he began to fear that silence would settle between them, she finally nodded. "I am."

"Are you going to fight for the maximum sentence?" The question hung in the air, loaded with anticipation.

She narrowed her eyes as if she weighed where this conversation might lead. "I am. He could have killed someone, and that's not just a possibility—it's a reality. Just think about it: he seriously injured the couple in the other car, leaving them with injuries that may forever change their lives."

He paused, momentarily taken aback. "But he didn't kill anyone." He attempted to grasp the full extent of her conviction, even as doubt crept into his mind.

"It's his second DUI, and only because we've managed to catch him this time," she said, her tone firm yet layered with frustration. She stood up gracefully, smoothing her skirt as she did, her movements precise and deliberate. "I'm sorry, Mr. McNabb, but that is all I have today. I'll see you in court."

Casper rose from his seat, a rush of sensations overwhelming him as he caught a whiff of her intoxicating perfume—a sweet blend that lingered in the air, causing his heart to race. He couldn't help but wonder what it was about this woman—this much younger woman—who had an effortless ability to distract him from his pressing objectives. His mind, usually sharp and focused on assisting his brother and alleviating the mounting pressures from their mother, was now engulfed in thoughts of her. The warm light reflected in her hair, framing her face just so, making it harder for him to concentrate on anything beyond the stirring in his chest as he watched her walk away, a blend of admiration and longing stirring within him.

"Nettie—" His voice faltered, uncertainty clouding his mind as he struggled to find the right words. The moment's urgency surged through him. He couldn't allow her to walk away, not like this.

With her hand poised to insert her keys into the lock, she paused and turned, her expression a mix of curiosity and exasperation. "Mr. McNabb—"

He dropped back onto the plush loveseat, the furniture creaking as he leaned forward, elbows resting on his thighs. Fingers tangled in his hair, he felt the frustration seep out in a breathless "Christ."

"You know, Mr. McNabb, I may curse from time to time, but I'd never use the Lord's name in vain. It bothers me when others do."

After a long, weighted moment, she sighed heavily, a profound sound that seemed to resonate in the open air. With a reluctant grace, she returned to her seat, the tension between them palpable. "What?" her tone sharp, cutting through the silence that enveloped them.

Casper turned his gaze toward her, desperately trying to project confidence while suppressing the tumult of uncertainty within him. He took a deep breath. "I can't let you just walk away."

Nettie stiffened noticeably and looked at him defiantly and cautiously. "Is that a threat?" she asked, her jaw tight as she clenched her hands in her lap, her knuckles turning white. The sight of her tension made him wince, aware that the stakes of the moment had escalated.

"No," he hurried to clarify, his heart racing. "It's not like that…. There's just something about you that draws me in.…"

She raised her brows, skepticism evident in her expression. "And?" she pressed, clearly unfazed by his attempt to explain. The air between them crackled with tension, leaving Casper grappling for the right words to bridge the growing distance between them.

He exhaled deeply, the weight of his admission hanging heavily in the air. "Okay. Here it goes. I want you."

For the first time in their meetings, she seemed taken aback by his words, a flicker of hesitation crossing her face, followed by a resolute calm.

"I know—" he began, hoping to bridge the gap she created.

"No. Mr. McNabb, while I can acknowledge that you are a good-looking man, more significant matters are at play here. You are more than a decade older than I am, and perhaps more importantly, you are the brother of a defendant." She rose from her seat with an air of finality, her posture firm and unwavering. "This is our last meeting, except in the courtroom. I must ask you to leave, Mr. McNabb."

Casper sprang to his feet, adrenaline coursing through him. "Nettie—" he began, with a blend of urgency and reluctance.

"Miss Broussard will do just fine," Nettie interjected decisively, her gaze shifting firmly to the front yard, where dusk seemed to swell with tension. "Max, he's ready to leave."

Nodding in acknowledgment, the sheriff's deputy strode purposefully toward them. But deep down, Casper felt the weight of reality pressing against him. He knew he had exhausted all the politeness and respect extended to him during this tense encounter.

"I guess, then, I'll see you in court, Miss Broussard," he stated, hinting a bit of resignation in his tone. He made his way down the steps, each footfall echoing the gravity of the situation, and approached his Jeep. He started the vehicle, listening to the engine roar to life. Still, he remained stationary, his mind swirling with confusion as the second deputy maneuvered their cruiser to create a clear path for his departure.

Casper stole one last glance at Nettie, who stood on her patio, her expression a mix of concern and determination as she watched him. As he pulled out onto the road, uncertainty gnawed at him. He hadn't anticipated this moment, and with it came the stark realization that his next move would not involve his brother's case—something he had been dreading yet felt compelled to confront.

No. Something was intriguing about Nettie that pulled at him, a magnetic allure he found impossible to ignore. He felt compelled to delve deeper, to uncover the essence of what made her so captivating. Yet, he knew he couldn't let this burgeoning attraction for a younger woman divert his focus from his paramount goal: getting his brother into rehab, a task that weighed heavily on his heart. However, this newfound curiosity about Nettie persisted, reminding him that he was at a crossroads. The opportunity to explore the enigmatic quality she exuded beckoned him, but he was acutely aware that he could not afford to be sidetracked from his responsibility. It was a delicate balance—his longing to discover more about her and his unwavering commitment to his brother's recovery.

In all his thirty-six years, he had encountered numerous women whose personalities varied widely and whose lives wove intricate tapestries of experiences. Each one had left a distinct mark on his memory. Yet, none had managed to divert him from the responsibilities that consumed him—be they military missions fraught with danger or civilian tasks rooted in everyday life. But now, as he had stood before Nettie, he had found himself unsettled. Something was captivating about her petite frame and vibrant spirit that threatened to disrupt his steadfast focus, making him question what made her so different from all the others he had known.

He found himself again at that crossroads, feeling the weight of an enormous responsibility pressing down on his shoulders. His resolve needed fortification, for he felt the intense pull between two competing priorities: advocating fiercely for his brother's case and nurturing a genuine relationship with Nettie. Until this moment, he had never tasted defeat. Every challenge he faced had been met with triumph. Yet, he realized that attempting to excel in both endeavors could lead to unforeseen consequences. Someone would inevitably bear the burden of his divided attention, and the last thing he wanted was for it to be Nettie—sharp-witted and spirited. Still, even more so, he could not allow it to be his brother, whose fate hung precariously in the balance as he fought on his behalf.

He realized how fucked he was no matter his next move.

CHAPTER TWELVE

"NETTIE, ARE YOU all right?" Max asked, concern etched on his face as he stood beside her, both watching intently as Casper—no, Mr. McNabb—drove away in his Jeep, the sound of the engine fading into the distance.

Their meeting had been an unexpected confrontation, unwelcome due to his unsettling connection to a pending case that weighed heavily on her mind. Despite her resolve to remain detached, his presence ignited a complex storm of emotions within her —feelings she was reluctant to explore or acknowledge. She couldn't help but feel vulnerable as she processed the reality that the man, eleven years her senior, had expressed a desire for her.

Was she merely some coveted youth trophy to him, something to be won? Or was it all part of a cunning manipulation designed to sway her away from pursuing justice against his brother? The thought gnawed at her conscience, filling her with doubt and confusion as she questioned her worth and the true nature of his intentions. Would she allow herself to become just another piece on his chessboard?

"Nettie?" Max asked in a whisper, almost as if he was afraid to disturb her thoughts.

Nettie shook her head slightly, trying to dispel the swirling thoughts that clouded her mind, and smiled. "I'm fine, Max. Why don't you and Ryan come in for some dinner? I can whip it up in no time." As she spoke, an echo of uncertainty tugged at her. She realized she wasn't entirely sure what she could prepare given her current pantry state. The last time she had stocked her supplies felt like ages ago, and the empty shelves in her refrigerator were a stark reminder. A thought of her freezer recalled it was nearly barren, save for a tub of ice cream, a comforting treat she kept for nights like this when her racing thoughts occasionally strayed from the grip of the law.

Max pondered for a moment, his brow furrowed. "We'd appreciate the meal, but we'll switch over before you have time to cook," he replied, his tone a blend of gratitude and concern.

Relieved at being excused from the duty, she took a deep breath and nodded, her mind drifting to the comfort of home. She inserted the key into the lock as she approached her front door, feeling the cool metal against her fingers. Max cleared his throat, instantly pulling her attention back to the present. She turned to him, a smile spreading across her face despite the tension in the air. "Change your mind already?" she asked, half-joking but hopeful that he might relent.

Max, however, shook his head firmly, his expression serious. "Nettie, you know I have to clear your house before you can enter," he replied, his tone leaving no room for debate.

Nettie's heart sank as she realized her earlier relief was fleeting. Temporarily lost in that relief, she had completely overlooked the potential danger lurking within her walls. The intrusion into her life—the precautions Max was taking—meant he truly cared for her safety, yet it felt invasive and stifling. She hadn't fully registered the weight of that responsibility or the implications of someone else's control over her personal space. It struck her with a mix of gratitude and frustration. She was grateful for Max's vigilance but frustrated by the sudden reminder of her precarious situation.

She stepped back, creating space for Max to slip past her on the concrete porch, and offered him a polite smile. "Please do," she said. As Max moved on, Ryan approached the porch with a purposeful stride, glancing back to ensure everything was in order.

With a sigh, she turned her gaze toward Ryan as he stood nearby. "Tough day, prosecutor?" he inquired.

The day's weight hung heavily in the air, prompting an unspoken understanding between them.

Nettie's first instinct was to deny her feelings, a reflex borne out of shock and disbelief. However, as the weight of the day pressed down on her, she felt an overwhelming fatigue wash over her. With a reluctant resignation, she sank into the comfortable embrace of a wicker chair, letting out a heavy sigh that seemed to carry the burdens of her emotions. "Yes," she admitted softly. Had it really been only that morning when the shooting had shattered her reality? The day had unfolded with relentless activity, each moment packed with the chaos of afternoon court proceedings and the formidable presence of Mr. McNabb. Amid all this turmoil, she had forced herself to shove the traumatic experience into the recesses of her mind, trying to ignore its haunting presence. Yet, it lingered, waiting to be acknowledged.

"Don't worry," Ryan said. "We won't let anything happen to you."

She smiled warmly at him, captivated by his endearing, boyish charm, which radiated an aura of innocence and enthusiasm. Ryan was almost the same age as she was, and memories of him asking her out on a date filled her mind—an invitation that had stirred a flurry of emotions within her. She believed she should be drawn to this kind of man—vibrant and close to her age instead of someone significantly older like Mr. McNabb.

Yet, a persistent whisper in her mind reminded her that Mr. McNabb was only eleven years her senior, a difference that felt minor in the broad spectrum of her life experiences. At just twenty-five years old, the weight of those eleven years felt daunting, as if they represented an insurmountable chasm in their worlds, filled with complexities and expectations that she was not sure she was ready to bridge.

Nettie felt an overwhelming wave of frustration wash over her. Why was her mind stubbornly fixated on Mr. McNabb? He was, in every conceivable way, her adversary in the courtroom. To her, he epitomized everything that obstructed her quest for justice, failing to comprehend the depth of her commitment to uphold the law. Even his brother, involved in the tangled web of their legal battle, was no exception to her disdain.

Max stepped out as the door swung open, his expression brightening as he smiled reassuringly at her. "All clear," he declared.

Thank goodness, Nettie thought, relief flooding her senses. She felt utterly spent, unable to take on another challenge that day. The warm glow of the porch light illuminated the scene, casting a soft light over the two deputies standing beside her, their faces taut with watchfulness. It enveloped her in a cocoon of cautious safety at the end of a long day.

"Thank you, both," she said with genuine gratitude. "I truly wish there was something I could do to express my appreciation more properly."

Max chuckled softly, a warm smile spreading across his face. "Well, Ryan would probably appreciate a date," he suggested playfully, his eyes twinkling with mischief.

Nettie's gaze flicked to Ryan, who immediately turned away, his cheeks turning a deep shade of crimson as the embarrassment washed over him. The moment was both amusing and endearing, capturing the camaraderie among them.

"But what we'd both like," Max continued, his tone shifting to a more serious note, "is for you to continue to trust us and to fight hard for the law." His words hung in the air, a reminder of the shared commitment they all bore.

She nodded, feeling a surge of determination. Upholding the law was a duty she could embrace wholeheartedly. It was her true calling. While sweetly tempting, the idea of a date with Ryan could wait. What mattered most was her unwavering resolve in the pursuit of justice.

"I can do that." She turned, the soft creak of the door punctuating her resolve, as she slipped inside her cozy house. The door clicked shut behind her, and she leaned against it, feeling its solid weight like a lifeline holding her steady. With her eyes closed, she inhaled deeply, savoring the familiar scent, and waged an internal battle to push away the thoughts swirling in her mind. The day had been long and taxing. She knew she needed to meditate, to work through the tension that clung to her like a second skin.

As she opened her eyes, the world came back into focus, vibrant and welcoming. She dropped her keys into a blue, seashell-shaped tray on a side table—a small, decorative piece that reminded her of sun-soaked beaches and tranquil waves. Her purse thudded quietly onto the floor, the day's burdens momentarily forgotten. She kicked off her heels, feeling the instant relief spread through her feet, and with a practiced motion, bent down to retrieve her navy blue shoes.

With a purpose, she made her way to the bedroom, eager to change into something more comfortable. She rifled through her drawer, selecting a soft, worn pair of pajamas—something cozy yet unpretentious, just in case the deputies decided to check on her later in the evening. A sudden thought struck her: she hadn't inquired who would relieve Ryan and Max for their evening shift.

But then she brushed the thought aside, convincing herself it didn't matter. If everything unfolded as planned, she wouldn't see them anyway—just Max and Ryan in the early morning light when she arrived at work. Yet, a subtle worry tugged at her mind. She was set to leave earlier than usual tomorrow. Well, perhaps only time could tell the outcome of the night ahead.

After meditating, Nettie was enveloped in indecision. The calming practice usually brought clarity, but tonight was different. Instead of diving into her usual routine of reviewing dense case files and meticulously preparing for court, she faced an unexpected void. Her boss had explicitly instructed her not to take work home tonight, leaving her with a rare evening.

The house was spotless, a testament to the diligent weekly house cleaner who had come by just two days ago, meticulously scrubbing every surface until everything sparkled. With her surroundings tidy, the only mess left was the clutter of her scattered and unresolved thoughts. She considered turning on the television, but scrolling through the channels usually made her feel more lost. Besides the evening news, which she found dull, she hadn't watched television in ages and felt utterly out of touch with what was popular.

Books filled the shelves in the living room, their spines well-worn, but the prospect of diving into another story held little appeal. Instead, an idea began to blossom —maybe a bubble bath would do her some good. It had been an eternity since she had indulged in such a relaxing luxury, and the thought of warm water soothing her body seemed irresistible.

Setting her mind on that comforting notion, Nettie went to the bathroom. She envisioned a glass of crisp white wine to sip while she soaked, soft music playing in the background to create an oasis of calm. As she prepared, she could almost taste the wine, its coolness contrasting with the warmth she was about to envelop herself in.

When the water warmed under her hand in the old, claw-foot tub, she added bath salts and a splash of bubble bath, watching as the water transformed into a frothy cloud of bubbles. The scent wafting up from the bath products was unfamiliar. It had been a gift from Joann last Christmas, and she hadn't thought to use it until now. Here it was September, and the bottle still sat unopened— a testament to her busy life and the neglect of small pleasures. But tonight, she would savor the moment, letting the warm embrace of the bath wash away the remnants of a long, taxing day and perhaps even reignite a part of herself that had been submerged beneath the surface for far too long.

As she settled into the warm embrace of the bathwater, the soothing heat enveloped her body, lulling her into a gentle state of relaxation. As she drifted off, her mind, instead of finding peace, was a swirling storm of emotions and thoughts. Images of Mr. McNabb flickered in her mind like shadows, his deep voice echoing the words he had spoken so earnestly: he wanted her. His intense gaze, filled with a mixture of desire and vulnerability, consumed her thoughts, stirring a blend of anticipation and confusion within her as she floated between sleep and consciousness.

CHAPTER THIRTEEN

NEAR HIS HOME, Casper suddenly slammed on the brakes of his rugged Jeep. The tires rebelled against the gravel of the seldom-used back road. Ahead of him, illuminated by the stark beams of his headlights, were two tiny shapes frozen in the middle of the road. Irritation bubbled up inside him—what was it with people and animals always getting in his way when he drove? On this secluded stretch of gravel, void of any other traffic, he quickly bounded from his vehicle, heart racing with concern as he slowly approached the two figures.

As Casper approached, the soft, frantic meows emanating from their little bodies reached his ears, revealing the truth well before he could clearly define their shapes: two very young kittens, hardly old enough to be away from their mother. Their fur was a mess, likely dusty from the road, and their wide, frightened eyes glowed in the dim light.

Realizing the mother cat might be nearby, he instinctively called out into the night, hoping to coax her from hiding. Deep down, he understood that a wild cat would likely avoid him, but the hope of catching a glimpse of her, to assure himself that the kittens were safe, filled his thoughts. Yet, as he looked around, dread gnawed at him; the realization hit him hard—they were not secure at all, stranded in the middle of the roadway, exposed and vulnerable to any incoming vehicle.

As Casper sensed the imminent danger of leaving them, his protective instincts surged like a tide. Realizing the situation's urgency, he sprang into action, moved by a profound sense of duty. With careful attentiveness, he knelt, reaching out gently to scoop up the vulnerable little bodies in his solid yet tender grasp. Each delicate movement was deliberate, ensuring he didn't startle them further, as he aimed to shield them from any potential harm that loomed nearby, like foxes and other wild animals.

"Hello, little kitties," he said softly as he cradled them delicately in front of the luminous glow of his headlights. The night enveloped them, but the Jeep cut a comforting light upon the two tiny creatures in his hands. He had a striking tuxedo kitten, its fur a glossy black broken only by a distinctive black line that perfectly mimicked a fashionable mustache. Beside it, a calico kitten, a tapestry of orange, black, and white patches, squirmed with eager curiosity.

The kittens, vibrant with energy, climbed up his shirt with surprising agility, their minuscule claws pricking at his skin like tiny needles. Instead of jerking away in discomfort, he welcomed their playful antics, allowing the soft, rhythmic brush of their furry bodies against his neck to bring a smile to his face. The purring resonated like a gentle engine, harmonizing with the stillness of the night, creating a sense of shared contentment.

"Oh, no. I can't have two cats," he informed them with a mix of amusement and resignation, fully aware they would remain blissfully ignorant of the gravity of his words. They gazed at him with wide, innocent eyes, their world a wondrous play of sights and sounds. "Let's get you home. Mom surely will want something to nurture now that my brother is out of her reach," he added, a hint of laughter as he imagined their new lives unfolding together in his bustling household.

Grateful for the protective cover of the top on the Jeep, Casper carefully gathered the two tiny kittens and gently placed them on the floorboard of the front passenger seat. Worrying about their safety, he wished for something better to secure them with—like a harness or a crate—but decided it would have to suffice for their brief journey home.

The curious, fluffy, and wide-eyed kittens began exploring their new surroundings. They eagerly scrambled into the passenger seat, their tiny paws seeking out the warmth of Casper's lap. Just as he would reach down to lift one kitten off, the other would nimbly leap over the center console, determined to nestle in against him. Their playful antics brought forth a light chuckle from him, a sound that reflected the joy they infused into his thoughts. Each squirm and mew was irresistibly adorable, and he couldn't help but smile.

When he arrived home, he let the kittens enjoy a little more adventure. As he stepped through the door, both perched on his shoulders like fluffy companions.

His mother appeared in the doorway with an incredulous expression. "You take those rodents right out of here!" she exclaimed, her hands on her hips.

Feeling exasperated and determined, Casper replied, "Ma, they're not rodents! They're kittens. I found them on the road and thought you might like a new pet to keep you company."

His mother's initial surprise turned to disapproval as she huffed in response. "Well, I don't! They probably have fleas crawling all over them. Get them out of this house this instant, Ash McNabb!"

Despite the warmth of the kittens snuggled against him, he felt a twinge of frustration, knowing that his attempt to bring joy home was met with resistance.

Knowing he had no choice but to leave if he wanted to maintain peaceful relations with his mother, Casper resigned himself. The air was filled with the comforting sound of the kittens purring contentedly in his ears, a balm to his troubled spirit as he stepped out the door. He took a deep breath, reflecting on his decision and its implications for his family dynamics.

Now what? He reached for his phone and dialed the only other person he'd spoken with since his return, hoping JD might provide a reprieve from this unexpected responsibility that had unexpectedly landed in his lap. With a grueling work schedule and frequent, prolonged absences from home, owning a pet was out of the question unless he had a reliable designated pet sitter—a role he had not arranged for and had no intention of seeking.

"JD," he said with a hint of urgency when his friend picked up the call. "I found two tiny kittens abandoned in the middle of the road. Would you—"

"Oh no!" JD interrupted before Casper could finish his thought. "We already have two cats at home. While I know my son and Cassie would absolutely adore having more, we aren't moving to a bigger space yet."

Frustration washed over Casper as he contemplated his options. "Well, then, what the hell do I do with them? I can't bear the thought of dropping them off at the shelter, especially since it's closed for the day," he replied, feeling the weight of the situation pressing down on him.

"Do you know anyone else who can take care of them?" JD asked, his tone serious but still supportive.

Casper racked his brain, desperately looking for anyone who could help. But as the minutes ticked by, he could think of no one suitable. Then, an idea suddenly struck him like a bolt of lightning. "I might have an idea," he said, a spark of hope igniting in his voice. "I'll reach out to you tomorrow."

JD chuckled softly. "Glad I could help you brainstorm a solution," he replied warmly before they ended the call, leaving Casper with new possibilities to explore.

Knowing he couldn't arrive with the flea-ridden kittens without a solution to alleviate their discomfort, he hurried toward the pet store, relieved that it remained open that evening. The soft glow of the store's neon sign welcomed him as he pushed through the glass doors.

Inside, he clutched the two kittens against his chest, their tiny bodies trembling slightly as they peered around with wide, curious eyes. The employees, a lively bunch with genuine smiles, immediately noticed the precious little furballs. They gushed over their adorable features and fluffy coats, their enthusiasm infectious. With their help, he filled his shopping cart with an array of essentials: flea treatments, soft bedding, nutritious food, and an assortment of toys to keep the lively duo entertained.

After what felt like he had spent nearly a month's pay on cat supplies, he finally made his way to the checkout. The cashier, captivated by the kittens, cooed at them as he paid, her fingers gently grazing their velvety fur. Satisfied and hopeful, he secured the little tykes in a sturdy, padded pet carrier, fastening it safely in the back seat of his Jeep. This time, they were snugly buckled in, ready for their new journey together, their future brighter with his newfound determination to care for them.

He held onto a flicker of hope that his plan would succeed. As he navigated the winding roads to his destination, he turned his attention to the tiny creatures in the cage behind him. The soft, fragile kittens seemed to sense his nervousness, their mews filling the air with curiosity and distress.

"Now, we don't really know how she'll react when she sees you, but I truly believe she has a big heart, ready to embrace new friends," he said reassuringly, glancing at the kittens who stared up at him with wide, innocent eyes through the bars on the front of the carrier. "There's a chance she might kick me out, but I trust she'll take you in. And if things don't go as planned, we'll find a way to work together."

The little furballs continued to meow, their desperation to escape the confines of their cage palpable as they pawed at the bars, eager for freedom.

As Casper parked his Jeep, a sense of unease washed over him. The warm glow of the streetlights illuminated the scene, but it also revealed a new presence. A new pair of sheriff's deputies now stood guard at Nettie's home, their imposing figures casting long shadows on the pavement. Would they allow him to pass? Casper felt a knot tighten in his stomach. He truly hoped they would.

Before he could cut the engine and take a deep breath, a burly, dark-skinned deputy approached, his expression a mixture of scrutiny and authority. "How may I help you?" he asked, his tone firm but not unkind.

Casper flashed what he hoped was his most disarming smile, which radiated warmth and sincerity. "I'm here to see Nettie," he replied, deliberately opting for the relaxed familiarity of her name to make the moment feel less intimidating.

The deputy raised an eyebrow, clearly unimpressed. "She's not expecting company tonight," he stated with a hint of skepticism, crossing his arms over his chest.

"No," Casper admitted, his heart racing a little faster. "She's not expecting me, but I have a surprise for her." He hoped this would lend some credibility to his visit.

The deputy's gaze narrowed suspiciously, the soft glow of the streetlight catching the corners of his eyes. "What exactly is this surprise?" he probed, leaning slightly forward as if to glimpse Casper's intentions.

Without hesitation, Casper gestured toward the backseat of his Jeep. The kittens' meows erupted in a symphony of tiny, pleading sounds. Their innocence was almost palpable, as if they understood the situation's urgency. "I brought some kittens!" he exclaimed, feeling the weight of how their furry little bodies might bring joy to Nettie.

The deputy shook his head, a hint of a smile creeping onto his face despite himself. "She needs a pet, but I'll have to clear you first," he replied, conferring with the other deputy who stood a few paces away. "Ask Miss Broussard if she's up for company," he instructed, nodding toward the entrance to the home.

Turning back to Casper, the deputy asked, "What did you say your name was?"

Casper felt a rush of hope mixed with apprehension as he prepared to answer, knowing that every word that followed would determine the outcome of this encounter. "Tell her it's Casper, and it's not about my brother's case or…or what we discussed earlier. Tell her I have a… peace offering."

CHAPTER FOURTEEN

A SUDDEN, JARRING noise pierced the tranquility of the bathroom, startling Nettie from her dreamy slumber in the tub. She blinked her eyes open, finding the bubbles that had once danced playfully on the surface long gone, leaving only the milky whiteness of the dissolved bath salts swirling around her. As the knocking sound erupted again, this time more insistent, Nettie felt an adrenaline rush. She leaped from the tub, splashing cool water in her wake, the droplets glistening in the room's soft light. With a sense of urgency, she wrapped herself in her oversized robe, its fabric soft against her damp skin, and hurried to the door, the rest of her body still glistening and unbothered by the chill of the air.

The third knock reverberated through the hallway, sharp and insistent. It was accompanied by a voice calling out to her with an urgency that hinted at desperation.

"I'm coming!" she called back, her heart racing as the knock echo lingered in her ears.

In a flurry, she darted to the mirror, glancing at her reflection to ensure her attire was both appropriate and presentable, adjusting the coverage over her breasts before heading toward the door, a mix of anticipation and anxiety bubbling within her.

Checking the peephole carefully, she caught a glimpse of the familiar deputy uniform, a sight that stirred a mix of anxiety and annoyance within her. Reluctantly, she opened the door just about three inches, enough to see him clearly while keeping her space intact. "Yes?" she asked cautiously, silently hoping he didn't expect her to invite him to step inside her home.

The deputy nodded, his face solemn yet polite. "Deputy Wright, ma'am. I'm afraid you have a visitor. A man calling himself Casper," he stated.

Unfrickenbelievable, she thought, an exasperated sigh welling up inside her. Did the man ever give up on pestering her? "I don't wish to see him—ever," she replied, her conviction clear as she hardened her expression against any possibility of swaying.

The deputy briefly swayed back and forth on his feet, a slight fidget revealing his discomfort. "I get that, ma'am. Truly, I do," he said with a nod. "But you might want to consider seeing him this one time. He has a peace offering, as he calls it," he added, implying that this could be more than just a casual visit.

She cast an appraising glance at her attire, her fingers brushing the soft fabric of her bathrobe. "I'm not dressed for company, so tell him to bring it to court."

The deputy shifted his weight, glancing at her and then at the ground, his brow furrowed. "I don't think he can do that, ma'am."

A wave of confusion swept over her. "What does he have for this…peace offering?" She raised an eyebrow, suspecting it must be something rather unique or fragile for the deputy to appear so hesitant, like a child reluctant to confess mischief.

"It's kittens, ma'am."

Her heart skipped a beat. *Kittens?* What was she supposed to do with a handful of energetic furballs? Why would he assume she needed live animals to care for amidst her chaotic and demanding schedule? True, cats could often fend for themselves, darting about with a grace that made them appear almost regal. Still, kittens were an entirely different matter—needy and demanding, with their adorable antics that often led to endless distraction.

Yet, as thoughts of tiny mewling creatures danced through her mind, she couldn't help but feel a glimmer of intrigue mixed with excitement at the idea of those little furballs. "Show him in," she said.

The deputy cleared his throat, uncertainty still evident in his countenance. "Did you want time to dress?"

Realizing she was still clad in her bathrobe, she couldn't help but laugh lightly, a sound that contrasted sharply with the serious nature of his presence. "Give me three minutes, then send him in." With that, she took a deep breath, ready to transform her disheveled appearance into something suitable for the unexpected visit.

As Nettie hurriedly pulled on jeans and a T-shirt, her heart raced with excitement and trepidation. She couldn't shake the nagging thought that inviting Mr. McNabb into her home might be reckless, especially without anyone else. Although she felt no real fear of him and didn't believe he intended her any harm, the weight of the situation loomed large in her mind. He was, after all, on the opposing side of a legal case.

This reality gnawed at her and refused to be dismissed. Ignoring it could lead to catastrophic consequences—the case could be thrown out of court entirely, or worse, her professional standing could be jeopardized, risking her disbarment.

Nettie took a deep breath, her thoughts racing as she buttoned her jeans. She could only pray that the deputies would keep their mouths shut about what transpired within the confines of her home. If word got back to her boss, she would undoubtedly be pulled from the case, and it handed off to her already overburdened colleague, who had more than enough on his plate. The thought of it caused her stomach to churn as she clenched her fists, vowing to navigate this precarious situation with all the cunning she could muster.

When a firm knock resonated through her cozy living room, she had just slipped her feet into well-worn, casual shoes that felt like old friends. Smoothing her trembling hand down the front of her T-shirt to calm her nerves, she walked eagerly toward the door. The earlier, resounding words of Mr. McNabb echoed in her mind, declaring with earnest intensity that he "wanted her." Why did those words send a giddy flutter through her stomach, igniting a curious blend of excitement and anxiety?

As she opened the door, her breath caught in her throat at the sight before her. Standing there was a sheepish-looking Mr. McNabb, his cheeks slightly flushed, clearly hesitant. He held up a gray pet carrier, from which the plaintive meows of two tiny kittens emanated, their soft cries tugging at her heartstrings. An overwhelming urge to scoop up the little creatures and cradle them in her lap surged through her.

"Come in, Mr. McNabb," she said. "I'm not entirely sure why you're standing there with live animals, but I'm curious about the story behind this unexpected visit." Her gaze shifted to the kittens, whose wide eyes observantly took in their new surroundings, her heart already winning over to their adorable charm.

Mr. McNabb stepped into the room, his presence immediately commanding attention. He took a moment to survey her, his gaze raking over her from head to toe, instilling a sense of vulnerability that made her instinctively retreat. Perhaps it had been a grave mistake to allow him entrance, she thought, as a shiver of unease coursed through her. The mewing kittens seemed to mock her unease, a clever distraction he might have orchestrated to draw her into another conversation about his brother's troubling case.

"I'm sorry to intrude," he said quickly, almost too hastily, as if trying to mask a deeper motive. "I don't know anyone else who could take them at such short notice, and the shelter down the street is closed for the day. Besides," he added, "I wouldn't feel right dropping them off there, not with their already overcrowding." His eyes flickered with a hint of urgency, urging her to see the dilemma he was portraying, yet another emotional layer added to the already complicated situation.

"I can appreciate that you took the time to consider my situation," she replied, steady yet tinged with a hint of frustration. "But I can't possibly care for live animals, not with the demanding nature of my work schedule." Her days were a relentless cycle of labor, beginning at the crack of dawn and extending long after the sun dipped below the horizon. Often, she would find herself tethered to her tasks for fourteen to fifteen grueling hours, leaving little room for anything else in her life. The thought of nurturing another living being that required regular feeding and constant attention seemed impossibly burdensome under her current circumstances.

"I took care of that." His tone was reassuring as he set the sturdy carrier gently onto the plush carpet that adorned the floor. With a smooth motion, he opened the door behind him, allowing two-night deputies to step into the room. They entered carrying an array of supplies: bags filled with premium cat food, a soft blanket for comfort, and an assortment of toys designed to stimulate a feline's curiosity. The sight of their arms brimming with the necessities for a cat's survival added to the weight of her reservations, making her wonder just how much care was being thrust upon her amid her hectic life.

As the deputies departed, Mr. McNabb warmly expressed his gratitude to them as if they were old friends parting after an extended visit. Nettie found herself with a growing sense of unease. What was happening in her life? Had she truly lost control, spiraling into a situation she never anticipated?

"I went ahead and purchased a dual automatic feeder for the kittens, ensuring they are fed even during your late nights at work. I also invested in a self-cleaning litter box.

It means you won't have to worry about any mess after a long day," he said, pridefully brimming.

Nettie couldn't help but acknowledge his thoughtfulness. He had clearly put significant effort into considering her needs before dropping off the kittens, not to mention the considerable amount he had spent on these essential items for their care.

"Still," she said, hesitating, torn between her desire to hold the tiny animals and the urge to keep her heart guarded, unwilling to form any attachments.

"Just hear me out," he implored. "I'm asking you to foster them until I can find a permanent home. I genuinely don't know anyone else who could assist me like this. And just to be clear, this has nothing to do with my brother's case if that's what you might suspect."

Nettie had briefly considered the possibility that he was trying to bribe or charm her into swaying the court's decision in his brother's favor. However, she quickly set that thought aside, recognizing through his sincere demeanor that his primary concern lay with the kittens' well-being rather than any ulterior motives regarding his brother's situation. The gravity of responsibility pressed down on her as she weighed her feelings against the innocent lives of the kittens before her.

"Let's see them," she said, her voice betraying her excitement despite her conscious resolve to resist. She felt a thrill, knowing that once she held one of the creatures, she would be irrevocably obsessed, which was precisely why she had never ventured into the shelter. Instead, she had contributed through the pet store's charitable fund, preserving her emotional distance.

Mr. McNabb's grin expanded, reminiscent of a child's delight in a candy store. He knelt, lifted the lid of the pet carrier, and carefully extracted two irresistibly adorable kittens, presenting the calico one to her with a flourish.

Her heart instantly leaped, overwhelmed by affection for the tiny creature. "Hello there, Callie," she whispered, caught off guard by her impulse to name the kitten—a blatant contradiction to her steadfast rule of not forming attachments. As the kitten's soft purring vibrated gently against her chest, a serene calm enveloped her, soothing her restless nerves.

She gestured for Mr. McNabb to sit on her rarely used gray couch. Despite her best efforts to maintain a professional demeanor, she struggled to shake off the thought of him as merely "Casper," still grappling with the barriers she had erected around their relationship. He settled across from her, a charming black-and-white kitten perched playfully on his shoulder, adding to the moment's warmth.

"I found them in the middle of the road," he said, then grinned widely, "kind of like I found you."

CHAPTER FIFTEEN

CASPER LEANED BACK, his eyes fixed on Nettie as he observed her reaction to his casual mention of their first encounter. He noted how she shifted uncomfortably, a vivid blush creeping across her cheeks. It probably stemmed from embarrassment, he mused, recalling how she had been anything but sober during their initial meeting—three sheets to the wind, as they say. Despite that entertaining introduction, she had astonishingly managed to survive a shooting and carried on with her work throughout the afternoon, demonstrating a resilience he admired. Now, here she was, standing at the threshold of accepting his modest peace offering.

Though she hadn't outright accepted the kittens yet, Casper felt an unwavering confidence that she soon would. After all, no woman—barring his mother, of course—could resist the charm of two tiny furballs, especially when those little creatures began to frolic and play together, their innocent antics pulling at heartstrings.

"Now, I realize they might have a few fleas, so I went ahead and purchased some flea shampoo. I thought I could lend a hand in scrubbing them up before they made themselves too comfortable on your couch," he mentioned casually, hoping to ease the tension.

Nettie raised an eyebrow, her expression a mix of surprise and skepticism. "You did, did you? Well, let me tell you, Mr. McNabb, I am more than capable of bathing them myself."

Casper raised a hand, a frown crossing his face as he cringed at her persistent use of his formal name. "Please, don't read anything into this. I merely wanted to help because I brought this burden to you in the first place. I am genuinely serious about finding a proper home for them. It's just that, quite frankly, I had no one else to reach out to tonight."

Her eyes narrowed, a sardonic smile creeping onto her lips. "And you, of all people, first thought of me? Your sworn enemy in the court system?"

The sharpness of her words pierced deep into his soul, but he countered by shaking his head. "No, this isn't about past grievances. This is about me bringing the kittens to a woman named Nettie. She's someone who could genuinely use some warmth and companionship after a long, draining workday. These little creatures might just brighten her spirits."

Casper glanced down at the squirming kitten, feeling the weight of its vulnerability as he contemplated the impact the two might have on Nettie's life, hoping to mend some of the fractures his actions had caused.

When Nettie sprang to her feet, an unmistakable sense of anxiety swept over Casper. He momentarily feared that she might unleash her frustration and send them all—him and the two kittens—straight to the curb.

However, in a delightful twist, she beamed and exclaimed, "Trade with me."

Eagerly, Nettie traded for the tuxedo cat while Casper cradled the tiny, fluffy creature she had affectionately named "Callie." With bated breath, he awaited her next move. She gently flipped the kitten over in her hands, inspecting it with curiosity, before turning it back to face her. "Hello, Madam," she greeted cheerfully as if the kitten were a noblewoman deserving reverence.

Wasn't her whimsical naming of the kittens an encouraging sign? Casper pondered this, feeling a rush of warmth at the thought. All he truly knew was that being near her was essential, regardless of the circumstances that bound them together. However, in his heart, he hoped his presence would bring her joy rather than face her wrath in a courtroom.

That hope, however, tethered him to the unsettling memory of his brother's sharp tongue. He could almost hear Aaron's disdainful tone labeling him as "working with the enemy against him" should he ever discover Casper's secret visit with the kittens. A wave of relief washed over him when he recalled how he had kept his mother blissfully unaware of his intentions. Had she known, she wouldn't hesitate to rush to the jail to inform Aaron of the so-called betrayal, undoubtedly branding his actions as traitorous.

But this was altogether different. It had nothing to do with the case and everything to do with her—Nettie, who shimmered with a light that drew him in against all odds.

"This has nothing to do with anything else," he asserted, though internally, he wrestled with the truth. The reality was that his intent was deeply intertwined with his growing affection for her. "I only wish to help," he added earnestly, trying to mask the flutter of nerves rising within him. "Let me assist you with washing the kittens. You can't manage them both simultaneously—they're far too wiggly and full of energy."

He stood there, allowing silence to settle between them as she weighed her options, contemplating whether to accept his offer of help or simply take the fluffy creatures away from him. In the end, their undeniable cuteness swayed her decision. Bless their little hearts. The tiny furballs were charming beyond measure.

"This is still unethical, Mr. McNabb," she finally replied, her tone a mix of reluctance and admission. "But I agree I need assistance, especially since the deputies won't come inside unless it's for a safety check on my home."

Not wanting to lose this fleeting chance, he quickly reached for one of the bags the deputies had brought inside. "Let me grab the kitten shampoo. The kitchen sink would be the most practical place. It offers more room." His gaze shifted to her as she hesitated, clearly uncomfortable. "Plus, there's no carpet, which helps prevent jumping mishaps—no risk of having creatures bounce from one kitten to the next before we take care of them."

His words trailed off, the gravity of his intent overshadowed by lighthearted sarcasm. Yet he wondered if she sensed his underlying concern for the fragile lives they were about to care for.

With her nod of agreement, he felt a surge of hope that perhaps this small act would help them build a closer connection between them while saving those innocent kittens from their fate.

With the cozy house's expansive open floor plan, Casper observed Nettie as she gracefully walked toward the kitchen, the tiny kitten, Madam, cradled gently in her arms. Madam meowed louder, the sound filled with urgency as if she were desperately searching for her sister, Callie. Not wanting to keep the two furry siblings apart for too long, Casper quickly followed her, a bottle of cat shampoo clutched firmly in his hand.

"We'll need some towels," he said, fully aware that she would have to venture outside the kitchen to locate towels large enough to dry the wet cats. "One to dry them off and another to help clean up the inevitable mess."

Nettie's eyebrows shot up in surprise, and a flicker of concern crossed her face. "What mess?" she asked.

Casper chuckled softly, the sound warm and lighthearted. "You've never washed squirming kittens before, have you?" There was a twinkle of amusement in his eyes as he imagined the chaos that would ensue.

Shaking her head, Nettie glanced down at the fluffy ball of fur in her hold, her expression shifting from concern to determination. She then carefully handed Madam over to him, ensuring the kitten felt secure. "Let me get them. Stay right here," she instructed firmly, her tone leaving no room for argument.

With that, she turned to dart off searching for the needed towels, leaving Casper to anticipate the delightful yet messy task of their miniature-washing adventure.

As the playful kittens clambered onto his shoulders, their tiny paws pressing against his skin as if they had claimed territory on their new feline perch, he couldn't help but admire Nettie as she walked away. The gentle sway of her hips, moving with an effortless and captivating rhythm, held his gaze momentarily. However, reality soon beckoned.

Turning his attention to the task, he prepared a warm bath for the kittens. He approached the faucet, twisting it carefully, and felt the water gradually warm to a gentle touch but remain cool enough to ensure the little ones wouldn't get scalded.

When Nettie returned, determined in her eyes, he instructed her with calm authority: "Please put one towel aside and lay the other on the counter surrounding the sink. It's probably their first bath, and they are likely to claw and flail in a panic to escape the water," he explained, trying to prepare her for the chaos that might ensue. "So, I'll hold them while you bathe them."

She nodded in agreement, a hint of excitement and trepidation evident in her expression. "That's fine," she replied.

With a gentle smile, he carefully removed Callie from his shoulder and cradled the little kitten. "Come on, little girl," he cooed softly. "Let's get you cleaned up for your new momma."

"Their new foster momma," she corrected gently, a smile touching her lips.

He felt a twist in his gut at her words, realizing what they implied. Inside, he understood that he was unlikely to get the kittens back once they bonded with her. So, he simply nodded, acknowledging the truth of her perspective. "Right," he conceded, the hint of loss looming over the moment's joy.

He carefully held Callie in the spacious kitchen sink, her tiny frame trembling with unease as he instructed Nettie to grab the long, flexible hose from the kitchen faucet. The warm water splashed into the sink, an ominous sound to the little kitten. As the hose sprayed the water over Callie, she let out an ear-piercing screech as if she were in grave danger, her sharp claws digging deeply into Casper's tough hands in a desperate attempt to escape the dreadful experience of water and the baffling ritual of a bath.

Nettie hesitated momentarily. When she finally turned off the water, Casper, trying to reassure the kitten and his friend, said, "It's okay. Not all cats take to water very well, but she's tough and will survive."

Nettie, biting her lip in concern, glanced at his hands, now scratched and trickling with tiny droplets of blood from the kitten's frantic escape. "But your hands—" she started, worry etched on her face.

He shrugged nonchalantly, stealing a glance at the wounds. "It's nothing to worry about. It's the price you pay when you take care of kittens."

As Callie gently wiggled and splashed in the warm water, her fluffy fur glistening in the streetlight that streamed through the window, Casper couldn't help but let his imagination drift. He envisioned Nettie's soft, delicate hands—hands that were always gentle and caring —gently scrubbing him clean instead. That tantalizing thought sent excitement down his spine and made his heart race with anticipation. Realizing he was sinking deeper into daydreams, lost in dreamy reverie, he cleared his throat loudly, trying to anchor himself back to the task at hand.

"By the way," he began, "the lady at the pet store mentioned that the kittens are around six weeks old. She recommended that they should be transitioned to solid food instead of being kept on continued bottle feeding, which is not ideal for their development." He paused, ensuring his words carried the weight of responsibility. "Just to be safe, I bought both soft and hard kitten food. I wanted to ensure they get all the nutrients needed to grow strong, healthy, and be well-fed and happy."

"It seems you thought of everything," she remarked, her gaze fixed on him as he gently dried off a sobbing Callie, careful to soothe her distress with soft words and a comforting touch.

"I tried my best," he replied, a hint of exhaustion in his tone but satisfaction in his efforts.

"Good," she said. "You'll have everything you need to care for them when you leave."

Shock washed over him like a wave crashing against a rocky shore. Leave? As in tonight? The very idea sent a shudder through his veins. "But, Nettie, I can't—" His words fell short, choked by disbelief and impending loss.

She raised a trembling hand, dripping with dampness, to interrupt him. Her expression was steely and resolute. "When you go back to Maryland—if you haven't found a new home for them," she insisted, despite the tears pooling in her eyes. "I'm serious about not keeping them. This isn't just a fleeting thought. It's a necessity."

He recognized this was not the right moment for a confrontation, so he offered a gentle smile and skillfully diverted the conversation. "There's a pet tent in one of the bags I brought. We should set that up to place Callie in while we bathe Madam."

"Can't we just put her bag in the carrier instead?" she inquired, nervously biting her lip.

Casper shook his head firmly, determination evident in his eyes. "No, they can't stay in the carrier all night. I figured a tent would be better since you won't have to worry about where they are. Plus, it'll keep them safe and secure. Setting it up is simple enough." He then moved into the living room, cradling the now contentedly purring towel-wrapped Callie in his arms, her whiskers twitching as she settled into comfort. "We'll also get the litter box set up along with food and water so she'll be all set to sleep by the time we finish bathing Madam."

"Wow, you know a lot about caring for kittens," she said.

Sheepishly, he smiled back, a hint of bashfulness in his demeanor. "Not really. I just took some lessons from the associates at the pet store. They taught me everything I needed to know. Here, you take Callie, and I'll set everything up." He stepped closer to her, captivated by the enchanting aura she radiated. As he did, an undeniable realization hit him—her scent was intoxicating, a fragrant blend that wrapped around him and sent a jolt of desire straight to his groin. Damn, she was incredibly alluring, especially with her hair cascading down her shoulders in beautiful waves tonight.

He hesitated momentarily, the tiny kitten nestled in his arms. She looked up at him, her large eyes sparkling with curiosity, and he couldn't help but notice the small gasp that escaped her lips as her breath caught in her throat. Without thinking, caught up in their chemistry, he leaned down, closing the distance between them, and softly brushed his lips against hers. A surge of exhilaration rushed through him, and he was grateful that she didn't recoil in shock or anger.

Encouraged, he attempted to deepen the kiss, feeling an overwhelming sense of rightness in the connection they were forming. Just as their lips met fully, a piercing screeching meow erupted from the kitten between them.

Casper jerked back instinctively, startled, his heart racing as he locked eyes with Nettie. Time froze, and they were suspended in a shared gaze filled with a storm of heat and confusion—an unspoken tension hanging heavy in the space surrounding them.

Nettie was the first to regain her composure. A gentle determination in her eyes as she looked at the tiny, crying figure cradled in Casper's arms. "I think I can take it from here," she said.

Clearing his throat to mask his uncertainty, Casper nodded slowly, his eyes lingering on the fragile baby, Callie, whose tear-streaked face poignantly reminded him of the emotions swirling in the room. He carefully handed Callie over to Nettie, feeling relief and unease. "I think you're right. I'll see you another time," he replied softly, the words tinged with finality.

With a heavy heart, he turned away, knowing that leaving now was the best choice for both—fearing that one more moment could lead to something neither of them was ready to face, something they might deeply regret.

Then, all hell broke loose around him.

CHAPTER SIXTEEN

THE SOUND OF gunfire erupted like thunder, deafening in its intensity, and he instinctively tackled and shielded Nettie with his body, feeling the rush of adrenaline surge through him as he tried to protect her from the relentless barrage of bullets. The air was thick with tension, and his heart raced, each pulse resonating with the frantic chaos surrounding them. As the cacophony of gunfire echoed off the walls, every instinct urged him to keep her safe at all costs.

His mind swam with confusion and doubt. Each thought swirling chaotically like a cyclone. How could he possibly think keeping the enemy safe was viable? After all, she was the one orchestrating his brother's imprisonment, shackling him in a dark cell while she feigned concern for his wellbeing. Yet, in this midst of turmoil, his sense of righteousness surged, asserting that the moral high ground somehow prevailed in this twisted situation. Despite the chaos, he knew that what was right, what was just, ultimately won out, illuminating the path forward amidst the shadows of betrayal.

As the echo of gunfire faded into the eerie silence that enveloped the room, Casper swiftly crouched, his heart pounding in his chest. His gaze darted toward Nettie, whose broad, frightened eyes were brimming with fear, and the tiny, fuzzy kittens scrambling desperately toward the safety underneath the couch. "Are you hurt?" he asked, his voice steady despite the swift beating of his heart.

Nettie glanced back at him with an expression that combined worry and determination. She shook her head vigorously, indicating she was unharmed but shaken by the ordeal.

Before he could fully process the situation, Casper returned to the task. He needed to quickly assess their surroundings, weighing the risks of danger still lingering in the air. "Once I give you the all-clear, get the kittens and check them. Stay here until then," he instructed, his tone low yet firm. "I'll check the deputies."

As Nettie lay motionless, a silent nod of understanding passed between them, her eyes glistening with unshed tears that threatened to spill over. The vulnerability reflected in her gaze tugged at his heartstrings, an ache that resonated within him. This wasn't just another day. It marked the second harrowing instance in which she had been targeted by gunfire. The trauma of those moments must have been overwhelming, enveloping her in a shroud of fear and uncertainty that he could hardly fathom.

Casper quickly reached down to his ankle holster, feeling the cold metal grip of the gun as he pulled it free. The silence around him was deafening, starkly contrasting to the rapid gunfire that had just erupted moments earlier. Adrenaline coursed through his veins as he sprinted toward the door, his heart racing with each step.

The deputies' lack of calls or updates sent a chill down his spine. It wasn't like them to remain quiet, especially after the chaos unfolding. He needed to know if they were okay. Casper pushed open the door with urgency, ready to confront whatever awaited him outside, his senses heightened and alert.

The first thing Casper noticed as he rushed into the front yard was Deputy Wright sprawled on the grass, his face contorted in pain and blood oozing from a terrible wound in his stomach. The crimson liquid pooled around him, slowly saturating the earth beneath him. Beside him, the other deputy was frantically applying pressure to the wound, his hands trembling as he desperately tried to staunch the flow of blood that threatened to spill more fervently. The air was thick with tension and urgency. "Are we clear?" Casper yelled, his voice rising as he sought reassurance from the deputy, his heart pounding with anxiety for the law enforcement officers.

The deputy knelt silently, his youthful gaze betraying the palpable fear, his wide eyes darting around as if anticipating danger lurking just out of sight. Fueled by a deep-seated mistrust of the seemingly inexperienced deputy, Casper took it upon himself to thoroughly inspect the grounds and the street beyond. He carefully surveyed every shadow and corner, ensuring the area was secure before he finally holstered his gun, its weight suddenly feeling more like a burden than a source of protection. With a steadying breath, he turned his attention back to the young deputy, ready to assist him in moving the unconscious form of Deputy Wright, whose fate now rested precariously in their hands.

Yet, who should he unexpectedly see? Nettie, the very woman he had explicitly instructed, to remain inside for her safety while he assessed the situation outside. Would she ever heed his warnings and listen to reason?

As he approached her, she held up her hands defensively, eager to explain herself. "I saw you holster your gun and dashed out here to Deputy Wright," she stated breathlessly, urgency in her voice. "The kittens are fine and in their tent." Her focus swiftly shifted back to the two deputies, her brow furrowing into a look of determination. "Give me your radio," she commanded, directing her order toward the young deputy with an air of authority that belied her stature.

As he complied, handing over the device, Nettie turned to Casper. Control radiated from her stance. Every gesture and tone of her voice indicated a woman who was entirely in charge of the situation. "This is ADA Broussard," she introduced herself. "I'm at my home location where we have one deputy with a gunshot wound to the stomach and another suffering from an arm injury. Mr. McNabb has cleared the scene and is providing protection until EMTs and backup arrive."

Casper felt a swell of admiration for her astute, quick thinking. He wanted to stand up and applaud her for handling the situation with such poise. But instead, he impatiently snatched the radio from her grasp. "Get inside, Nettie! They could return at any moment," he insisted as he scanned the surroundings in search of potential dangers.

Nettie stomped her foot—literally stomping her foot like a petulant child thrown into a situation beyond her control. "I will not. Not when I can lend assistance," she declared defiantly, dismissing Casper with a wave that cut through the tension in the air.

Kneeling beside Deputy Wright, she focused intently on the task at hand. "Lift your hands," she instructed the young deputy with an urgency that brooked no argument. He complied, his movements shaky, as Nettie swiftly positioned an article of clothing—over the wound, applying pressure with her own hands to staunch the bleeding.

"How bad is your arm?" she asked, searching the deputy's eyes for the signs of pain.

Casper read the name badge. Deputy Hollis seemed to realize the extent of his injury. His gaze fell to his arm as if it were a foreign object, and he instinctively covered it with his hand, trying to minimize the gravity of the situation. "It's fine, ma'am," he replied, though the waver in his voice betrayed the truth of his injuries.

As is often the case in emergencies, the firetrucks were the first to arrive on the scene, flashing their lights and blaring their sirens. They were swiftly followed by their dedicated EMTs, who hopped out of the vehicles with serious expressions etched on their faces. Casper, still reeling from the chaos, cleared the way for them, watching intently as they immediately turned their attention to the two injured deputies lying on the ground.

His frustration boiled over, and every ounce of his patience drained. With a determined grip, he snatched Nettie's arm and yanked her toward the front door of her home. "Get inside," he commanded, urgency lacing his tone as he pushed her away from the unfolding crisis outside.

She abruptly jerked her arm away from him, her eyes wide with fear and determination. "No. I'm safe now," she declared.

"It's not that," he said, shaking his head slowly, concern etched on his face as he struggled to find the right words to convey his feelings.

To emphasize the gravity of the situation and distract from the charged moment between them, Sheriff Beau Necaise waltzed up, his boots stomping lightly on the gravel. "Well, well, what have we here?" he announced, his tone a blend of curiosity and authority, casting a glance between the two with a knowing smirk.

Not yet grasping the desperation of their situation, Nettie frowned as she redirected her attention from the frantic activity to the sheriff standing before her. Ignoring the sheriff's comment, she responded, "I'm fine. Thanks for checking. How is Deputy Wright?" she asked, genuine concern for the law enforcement officer was evident in her tone.

As Casper glanced at the ambulance, the tug of urgency pulled at his heart. He noticed the doors being forcibly shut, signaling the seriousness of the situation. He turned to Nettie, trying to instill a sense of hope despite the palpable tension hanging in the air like a heavy fog.

"Oh, he'll be fine," Sheriff Necaise reassured her.

After narrowing his eyes at Casper, Sheriff Necaise returned to Nettie and asked, "Is there anyone I should call for you? Perhaps a friend or family member?" His tone ensured she felt supported amidst the turmoil.

Nettie shook her head firmly, her expression resolute but lined with worry. "No," she replied sharply.

"Don't worry," Beau said. "We'll get those windows boarded up for you," he promised with a steady voice, projecting an air of reassurance that he hoped would reach her deeply.

As they stood together, Nettie gazed at her home, seeing the physical manifestation of her troubles. Her shoulders sagged. "Thank you," she murmured, her vulnerability creeping into her tone and breaking through her earlier facade of strength. The woman who usually took charge under challenging situations felt momentarily defeated, reduced to a quiet figure engulfed in uncertainty.

The atmosphere shifted with palpable tension as the District Attorney decided to align himself with the group. He turned to the sheriff, offering a respectful nod that acknowledged the authority and gravity of the situation. After this gesture of solidarity, his gaze meticulously darted back and forth between Casper and Nettie as if weighing their reactions and assessing the dynamics at play. His expression revealed an undercurrent of contemplation about the implications of this alliance.

In that tense moment, Casper observed a profound shift in Nettie's demeanor. It became clear to him that she grasped the gravity of their circumstances, recognizing that the chaos around them was more than just the sound of bullets whizzing through the air or the sight of a deputy in distress. The realization hit her hard. She was on the brink of being ousted from a critical case due to allegations of misconduct, which threatened her career and reputation. This revelation added an unsettling layer to the already difficult situation they faced.

CHAPTER SEVENTEEN

NETTIE GAZED AT her boss, a knot tightening in her stomach as she realized the situation had escalated far beyond mere chaos. It wasn't the kind of turmoil that involved gunfire or immediate danger, but the damage to her heart was just as real. She could sense the impending judgment in her boss's eyes—he would never comprehend Mr. McNabb's presence in her home, regardless of the circumstances that led to it. Deep down, Nettie knew she had no viable excuse for letting him in without the presence of opposing counsel. It was a decision she had made hastily, and she could already feel the repercussions looming, ready to strike when she least expected it.

"Nettie," DA King said, "are you all right?"

She felt the urge to scream, a primal instinct bubbling beneath the surface. What kind of question was that? She had been shot at not once but twice in the span of a single day, her career hanging precariously in the balance. The weight of the situation pressed heavily on her chest, making it hard to breathe.

As her boss looked at her expectantly, she wrestled with the truth. She couldn't bring herself to lie and claim that Mr. McNabb had just arrived—everyone knew the deputies would contradict her. Yet the thought of fabricating a story twisted in her gut. She had always despised dishonesty. So, she settled for a half-truth, forcing a strong tone despite the tremor in her voice. "I'm fine. Just shaken." Even she could hear the residual unsteadiness in her words as if the threat still loomed over her.

"Nettie, Mr. McNabb, I will need to take your statements," Sheriff Necaise declared as he surveyed the two with a sharp gaze.

"Of course," Nettie replied, stepping forward with determination.

"I have a question," District Attorney King interjected, his tone dripping with disdain. "What exactly brings you here, Mr. McNabb?"

Nettie observed Mr. McNabb closely, noting how he shifted from the image of a resolute warrior poised to face any challenge to a charming man whose boyish grin seemed to erase years from his face. With a playful chuckle, he answered, "Kittens."

Startled by Mr. McNabb's unexpected response, DA King arched an eyebrow in disbelief. "Kittens?" he asked as if struggling to comprehend the significance of the answer.

Mr. McNabb's earlier grin vanished, replaced by a deep furrow in his brow. He took a moment to gather his thoughts, inhaling deeply before releasing a heavy sigh as though he were carrying an immense weight on his shoulders. "Yes, kittens," he repeated, the gravity of his situation evident in his tone. "I discovered them abandoned on the road and had nowhere else to bring them."

DA King's expression tightened, skepticism flickering in his eyes. "And your immediate thought was to call ADA Broussard at this late hour?"

Mr. McNabb narrowed his gaze, his frustration palpable. "No, I didn't think of her first. She was, quite frankly, my last resort."

Nettie shifted uncomfortably, her heart sinking as she processed his admission. The revelation stung more than she anticipated. The fact that he hadn't considered her his first option stirred an unsettling mix of emotions within her. Though she tried to dismiss it, the notion lingered, casting a shadow over her thoughts.

"Are you finished, counselor?" Sheriff Necaise's voice cut through the tension as he addressed DA King, effectively rescuing Nettie from the deep waters of her explanation about their visit.

A knot tightened in her stomach at the thought of what would happen if Sheriff Necaise discovered the secret she shared with Mr. McNabb—Casper. Just moments before, they had shared a fleeting kiss that could land her in serious trouble.

DA King's sharp gaze swept over Nettie and Casper again, studying their expressions as if trying to decipher their unspoken secrets. "Not right now," he replied coolly, his tone chilling the air between them. "Nettie, I'll need you in my office first thing in the morning." With that, he turned on his heel, striding purposefully away toward the blinking lights of his car parked in the distance.

Sheriff Necaise sighed heavily, his brow furrowing as he turned to face Nettie and Casper. "This doesn't look good," he said, a hint of concern lacing his words as he placed a reassuring hand on Nettie's shoulder. "I'll do what I can to keep it innocent, but the way it appears...well, it doesn't leave much room for interpretation."

Nettie shook her head, a spark of determination igniting in her eyes. "Don't worry about it, Beau. I can handle DA King."

"Well, kiddo," Beau said, "this officially marks the end of our agreement. You're not just going to have guards. You're going into protective custody now."

"But—" she began to protest, her brow knitting together in a deep frown of confusion. The weight of her thoughts pressed down on her as she grappled with the situation. She understood it was for the best, especially given the looming danger surrounding her. Yet her unwavering commitment to her work and the desire to spare her colleague from additional burden hung heavily in the balance of her decision-making. Each reason swirled in her mind like storm clouds, battling for clarity as she stood at this crossroads.

"Let us handle this," Casper interjected, appearing to surprise himself. He cleared his throat, the tension between the group palpable as he continued. "You're already stretched thin, and with two of your deputies injured, it's not safe for you to manage this alone. Hamilton Investigation and Security has a proven track record in protecting clients. We could take over her protection duties, allowing her to focus on her work remotely, away from the danger."

Beau's gaze shifted to Casper, a furrow of concern on his brow. "We can't afford any high-end security," he stated.

Casper shook his head, his expression resolute. "We take on numerous pro bono cases each year. This one will be no different," he insisted firmly.

Beau raised an eyebrow, curiosity piqued. "Are you able to make that agreement?" he asked, probing for assurance.

"I am," Casper replied confidently.

Turning to Nettie, Beau sought her opinion. "Nettie? How do you feel about that?"

Nettie paused, the thought of being whisked away into virtual anonymity with unfamiliar faces gnawing at her. "I—" she started, grappling with her feelings.

"Good," Beau interjected with an encouraging smile, eager to move forward. "Let's work out the details."

"He can't be someone protecting me," she piped up, her eyes narrowing in determination. "That is non-negotiable."

Casper's gaze met hers, a reassuring smile spreading across his face. "Don't worry about it. I won't be bothering you again," he said, his tone light as if to ease her concerns. He turned to the sheriff, professionalism dripping from him. "Coastal Investigations will keep her safe until the team arrives tomorrow."

Beau nodded thoughtfully, his brow furrowing slightly. "I'm good with that. JD and Cassie can handle it," he replied confidently, glancing toward Nettie. "Especially now that they've got assistance from that former FBI guy."

Nettie felt a surge of frustration rising within her. She opened her mouth to voice her concerns, intending to assert her presence in the plans around her. But as she took a deep breath, she hesitated. With the weight of two shootings hanging over her, the power to make decisions felt stripped away.

A tremor coursed through her stomach, a visceral reminder of the fear that had gripped her since this morning. Someone had targeted her not once but twice in a single day, and the chilling reality struck her hard: not just one but two attackers had conspired against her. The first shooter was safely behind bars, but the thought of another lurking in the shadows sent icy fingers of dread creeping up her spine.

What had led her to this nightmare? What terrible fate had befallen her to warrant such a deadly pursuit? And the most haunting question of all—who sought her demise?

A sudden realization washed over her. Casper had been conveniently present both times—at the courthouse, standing firmly by her side and within the familiar confines of her home, a steadfast guardian. The timing of his appearances felt almost too perfect, too orchestrated. As her weary mind began to race with unsettling thoughts, she couldn't shake the nagging suspicion that there was more to his acts of protection than mere coincidence. Had he, in some twisted way, engineered the very incidents that put her in peril so that he could swoop in and be her savior? If that were true, didn't it mean she would owe him a debt, one he could call upon in court?

Logic teetered on the edge of her consciousness, but the eerie coincidences tangled with her jumbled thoughts like a dark web. She felt trapped in a labyrinth of uncertainty, each turn leading her further into a reality that could very well haunt her. It was a bitter relief that he wouldn't be part of her protective detail. On one hand, it was a necessity—a boundary dictated by their court relationship. On the other hand, an undeniable longing stirred within her. She missed the warmth of his presence, especially when they had washed the little kitten together, laughter echoing between them, or that fleeting kiss that sent shivers coursing through her.

Was that kiss merely a tactic to sway her emotions, to tilt the scales in his favor during the trial? The more she pondered, the more tangled her thoughts became. If—no, she forced herself to think of him as Mr. McNabb, not Casper—the enigmatic figure she thought she knew was indeed orchestrating these dangers around her, what kind of peril would his colleagues unleash?

"Don't worry, Nettie," he assured her calmly, almost soothingly. "We'll take great care of you."

But therein lay her concern. Those very words filled her with an unsettling dread.

CHAPTER EIGHTEEN

CASPER OBSERVED THE subtle shift in Nettie's demeanor as various emotions flickered across her face like a fast-moving shadow. Confusion, tension, perhaps even fear, played in her eyes, leaving him to wonder if he had somehow sparked her anxiety. The thought made his stomach twist. Surely, she couldn't be afraid of him. He was determined to keep his distance, especially with the prospect of entering protective custody looming and the meeting with her boss scheduled for the morning—albeit conducted through a screen.

"Just give me a moment," he said softly to the sheriff and Nettie, a hint of urgency in his voice. Turning away from their scrutiny, he deliberately walked a few paces farther, seeking a private space for the conversation. Pulling his phone from his pocket, he scrolled through his contacts until he found the familiar name that gave him relief.

"Please tell me I can send some of these boneheads your way. They are driving me crazy, clambering for work when I orchestrated them a holiday." Jesse Hamilton's voice burst through the line before Casper even had the chance to say hello. Jesse's exasperation was palpable, a welcome distraction from the turmoil swirling around him.

"Send them right away. She needs protective custody," Casper declared. The weight of responsibility pressed heavily on his shoulders. He couldn't allow anyone else to bear the burden of her safety.

"I can arrange that. Who do you want on the team?" Jesse inquired, ready to mobilize at a moment's notice.

Without a moment's pause, Casper replied, "Doc, Pup, Cowboy, and Nemo. Make sure Pup brings the dogs with him. We've only had gunfire, but I refuse to take any chances." He paused, a sense of urgency washing over him. "And Devon needs to find a secure location where she can work remotely. It's crucial if we're ever going to get her into protective custody."

"What about you?".

Casper rubbed the back of his neck, a wave of disappointment washing over him as he admitted, "I can't be part of the protection detail." The realization stung more than he anticipated. But then, a spark of inspiration ignited within him. "I'll lead the teams instead."

Jesse chuckled lightly, a hint of admiration in his voice. "I expected nothing less from you."

"Can you get them here by tomorrow morning?" Casper pressed, urgency creeping back into his tone.

"Casper, I could have them here in a few hours if needed. But tomorrow morning would be the best timing," Jesse assured him.

After ending the call with Jesse, Casper swiftly dialed JD's number, his heart racing with urgency. When

JD picked up, Casper rushed to speak, "I need you and Cassie tonight for a protection detail. Can you do it?" The words tumbled out, laden with the weight of the situation.

"Let me find a sitter for Henry Kyle, and we'll be there as soon as you need us," JD replied.

Casper took a deep breath, his mind racing as he thought about the best place to hide Nettie for the night. "Where's the safest spot to stash her? The teams will arrive in the morning with an address for a secure location, so we need somewhere for tonight." A pang of regret hit him. He realized little about the town's growth since his last visit. The once-quiet streets were now lined with vibrant casinos, bustling businesses, and hotels filled with tourists. He mentally cursed himself for not keeping up with the changes.

"I'll take care of it," JD assured him. "But are you sure it's wise to be there, given the case and everything?"

Casper hesitated, aware that he shouldn't be inserting himself into the situation, but the thought of leaving Nettie unprotected was unbearable. "I have to be there," he said, determination hardening his resolve. The instinct to ensure her safety thrummed intensely within him, a primal urge that overshadowed his concerns for his well-being. Until he could guarantee her safety, he couldn't allow himself to step away. The reason for this fierce protectiveness eluded him, but it felt like an unshakeable vow, compelling him to remain by her side.

"Oh, make sure to find a place that welcomes pets," Casper suddenly recalled a sense of urgency in his voice. "She has two adorable kittens." The image of the little felines shuffled through his mind. He couldn't bear the thought of them being away from her. Deep down, he sensed that she desperately needed their companionship to help her navigate the storm brewing on the horizon. He couldn't pinpoint what lay ahead, but he was all too familiar with the presence of villains, and experience told him they rarely backed down.

JD chuckled softly on the other end of the line. "So, you found a place for the little ones."

Casper nodded, even though JD couldn't see the gesture. "Yes, she's going to be their foster mom." A warm smile spread across his face as he recalled her infectious enthusiasm when she quickly named the tiny creatures. "Although after seeing her with them, I believe they'll end up being foster fails."

"They almost always turn out that way," JD replied with a knowing laugh. Clearing his throat, he added, "Now, give me the address. We'll be there in less than an hour."

Casper quickly recited the address he had memorized, feeling a rush of determination as he hung up the call.

As Casper made his way back, he noticed that the sheriff had stepped away, engaging in a low conversation with one of his deputies, their voices a murmur against the backdrop of the bustling area. Nettie hung up her phone and turned to him, an expression of mingled relief and frustration gracing her features. "Okay, my boss has given the go-ahead for the virtual court hearings, but he's not thrilled about it. He's curious about where I'll be stationed during all this."

Casper shook his head, a firm resolve anchoring his response. There was no way he would disclose her protective address, not to anyone or her boss. "No can do. He'll have to remain in the dark like everyone else."

Nettie crossed her arms, defiance written all over her. "What about my paralegal? I meet with Janet several times a day to prepare for cases. Surely, I can let her know where I am."

He shook his head again, his tone leaving no room for negotiation. "Virtually is your only option."

A spark ignited in Nettie's eyes as she placed her hands on her hips, her posture radiating fierce determination. "What if I decide to go with the sheriff instead? Maybe he'll be more realistic about this situation."

Watching the fiery passion in her gaze stirred something within Casper, a complex mix of admiration and concern that he knew he shouldn't indulge. "You heard the sheriff," he replied. "He doesn't have the staffing to handle this and wouldn't allow it either. It's called 'Protection 101.'" His tone was firm, masking his warmth at her spirited nature.

"Fine," she huffed, her tone reminiscent of a petulant child who realized, deep down, that the argument was lost.

"Fine," he echoed, a smirk dancing across his lips. There was something undeniably alluring about her during their debates. It fueled his anticipation for seeing her in court. He could already envision her as a fierce prosecutor, igniting the room with her passionate arguments.

"Who is JD?" she inquired, her brows furrowing in curiosity. "Is it Cassie McKay's JD? I know her but have never had the chance to meet him."

Casper nodded, the corners of his mouth lifting in a knowing smile. "Yes, that's him. They should be here shortly. Let's get you inside to tidy up the chaos before they arrive. We can also offer some comfort to the kittens. Madam needs a flea bath, and now that they're reunited, Callie could use another one too—those pesky fleas tend to leap from one to the other."

Nettie gasped, covering her mouth in alarm. "Oh no! Can I take them with me? I can't bear leaving them alone for an unspecified time, even though you bought those automatic feeders."

Casper couldn't help but admire how her heart swelled with concern for the helpless little kittens. She was a kind-hearted woman, caught in a difficult situation that he knew stemmed from her demanding job—one he recognized she excelled at with unwavering dedication. "You can."

Nettie released a deep, weary sigh that Casper interpreted as a sign of relief. "Great," she murmured. She turned on her heel and ascended the stairs leading to her home, the weight of her day visible in her movement. Pausing halfway up, she cast a lingering glance at her front door, where the jagged scars of bullet holes marred the wood—reminders of a harrowing experience. With a visible slump of her shoulders, the sight seemed to drain the color from her face.

In that fleeting moment, Casper felt a surge of conflicting emotions, a blend of desire and compassion, urging him to envelop her in a warm embrace. He longed to tell her everything would be fine, to instill a sense of safety that he struggled to believe in. But deep down, he knew he couldn't make such promises. He had never been able to promise her certainty, and he never would. Nonetheless, he resolved to do everything within his power to create a semblance of security for her, determined to fight for her peace of mind with every ounce of strength he had.

Casper ushered her inside, the door creaking ominously as he maneuvered past the jagged remnants of the door frame, where splinters jutted out like the teeth of a broken smile. "Let's get the kittens ready," he said, hoping to divert her attention from the palpable danger that loomed over her.

She nodded, her silence weighing heavily on the air. It bothered him more than he cared to admit, but he pushed it aside as they swiftly began bathing the kittens. Their soft fur soaked up the warm water as they squirmed playfully, oblivious to the tension.

As Nettie moved about the house, gathering her clothes and essentials, JD and Cassie arrived, bringing a sudden rush of urgency into the space. Casper extended his hand, offering a firm shake to JD and then to Cassie, his expression a mix of gratitude and unease. "I'm so appreciative you could do this on such short notice."

JD nodded, his brow furrowing. "It was surprisingly easy to slip past all the law enforcement outside. She needs to be in custody—this is just too chaotic."

Cassie grimaced, concern etched on her face as she glanced around the disheveled room. "Where is she? This must be harrowing for her," she asked gently.

Casper gestured toward the closed bedroom door. "Packing," he replied, his tone heavy with unspoken worries.

Cassie nodded, determination setting her jaw. "I'll go help her," she said, striding confidently toward Nettie's bedroom, her footsteps fading as she moved out of earshot, leaving an air of anxious anticipation in the room.

"What's up?" JD asked, his keen eyes studying Casper's troubled expression, a hint of concern etched on his brow.

Casper took a deep breath, the moment's weight heavy on his shoulders. "I need to prepare Bryce for what's coming and my brother's hearing first thing in the morning."

JD raised his eyebrows, a look of urgency crossing his face. "I wouldn't wait. Bryce needs to hear this news as soon as possible—he must brace himself for any fallout."

Casper tilted his head slightly, contemplating JD's words with furrowed brows. "What kind of fallout do you think we're looking at?"

JD frowned, his gaze shifting away as if reluctant to spill the harsh truth. "She'll probably be removed from the case. If that happens, it'll likely create a rift between you two. She'll resent you for it."

Though he knew he should remain indifferent, the thought of Nettie harboring any hatred toward him gnawed at Casper. He couldn't bear the idea, even if pulling her away was for the best. "Is there anything I can do to change that outcome?" he asked, a flicker of desperation in his voice, despite knowing deep down that Nettie's more lenient colleague would probably grant his brother bail.

"No," JD replied with resolute finality. "Nothing at all."

CHAPTER NINETEEN

"BUT, MR. KING—" Nettie implored during the video call with her supervisor and District Attorney, Kevin King.

"No, Miss Broussard. You have jeopardized the reputation of the entire District Attorney's office," he replied sharply, his tone cold and final. "You are removed from the case immediately, and I will be scrutinizing all your current cases for any signs of misconduct. I won't tolerate this kind of behavior. I knew hiring someone so young would be a risk. Make sure this doesn't happen again in the future." With that, he abruptly ended the video call, the screen fading to black.

Nettie sat alone at the desk in the hotel room, her heart racing and mind reeling, utterly stunned by the weight of his words. The following silence felt oppressive, a crushing reminder of how quickly things could unravel.

She fought to hold back the tears that threatened to spill over after receiving her first disciplinary action. Anger surged through her like a storm, fierce and unrelenting. Yet, her ire wasn't directed at DA King. No, her wrath was reserved for Mr. McNabb—Casper. He had maneuvered this situation with deliberate intent, successfully plotting her removal from the case in which she had so passionately invested herself.

With a heavy sigh, she closed her laptop, the screen flickering to darkness as she surveyed the stark, impersonal hotel room surrounding her. The bland walls held no comfort, and a profound dread washed over her as she sat amidst the sterile furnishings. She wondered how long she would have to endure this isolated existence. Until now, she had taken her safety for granted, convinced those around her would always look out for her. Beau had been her steadfast protector, but in her quest for alliances with Casper's friends, she had foolishly severed that safety net.

Was that a wise choice? Doubt gnawed at her. The unsettling realization struck her that it was entirely possible Casper was orchestrating the very shooting incidents she feared, positioning himself as her savior while covertly ensuring that her every misstep would be catalogued and exaggerated—ultimately aimed at ousting her from the case or discrediting its legitimacy entirely. The room felt smaller, the air thicker, as the shadows of betrayal loomed larger.

Nettie stood in the dimly lit room, a swirl of emotions battling within her. She took a deep breath, summoning the courage to change her life. Stepping toward the door, she grasped the handle and pulled it open, her heart racing as she called for Cassie, who lingered in the hallway, her expression curious.

Cassie had bright eyes and a warm smile that instantly put Nettie at ease. As she entered the room, JD, a tall figure leaning against the wall near the elevator, glanced over with a furrowed brow. "Everything okay?" he asked, genuine concern creasing his forehead.

Nettie's heart sank at the question. No, everything was far from okay. She longed to scream her troubles into the air, to let it all out in a torrent of emotion. Yet, she swallowed the urge, forcing a smile to her lips and nodding. "It's fine. I just wanted to chat with Cassie about something important."

She glanced at JD, appreciating the worry etched on his face, but her trust didn't lie with him—he was still a stranger. Instead, her gaze settled comfortably on Cassie, whose loyalty felt like a lifeline in this sea of uncertainty.

"We'll be okay," Cassie reassured JD. A playful smile danced across her lips as she glanced back at him, her fiancé, before stepping into the dimly lit room and gently closing the door behind her. The air was thick with tension, and with a mix of concern and warmth, her eyes searched Nettie's face, unveiling the unspoken worries that made her feel exposed and fragile. "What's wrong?" she asked, her tone dripping with empathy.

Nettie sank onto the edge of the bed, its frame creaking slightly, even under her light weight. She gestured toward the armchair opposite her, inviting Cassie to sit. "Lots," she whispered.

Cassie let out a light chuckle, the sound almost musical in the heavy atmosphere. "I can imagine." As she settled into the chair, she fiddled with an inconspicuous earpiece that had evaded Nettie's notice until now.

Nettie's heart raced. "Is he listening?" she asked, her chest tightening with anxiety. The thought of her private thoughts being overheard made her skin crawl. She wanted this conversation to be just between her and Cassie.

Cassie shook her head reassuringly, a gentle smile lighting up her features. "No, I just cut him off. I can hear him, though, just in case we need to." There was an unspoken weight in the room. Cassie's brief pause suggested deeper layers to the story. She chose not to elaborate on whether someone lurked outside, poised to cause trouble again. Of course, she expected Casper would be her savior before anyone else could intervene.

"What's the date for your wedding?" Nettie blurted out, the question spilling from her lips before she could rein it in. It wasn't what she had intended to ask. She was using the inquiry as a diversion to shift focus from the turmoil swirling in her mind.

Cassie arched an eyebrow, her expression mixed with mild surprise and amusement. "As soon as Mom and Levi return from their whirlwind trip abroad," she replied, her tone casual, though there was a hint of excitement in her voice.

Nettie nodded, though her attention was only half on Cassie's words. A cloud of worry hung over her, pressing down on her like a weight. "What do you know about these men who are supposed to protect me?" she asked, forcing herself to focus.

Cassie uncrossed her legs and leaned forward, concern flickering in her eyes. "Is that really what's bothering you? You're unsure if they can keep you safe like the sheriff's department can?"

Nettie swallowed hard, feeling a lump rise in her throat. "Yes, exactly. I mean, I don't know them at all. I need to be sure I'm not stepping into a situation that could be dangerous." The uncertainty gnawed at her as she spoke, each word steeped in the weight of her fears.

"Well," Cassie began, a hint of gratitude lighting up her expression. "They saved my life, so I trust them completely. Casper took the lead, rallying a few women from the family who were just as fierce."

Nettie's eyebrows shot up in disbelief. "You never mentioned that before."

A soft chuckle escaped Cassie's lips, a fleeting memory dancing in her eyes. "Well, it's not like we've had the chance to catch up since then. But anyway, the story is quite wild. Some deranged woman kidnapped me, hell-bent on killing me unless she got JD's son, Henry Kyle." Cassie waved her hand dismissively, her tone shifting. "It's a long, tangled saga for another time. Right now, what's really gnawing at you? Why the mistrust about HIS?"

"Because," Nettie inhaled deeply, her breath steadying her racing heart, "I believe Casper is behind the shootings."

Nettie's brow furrowed in deep concentration as she observed Cassie's reaction.

"What do you mean? Wasn't he there during the shootings?" Cassie's eyes widened with disbelief, as she leaned in closer, eager for answers.

Nettie nodded slowly, a grimace crossing her face. "Exactly. He was there to save me during both shootings. Conveniently there, I might add. It's almost too perfect. He effectively got me removed from his brother's case." The weight of her accusation hung heavily in the air, a palpable tension swelling between them.

Cassie leaned back in her chair, crossing her legs in a defensive gesture, her expression shifting from surprise to skepticism. "I don't know. I can't imagine Casper doing something like that. Why do you think he orchestrated the whole thing? He put himself at risk, too. Didn't he get shot the first time?"

Nettie knew that was true. He did take a bullet during the first incident, a mere graze, really, but she couldn't shake the nagging doubts that crept into her thoughts. Yes, she recalled the way he had grimaced in pain, shifting uncomfortably as he tried to find a position to ease the sting. Yet, he'd still been there by her side during the second shooting, that undeniable stark proximity a haunting reminder of their shared ordeal.

Frustration gnawed at her, and she bit her lip as she gathered her thoughts. "I don't know…. It just feels too coincidental. And look how it all turned out. I was removed from his brother's case. Just like that."

"Oh, Nettie. I'm so sorry to hear that," Cassie murmured, her tone softening, concern knitting her brow.

"I want you and JD to take on the responsibility of protecting me instead. I can't bring myself to trust anyone Casper assigns to this task."

Cassie's shoulders sagged under the weight of Nettie's request. "I wish we could help you, Nettie. But

JD and I can't manage twenty-four-hour protection. Our responsibilities include caring for Henry Kyle and managing a heavy caseload," she replied with a soft smile that didn't quite reach her eyes. "And from what I've heard, Casper won't be involved in the protection detail anyway."

Nettie's brow furrowed in agitation. "But those are Casper's men. His colleagues. Surely they would follow his lead, allowing him to be close enough to interfere if he wanted to," she said. The urgency of her situation consumed her thoughts—this was about her life, and she felt as though the ground beneath her was crumbling.

A glimmer of thought crossed Cassie's face as she paused, her expression shifting to one of concern. "Hang on a second. Didn't you receive those threatening notes before his brother was arrested? Before Casper even showed up?"

Nettie's mind raced as she slowly nodded, grappling with the implications of Cassie's words. The connection seemed tenuous, slipping through her fingers like sand. "Maybe they aren't connected," she contemplated aloud, the uncertainty gnawing at her. "After all, the first shooter is in custody. He never claimed credit for writing the notes."

Cassie leaned forward, her tone grave. "From what I understand, he's not revealing much at all." The ominous thought hung between them.

With an intense whirl of anxiety swirling within her, Nettie fixed her gaze on Cassie and declared, "I need you and JD to dig into Casper. I want to uncover every detail about him and his brother. Something about them sets off alarm bells in my mind, and I must ensure I'll be safe under HIS protection."

Cassie, her brow furrowed in concern, gradually nodded as she searched Nettie's face. "We can look into it for you if it helps ease your mind."

Though Nettie appreciated the offer, an unsettling doubt lingered within her. Would knowing more really bring her the reassurance she craved? Deep down, she sensed that the danger she felt was more than just a personal threat. It loomed larger, casting a shadow over much more than her safety.

"Do it," Nettie urged. "Gather everything you can on them, and make it quick. If you hit a wall, don't hesitate to call Beau for backup."

Cassie raised a hand, a cautious gesture that cut through the tension in the room. "Hold on a second. Let's not bring in the sheriff just yet. We should do our digging first. I promise we'll have the information for you quickly."

Nettie exhaled a heavy sigh that seemed to release some of the tension in her chest. The burden she'd been carrying felt a bit lighter as if the world's weight had shifted on her shoulders. "All right then," she said, her tone turning serious. "Now, catch me up on Henry Kyle and his antics."

CHAPTER TWENTY

CASPER LOOKED ACROSS the room at his brother and said, "You have a new prosecutor assigned to your case. It's ADA David Baker."

Aaron's brow furrowed in confusion. "What happened to the hot chick?" he asked, leaning back in his chair. "I mean, I'm not complaining—she was a fierce competitor, but I'm genuinely curious."

Feeling a mix of irritation and restraint at his brother's casual remark, Casper took a deep breath to calm his frayed nerves. "She was removed," he replied, the gravity of the situation weighing heavy in his words.

"Maybe now I can finally secure bail and escape this hellhole," Aaron murmured.

Casper nodded in agreement, but a knot of worry twisted in his stomach. He had heard that ADA Baker was notorious for swiftly closing cases, often prioritizing a swift judgment over the possibility of rehabilitation. Casper couldn't shake the feeling that his brother needed more than just freedom. He needed a lifeline to combat his addiction and reclaim his life.

"Time's up," a deputy announced, his voice carrying a stern finality that echoed against the cold, unforgiving walls of the room.

Casper rose slowly from the hard, uncomfortable chair, a heavy weight settling in his chest. "Bryce will get you out on bail," he reassured, keeping his tone steady despite the frustration brewing.

Aaron glanced up, his brow furrowed in distress, the worry etched deeply in his features. "But I don't have any money," he whined. "Neither does Mom."

Casper rubbed the back of his neck with a resigned sigh, feeling the tension creep into his muscles. He knew, with a sinking certainty, that he would have to cover his brother's bond. Deep down, he longed for his brother to take responsibility and contribute somehow, but he couldn't ignore the bond of family that compelled him to act. "I'll cover it," he finally conceded, the words heavy on his tongue.

"Thanks, man," Aaron replied, relief washing over his face, though it only added to Casper's mounting irritation.

A surge of frustration swelled within Casper. He knew well that this generosity would likely go unappreciated, and his brother would make no effort to reimburse him. The thought gnawed at him, even as he resolved to do whatever was necessary to get Aaron out of this place.

As Casper stepped out into the brightly lit corridor, he encountered Bryce, and the two men made their way toward the courtroom in an uneasy silence. The atmosphere was thick with unspoken tension, each lost in their thoughts. It was Bryce who eventually shattered the quiet. "Your brother's case is second on the docket, so the wait won't be long," he said, his tone steady but lacking its usual cheerfulness.

Casper nodded absently, his mind swirling with concerns about how ADA Baker might approach the case. He couldn't help but compare that to the strategies he would expect from Nettie, a familiar worry creeping in. Suddenly, it hit him just how much he had been preoccupied with thoughts of her—again, the entire night had been consumed by anxieties about her safety and the unknown threats that seemed to loom around her. His heart tightened at the thought of who might be plotting to harm her, overshadowing all else in his mind.

The courtroom proceedings unfolded in a manner that aligned perfectly with Casper's anticipations. As the atmosphere was tense, Bryce confidently stepped forward to advocate for his brother's release on bail. After a brief pause, the judge nodded in agreement with a discerning gaze, granting the request and setting the stage for a hopeful turn in the family's fortunes. Afterward, Casper posted it, and once his brother was free, the tightness in his chest eased, knowing his brother wouldn't be in a cell.

Aaron, all smiles, settled into the passenger seat beside Casper as they made their way to their mother's home.

When they arrived, the front door swung open, and their mother stepped out, her eyes sparkling with warmth and love. She rushed forward, wrapping her arms tightly around Aaron and comforting him. "Oh, my sweet boy," she murmured. "I'm so glad you're finally home," she gushed without greeting Casper.

Accustomed to fading into the background while Aaron took center stage, Casper made his way to his room with heavy steps. The air felt thick with anticipation as he prepared to change into something more tactical. He was about to meet his fellow agents, arriving in town shortly. The weight of responsibility pressed down on him. He needed to brief them thoroughly before they assumed control of Nettie's safety. The task's urgency gnawed at him, especially with the unsettling thought that he might soon be unable to see her again.

That idea spiraled in his mind like a relentless echo, leaving an unsettled knot in his stomach. He yearned for her presence—a force that pulled him even when he knew he should distance himself. Nettie was no longer the enemy he once perceived. The lines had blurred, and now she was simply...Nettie. The woman who had once been at odds with Aaron had shifted in his heart, and the thought of never seeing her again felt like an impending loss he was not ready to face.

A sinking feeling settled in Casper's stomach like a heavy stone as he heard the unmistakable sound of the front door creaking open and then shutting with an echoing thud. Aaron had slipped away again, most likely to pursue his reckless lifestyle, a pattern that had become all too familiar. But Casper couldn't afford to dwell on his brother's choices. The urgency of securing Nettie's safety loomed larger than his worries. His brother's antics would have to take a backseat, at least for the moment, especially after he'd just been released on bail. Casper could only hope that Aaron would stay out of trouble and refrain from making any reckless decisions that might land him back behind bars, risking the precious chance he had been given.

Clad in his familiar black tactical pants, snug black T-shirt, and sturdy combat boots, Casper secured his sidearm in the holster at his hip. He reached for his well-worn ball cap, a gesture that felt almost ritualistic, before stepping out of his room and into the dim light of the living room.

There, on the couch, sat his mother, her shoulders shaking silently with quiet sobs. The sight of her pain wrapped around his heart like a vise. He knew all too well that she wouldn't welcome his hug. In moments like these, she would often draw away. Yet the instinct to comfort her tugged insistently at him, a reminder that she would always be his mother despite the distance between them—though there were times she might wish otherwise.

With a quick, almost frantic motion, she wiped the tears from her cheeks, her eyes glimmering with sorrow and surprise as she stood to face him. "Where are you going? And wearing a gun, I might add," she said, her tone stern and argumentative.

"To work," he muttered, barely glancing at her as he swirled past and stepped out into the bright afternoon. The Jeep's engine roared to life with a familiar growl, and the moment the Bluetooth connected, he spoke with purpose. "Call Jesse Hamilton." The phone rang, filling the vehicle with urgency as he shifted into gear, leaving the familiar comfort of his mother's house behind for the open road to the airport.

"How'd it go?" Jesse's voice crackled through the speaker, bypassing the usual pleasantries with a directness that matched Casper's mood.

"He's out on bail and already back behind the wheel." As he navigated the highway, the asphalt stretched before him, the magnolia trees swaying gently in the breeze as he traveled along I-10 toward the Gulfport/Biloxi Regional Airport.

"Shit. Well, you can't do everything for him. He's got to want to do it," Jesse cautioned, a hint of frustration lacing his tone.

Casper's eyes were fixed on the winding road ahead, each bump and dip drawing his thoughts deeper into a swirling tempest of concern that weighed heavily in his chest. "I can't focus on him right now," he muttered, the words almost lost in the engine's hum. "When are the guys arriving?"

"ETA-20 minutes. I arranged for them to take the private jet," Jesse replied, his tone casual yet firm.

A smile tugged at the corners of Casper's mouth, lifting his mood more than he expected. "Wow. I feel special."

"Don't get too comfortable," Jesse cautioned with a sly grin. "The pilot needed the flight hours, and we didn't exactly require him for any grand mission."

"So, you're sending me a bunch of pampered agents. Is that what you're saying?" Casper teased, a sense of lightness washing over him. While the agents would still face the rigors of their work, the thought of them enjoying the lavish perks of a private flight—complete with a dedicated pilot and attentive steward—sparked a flicker of delight within him.

Jesse let out a light chuckle, the sound a teasing familiarity. "You'll have to figure that out for yourself," he said. "Listen, we've been in touch with the sheriff and coordinated our equipment to ensure the men won't run into any problems while protecting…your lady."

Casper's lips pressed into a tight line, a low growl escaping him. "She's not my woman. She's just… someone who needs our help." The weight of his denial hung heavy, his tone a desperate attempt to keep his emotions in check.

"Sure, keep telling yourself that."

Deep down, Casper felt a tumult of conflicting emotions—the longing for her—a visceral aching urge— gnawed at him. Yet, labeling her as "his woman" felt like a degradation he couldn't allow. She was far more complex than that, an enigma he couldn't quite define.

"The exchange will happen at the airport," Jesse stated, shifting to a more serious tone.

Stunned by the sudden shift in plans, Casper straightened in his seat, his mind racing. He turned onto Airport Road in Gulfport, the familiar scenery feeling foreign and urgent. "When did this change?" he asked, disbelief mingling with a surge of anticipation as the reality of the situation sank in. "Why didn't he tell me this sooner?" he questioned.

"Because he knew you were preoccupied with your brother," he explained, his tone steady and reassuring.

"But don't worry. Once the men take control, you'll be in charge."

Feeling a spark of trust in JD and Jesse, Casper nodded, determined to stay focused. "All right, we'll transfer her to the designated spot. That should work. They'll get lost in the airport traffic." He held back his thoughts about the sparse airport buzz—traffic was generally only heavy during the arrival of a large plane—but he was confident they could find a way to make this plan succeed.

"What else do you need from me?" Jesse asked, ever the supportive partner in their complicated dealings.

"Just the background that Devon was working on," Casper replied, maneuvering the jeep into the parking garage. The fluorescent lights flickered overhead as he parked near the baggage claim at terminal two.

"The men have it handled. Just give me a call if you run into any issues. Oh, and Casper?"

"Yeah?" he responded, shifting his focus to the conversation, the engine's hum fading into the background.

"Don't screw this up," Jesse cautioned. "Your dick might want one thing, but logic might be pointing in another direction." With those weighty words, Jesse ended the call, leaving Casper to grapple with his thoughts in the stillness of the parking garage.

As he stepped into the bustling terminal, the sharp clink of metal caught his attention. Security personnel quickly intercepted him, eyeing the weapon with caution and authority. Frustration bubbled within him. He should have anticipated this inconvenience and left the gun behind. But duty called, and the firearm was an inseparable part of his uniform.

Just as the guard prepared to contact the sheriff for verification, JD approached confidently, accompanied by Cassie and Nettie. "He's with us, Jim," JD announced, his tone reassuring.

Jim turned to JD, a smile breaking across his face, before shifting his gaze back to Casper. "Hell, boy, why didn't you just say so?"

Casper shook his head, a hint of disbelief coloring his expression. JD had more connections and influence than he had anticipated. His attention was soon drawn to Nettie, who stood comfortably by Cassie. His breath hitched in his throat at the sight of her. Dressed casually in snug capris and a fitted T-shirt, she effortlessly showcased her sun-kissed arms and toned calves. A gentle breeze played with her hair, causing it to dance softly around her shoulders, and he found himself momentarily speechless, captivated by her effortless beauty.

JD nodded toward the escalator, his eyes lighting up. "Here come the boys."

Casper turned, and his gaze quickly landed on the unmistakable presence of four men, all dressed similarly to him. They maneuvered through the terminal with purpose, their eyes scanning the surroundings, surveying every detail with a keen, practiced vigilance.

Just as he was about to pivot back to Nettie, an unwelcome sound pierced the air—familiar yet distant, echoing from a time he thought he left behind. "Ash. Ash McNabb!" Marie Edwards called out, her tone a mixture of relief and urgency. He turned to face her, recognizing the weathered features of a woman he hadn't seen in over a decade.

Her warm smile wavered as she gestured to the teenage girl beside her. The girl had striking blue eyes that sparkled with curiosity and blonde hair that cascaded down her shoulders, reminiscent of a sunlit summer day. "Kayla, this is your father," Marie introduced with pride.

The moment hung in the air like a fragile glass ornament, and when he heard a sharp breath from Nettie, it felt as though the ground beneath him had crumbled. A rush of shock and disbelief coursed through him, instantly turning his world upside down. "Kayla Marie," he muttered, grappling with the reality that this girl—this young woman—was his daughter.

CHAPTER TWENTY-ONE

NETTIE STOOD FROZEN, her heart racing as she watched the disbelief wave wash over Casper's face. His eyes widened, reflecting a mixture of shock and confusion as he stared at the woman and the teenage girl she had just identified as his daughter. A flurry of questions surged, akin to those an investigator might ponder: Had this woman spoken the truth? Was Casper—this man she had come to respect—careless enough to father a child and then vanish from their lives? This wasn't just professional curiosity. It was a storm of jealousy disguised as concern. But she quickly reminded herself that she held no romantic feelings for him. No, that was a lie, a feeble attempt to mask the truth.

Around them, Casper's loyal men formed a protective barrier around JD and Cassie, their imposing figures casting long shadows that enveloped the duo. Nettie felt the weight of their presence. It was both comforting and stifling. She understood the necessity of their vigilance, especially since she had not anticipated the danger lurking behind her unexpected visit to the airport—a place she hadn't planned to go at all.

"Yes, honey," the woman pressed on. "She's your daughter. You never should have left us."

Nettie's breath caught in her throat, a sharp gasp escaping her lips as the words hung heavily. Had he abandoned a pregnant woman? The realization twisted in her chest, shattering the idealized image she had held of the man who had risked everything to save her life—not once but twice. Had the hero she envisioned been merely a mirage born of her imagination? Is it possible that the complexities of humanity overshadowed the gallant facade? The thought gnawed at her, igniting a mix of disappointment and confusion.

"And," Marie continued, "we need you."

Casper shifted his gaze between Marie and Nettie. His eyes, imbued with an intense focus, finally locked onto her. "Cowboy. Nemo. You two, grab the crates coming off the belt." His voice was firm, but his attention remained fixed on Nettie, the tension palpable between them. "Doc, you're in charge. Take whatever steps are necessary to fulfill our mission. I'll catch up with you later."

Nettie, a storm of emotions swirling inside her, felt an overwhelming desire to scream that Casper wouldn't be seeing her again. Yet, ignited by an undeniable attraction, another part of her compelled her to stay silent. The conflict between her seething anger and heated desire raged within her, leaving her frustrated and yearning for clarity amid the chaos.

Before his intense gaze finally broke away from hers, he leaned in closer and intoned, "Trust me." With a swift motion, he pivoted to face the woman standing to the side. "Marie, what in the world are you talking about?"

Nettie stifled a laugh at the shock that flickered across Marie's features, but the weight of her concerns quickly overshadowed any amusement. If Casper was indeed the mastermind behind the attacks on her life, then these men were hiding secrets that could not be ignored. The notion of their "mission" sent tendrils of fear curling around her usually self-assured demeanor.

"Hey, JD. Cassie," the sturdy man beside her rumbled. "Nettie—would it be all right if I called you that?"

Nettie nodded, her curiosity piqued despite her apprehension.

"Nettie, I'm Doc," he introduced himself, gesturing to the tall figure behind her. "This is Pup."

Pup, his expression a mix of curiosity and mischief, raised his eyebrows and asked, "Now?"

Doc let out an exasperated sigh, his patience clearly thinning. "Yes, now you can check if the dogs are ready."

Nettie opened her mouth to question this abrupt command when Doc anticipated her words and silenced her with a wave. "He's our dog handler. Well, one of them. But the handler for our team."

"Dogs?" Nettie echoed with disbelief as she tried to absorb the weight of the situation. The very idea that her safety was perceived to be under such dire threat that powerful men felt compelled to deploy dogs as part of their security measures left her feeling unsettled. The notion seemed almost excessive, especially when she considered the possibility that Casper had orchestrated the recent shootings to intimidate her into stepping away from his brother's case. He had achieved his goal—so why the elaborate measures, including the security team and the canine guardians?

A whirlwind of conflicting thoughts swirled in her mind, crafting a storm of confusion. If Casper had been behind those attacks, what could have motivated this ongoing charade of protection? Yet, if her instincts—usually sharp and reliable—had failed her this time, then perhaps a genuine threat lurked in the shadows, one that these men were pledged to guard her against.

Each time Casper had come to her rescue, whether his actions stemmed from a calculated plan or pure luck, it became increasingly clear he had no intention of ending her life. Logic dictated that these men would carry out their duty with similar restraint. But despite her belief in rationality, an underlying unease remained. She still felt an urgent need for the background check, which Cassie had diligently been working on. More than anything, she wanted to peel back the mystery surrounding Ash McNabb, yearning to uncover every detail of his life that could be unearthed.

The two men Casper referred to as "Cowboy" and "Nemo" approached their sturdy frames dutifully bearing a substantial black crate. Nettie felt a surge of curiosity and apprehension as she pondered the mysterious contents concealed within its opaque exterior.

Looking intently at the nearby guard, Doc shifted his stance and inquired, "May we arm ourselves?"

The guard exchanged a glance with JD, who subtly nodded in response.

"They're assuming her protection," JD informed the guard.

"Go ahead, but I'm staying with you until you leave the parking lot," the guard replied, his expression firm, underscoring the gravity of the situation.

"We can deal with that," Doc affirmed, determination hardening his features. His gaze drifted to Casper. The man stood huddled, conferring with Marie, their discussion a hush in the bustling ambiance. Meanwhile, the teenager watched with wide eyes, intrigue flickering as she took in the imposing figures of the men guarding Nettie.

Nettie stood frozen, her eyes wide as she watched the men deftly unlock and pry open the heavy wooden crate. The pungent scent of metal and oil wafted toward her, mingling with the tension in the air. Inside lay an unsettling array of weapons—gleaming handguns and rugged rifles meticulously arranged, as if awaiting inspection. A chill ran down her spine, and her hands involuntarily quivered as the gravity of the situation sank in. The men clearly believed her life was in imminent danger, a realization that sent ripples of fear coursing through her.

Doubt crept into her mind. Perhaps she had been mistaken about Casper orchestrating the recent incidents. Yet, the nagging thought that she had crossed paths with danger on two separate occasions was a coincidence too profound to dismiss.

"Nettie," Cassie said. "I'll have that report to you today."

Nettie's heart sank further. The comforting presence of Cassie and JD, who had offered her solace in a chaotic world, was slipping away. The fact that she was left in the care of men associated with HIS—a name that echoed dread—left her feeling more isolated than ever. A desperate urge to call out for JD and Cassie welled inside her, a primal instinct to flee from the uncertainty surrounding her. But she restrained herself, knowing they were bound by duty and unable to prioritize her safety.

"Thanks," she managed to say, her voice trembling slightly. "Thank you for sitting with me last night." She turned to JD, a flicker of gratitude in her weary eyes. "And it was nice to see you."

"Don't worry," JD replied, as if he recognized the fear etched on her face. "They're professionals. No one will get to you through them. They'll keep you safe."

Despite his calming words, her unease gnawed at her, reminding her of the stark reality outside their temporary refuge.

Nettie observed with curiosity and apprehension as each man donned his gear with purpose. They inserted small devices into their ears one by one, and she speculated that they were communication systems or something of that sort. High-tech surveillance equipment wasn't her area of expertise. They could have been tuning into a football game for all she knew. Still, her instinct told her that her initial guess was likely on point.

"We've got her," Doc announced confidently to JD and Cassie. The two men who had just unloaded the heavy crate maneuvered it again into position. "We've arranged for a rental to be delivered to the terminal, so we won't have to travel far for transportation."

JD nodded, his expression serious. "Jim, I'd like you to meet the team from Hamilton Investigation and Security. They're the brave souls who saved Cassie not long ago."

The guard offered a respectful nod in response, his demeanor betraying a sense of camaraderie. "Take care of this lady," he instructed, his tone firm and protective.

Nettie turned to him, confusion flickering across her features. Although she had no recollection of ever meeting this guard before, there was an undeniable air of respect surrounding him.

Sensing the uncertainty radiating from her, Jim stepped closer. "We all know who you are, Miss Broussard. You inspire not just the force but every guard out there. Your relentless pursuit of true justice—refusing to settle for a quick closure—sets you apart. We appreciate you deeply and are dedicated to ensuring nothing happens to you."

Unsure how to respond to such an unexpected compliment, Nettie smiled faintly and said, "Thank you."

Before any further conversation could unfold, Doc and the men guided her toward a sleek black SUV that had just rolled up to the bustling terminal pickup area. A flicker of curiosity crossed her mind—why was it always black SUVs that accompanied the security details? But she quickly brushed aside the thought. There were more pressing matters than pondering their vehicles' color.

As the team loaded two sizable kennels and an imposing black crate into the rear of the SUV, Nettie felt a sense of urgency. She was ushered into the back seat, where Cowboy, clad in a distinctive cowboy hat, settled beside her. To her right was Nemo, his warm presence grounding her in the moment. Pup took the wheel while Doc occupied the passenger seat, a reassuring figure amidst the tension.

Turning back for a final glance at Casper, she noticed his intense gaze locked onto her—an unspoken bond stretching taut between them. As the SUV pulled away, the reality of their separation weighed heavily on her. He had vowed to distance himself from her protection, leaving her with the bitter truth that she might never see him again. The thought churned in her mind, a painful acceptance that felt too soon.

CHAPTER TWENTY-TWO

CASPER'S MIND DRIFTED away from Marie's sweet, syrupy tone as he fixed his gaze on Nettie and his men, who were already pulling away, leaving him to grapple with this unexpected turn of events. He turned back to the duo, a flicker of doubt gnawing at him regarding Marie's explanation. "Let's find a quieter spot to talk, away from all these curious ears," he proposed.

"Sounds perfect," Marie replied, a hint of longing in her eyes. "Especially since they didn't serve us breakfast on the flight."

"Where did you park?" he asked, a knot forming in his stomach as he braced for her response.

"Oh, we didn't park anywhere, darling. We just flew in from Chicago," she said nonchalantly as if that information wouldn't send his heart racing.

"A rental, then?" he pressed, knowing he was being roped into acting as their chauffeur for whatever destination they had in mind.

"Nope, no rental. We were planning to catch a ride to your mom's house to find you," she replied, her tone casual, but the implications hung thick in the air.

"That was quite a gamble," he replied, disbelief coloring his words. "Especially considering I don't even live here anymore."

"And yet," Marie countered, a knowing smile creeping onto her lips, "here you are."

Yes, Casper thought bitterly, here he was—caught in a tangled web of memories, facing the woman who had shattered his heart in their teenage years, and now, standing beside her was the girl who claimed to be his daughter.

As they crowded into his rugged Jeep, the air buzzing with anticipation, Casper stole a sideways glance at the girl who had yet to utter a word. He turned to her and asked, "Kayla, how old are you?"

Kayla lifted her chin defiantly, her expression a mix of pride and rebellion. "Sixteen," she replied.

Sitting in the front passenger seat, Marie quirked an eyebrow in amusement. "Huh," she commented dryly. "Going on thirty."

Kayla redirected her gaze to her mother, a curious spark in her eyes. "Okay, so I've met him. May I have my phone back now?"

With a resigned sigh, Marie rummaged through her purse and produced a sleek, modern cell phone, handing it over to her daughter. "She wouldn't come unless I took away the one thing she holds dear—that cursed cell phone," she said with a hint of exasperation.

"I'm going to be an influencer," Kayla declared, her excitement bubbling through her words as she cradled her phone like a prized trophy.

Casper observed the dynamic between mother and daughter, a curious blend of tension and affection. He couldn't help but wonder why Marie had chosen this moment—of all moments—to introduce them. Questions swirled in his mind, but he hesitated to voice them before Kayla. Yet, he realized he needed clarity. "It's still breakfast time, so only a few spots are open," he said thoughtfully, "but I know a place where we can talk."

Casper navigated the winding roads toward Gulf Island, a quaint enclave synonymous with JD and Cassie. As he approached a charming little breakfast spot renowned for its decadent omelets, the sun hung low in the sky, casting a warm glow over the rustic establishment. Since breakfast hour was nearing its end, he was relieved to find the place relatively empty, offering a cocoon of privacy for the critical conversation ahead.

As he stepped out of his Jeep, his gaze landed on Kayla, who was meticulously documenting her surroundings, her eyes glued to her phone with the focus of an artist at work.

"She's live, most likely," Marie remarked, irritation lacing her tone. "She's always live. It's like living inside a reality show—complete with the drama."

Casper shot her a raised eyebrow, curiosity blooming. "And you just let this happen?"

Marie let out a frustrated sigh. "What choice do I have? Just wait. You'll see for yourself."

Unease fluttered in Casper's stomach, but he suppressed it for now, focusing instead on finding a cozy table once they were inside. "Kayla," he called gently, waiting for her to break away from her screen. When she finally acknowledged him, she smirked into the camera and said, "This is supposedly my dad. The one who abandoned me and Mom when she was pregnant."

A surge of anger coursed through Casper at the distortion of truth. He quickly reached out, snatching the phone from her grasp, and decisively ended the live stream.

"Hey!" Kayla protested, lunging for the device. "Give me that back!"

"No," Casper responded firmly. "Not when you're spreading lies like that. Right now, we'll sit down and have a nice meal." With that, he tucked her phone securely into his pocket and guided her through the restaurant's entrance, the door swinging closed behind them, blocking out the chatter of the outside world.

Once settled into their seats, Kayla leaned forward, her eyes sparkling with determination as she asked for her phone again. Casper shot her an admonishing glare. "Not at the table." The words slipped out, reminding him of his mother's persistent nagging, and he cursed himself internally. The last thing he wanted was for their private exchange to be splattered all over Kayla's social media feeds. The thought of it going viral sent a shiver down his spine.

A hollow sensation nestled in his stomach as he scanned the menu where hunger once resided. It starkly contrasted the warmth that had flickered in Nettie's eyes when they last parted. Memories of her and the crew leaving the airport rushed back, quickly overshadowed by Marie and Kayla's uneasy presence. Any connection he once felt with Nettie had faded into the background, eclipsed by the chaotic swirl of emotions brought on by their sudden arrival.

As the morning sun streamed through the window, casting a warm glow over the table, a heated debate simmered between Kayla and Casper over the day's breakfast choices. Casper, growing increasingly frustrated by Kayla's obstinate attitude, sensed that her constant whining and pleas for her phone were a ploy to provoke him. He tuned out her complaints and shifted his focus to Marie, his expression firm and expectant. "Now, Marie, explain."

With a hesitant breath, Marie began, her lip trembling slightly. "Well," she said, glancing at Kayla before continuing, "when you left for boot camp, I was pregnant."

Casper's eyes narrowed in disbelief, his brow furrowing as the shock of her words settled in. "And you failed to tell me for what, sixteen years?" he shot back, incredulity lacing his tone. "As I recall, you weren't waiting for me after I finished my training. You had already moved on with an Air Force captain."

Across the table, Kayla's eyes widened in astonishment, her mind racing as she processed the shocking revelation. It was painfully clear to her that the tale Marie had concocted at the airport was an elaborate fabrication.

Sensing the moment's weight, Marie stole a sidelong glance at her daughter and let out a nervous giggle that fell flat in the charged atmosphere. "That's not how it was, Ash," she stammered, her voice lacking the conviction it needed.

Casper raised his eyebrows, leaning back in his chair as he crossed his arms defiantly over his chest. "Then tell me how it was, Marie," he demanded, his tone unyielding as the tension in the room thickened.

"Well," Marie said, as she wet her lips, "you never wrote. I thought maybe you had changed your mind about marrying me, so I had no choice but to find someone else to help take care of our child."

Casper clenched his fists, summoning every ounce of calm he could muster. "I wrote to you daily and mailed out letters twice a week with each day's message." His heart raced, fueled by anger and frustration.

Marie averted her gaze, fingers nervously twisting the napkin in her hands—his mind raced to recall that telltale sign, a surefire indicator of deception. Why was she lying?

"Bullshit," he snapped, unable to contain himself. "You might not have received every single one, but you got some. The mail service can't be that derelict in their duties."

"Okay," she finally conceded in a whisper, "I may have received one or two."

"Let me guess," he pressed, anger simmering just below the surface as memories of the past surged back. "I wouldn't make enough for you as a private, so you looked for an officer instead. And since this base is nearby, an Air Force man fit the bill nicely?"

"You're making me sound like a terrible person, Ash. That's not how it was." Her voice trembled as she spoke, a mix of defensiveness and guilt.

"Sounds about right to me," chimed Kayla, taking a sip from her brightly colored straw, the sugary soda fizzing against the ice.

Marie swung her gaze toward Kayla, irritation etched on her face. "You stay out of this."

"Sounds like I'm a big part of this," the girl retorted, biting back tears. "Remember, I'm the consequence of your actions. Isn't that what you always said, Mom?"

Casper felt a wave of nausea wash over him at those words. How could a mother say such a thing to her child? It was an unfathomable betrayal, and yet it echoed his painful memories of a mother who had been just as cold and calculating.

"Kayla, now is not the time to argue with me," Marie urged. The room crackled with tension as the two women faced each other, steam practically rising from Kayla's narrowed eyes.

Casper could feel the weight of the atmosphere pressing down on him. "So what do you want?" he asked, a wariness creeping into his voice. He'd learned by now that Marie always had an angle, a move waiting in the shadows. In his youth, he had overlooked her cunning charm, blinded by the depth of his infatuation. But maturity had peeled back the layers, revealing her strategies for what they truly were—manipulative and self-serving.

"Why, I want you to take Kayla and me in," Marie declared, her words tinged with a false excitement that made Casper's stomach churn. "It's time you got to know your daughter."

Casper's heart plummeted. The revelation hung in the air like a storm cloud threatening to burst. If Kayla was indeed his daughter—a realization that both thrilled and terrified him—he would willingly welcome the rebellious teenager into his home. But the thought of inviting Marie back into his life felt like swallowing gravel.

His phone vibrated sharply in his pocket as he contemplated how to respond, pulling him from the spiraling thoughts. He pulled it out, feeling Kayla's piercing glare burn through him like a laser.

With a sense of urgency, he glanced at the screen, his breath hitching as he read the text from the sheriff: "Shooter dead. Stabbed in cell." The news washed over him like a wave, leaving him breathless. How would this new development change everything?

CHAPTER TWENTY-THREE

NETTIE SHIFTED UNEASILY in the cramped back seat of the vehicle, feeling the palpable tension that hung in the air like thick fog. The men surrounding her were utterly stoic, their faces etched with seriousness as they stared intently out of their windows, scanning the landscape for any signs of danger. The only sound breaking the silence was the occasional whimper of the dogs in the cargo area, their restless energy adding to the atmosphere of unease.

Desperate to break the heavy silence, Nettie took a deep breath and said, "So…." She trailed off and was unsure how to lighten the mood.

Doc turned his head, his expression revealing a flicker of curiosity. "Yes?" he replied, his tone encouraging yet cautious.

"Where are we headed?" she blurted, her heart thumping as she sought to break the tension.

"To a safe house," Doc answered, raising an eyebrow as if the answer should have been obvious. "Anything else?"

Nettie hesitated, feeling a rush of embarrassment for her previous question. But one more thought slipped out before she could stop herself. "Is Casper one of the good guys?" The moment the words left her lips, she almost wanted to cover her mouth in shock at her curiosity.

To her surprise, the men shared a soft chuckle, breaking some tension.

"I mean—" she began.

"I know what you mean," Doc said gently, a knowing look in his eye. "Believe me, they don't get any better than Casper when it comes to good guys." With a thoughtful nod, he returned his gaze to the world rushing by outside.

Feeling increasingly self-conscious after her slip, Nettie settled into the cramped space between two muscle-bound men, her fingers twiddling as boredom crept in. She gazed at the passing scenery, wishing she had brought a case file for work. Her boss must be in a frenzy without her contributions, considering they had promised she would be available to work remotely during these hours. After all, it was the peak of work hours for both the courthouse and the DA's office, and she felt the weight of her absence pressing down on her.

"We're here," Pup announced, steering the vehicle down a winding, tree-lined drive. The gravel path crunched beneath the tires as they approached an impressive house, its elegant facade framed by towering oaks and whispering pines. In the back, a serene pond glimmered under the afternoon sun, its still surface reflecting the vibrant hues of the surrounding foliage.

Nettie couldn't shake the disbelief that washed over her. The stunning residence felt more like a luxury getaway than a safe house, an impression that left her uneasy. This level of comfort was beyond her means. Just then, a nagging thought struck her—she realized they had never discussed who would foot the bill for her security. The sheriff's office certainly wouldn't cover it, and Casper seemed an unlikely candidate. She typically managed her expenses with care, but this? "Um, is this really a safe house? Because it feels more like a vacation retreat."

Doc, with his calm demeanor, nodded reassuringly. "It is indeed a safe house. The owners are currently on vacation, and we use their home in their absence."

A twinge of fear nudged Nettie as she asked, "Do they know we're here?"

The men burst into laughter, a sound that rubbed her the wrong way. She couldn't stand when they shared those moments of amusement at her expense.

"Of course they do," Doc replied, still chuckling. "Think of it like one of those modern options for lodging, where you stay in someone's home instead of a hotel."

"But I'm not on vacation, and I can't afford to rent a place like this," she exclaimed, her anxiety rising.

"Didn't Casper mention it? This is pro bono," Doc said, stepping out of the vehicle.

As they emerged, Doc and Cowboy flanked her, their imposing figures casting long shadows in the fading daylight. Meanwhile, Pup moved to the back of the vehicle, the familiar sounds of rustling leashes and eager barks signaling the release of his dogs. At the same time,

Nemo, a silhouette with a rifle cradled in his arms, strode away, losing himself in the woods surrounding the house.

Nettie felt a surge of frustration. She wasn't the type to accept charity, yet she remembered Casper's words echoing in her mind. Though she had never truly believed he possessed the authority to make such decisions, she had underestimated him.

"Do you think I'm still in danger?" she asked.

Doc nodded gravely, his eyes darkening with concern. "You were shot at even after the initial shooter was taken into custody. Someone is after you."

"Or Casper," Cowboy interjected, his Southern drawl thickening the air with an unexpected layer of unease.

Nettie turned her head sharply, her heart racing as the implication hit her like a freight train. "What?"

"Nothing," Doc replied swiftly, trying to dismiss the weight of Cowboy's words.

"No, he said 'or Casper.' What did he mean?" The concern for Casper's safety twisted in her gut, confusing her more than ever. Why did she suddenly care about someone who had inadvertently dragged her into this perilous situation?

"Listen," Doc said, his tone firm yet gentle. "You're the one who's been receiving threatening notes. Casper lived in Maryland. He wasn't expected down here, so Casper's not in danger. Besides, the shooter claimed to be after you."

"Oh." The realization washed over Nettie like cold water. While she understood the logic, it did little to quell her rising dread. The idea that someone wanted her dead felt surreal, a nightmare she couldn't shake off. She believed there had been attempts on her life, but what had she done to provoke such vengeance? The haunting question lingered in her mind, gnawing at the edges of her sanity.

She and her vigilant guards lingered in the shadows of the imposing SUV, its dark frame blending seamlessly with the dim surroundings while Pup and his dogs scoured the area for any sign of trouble. Nettie felt a knot twist in her stomach as she glanced anxiously around. She had no clue where Nemo had slipped off to, but an unsettling feeling crept over her, whispering that his departure had to do with the urgent need for security. The presence of the men flanking her should have offered some reassurance, yet the vulnerability of being exposed in the open gnawed at her. Had someone followed them? The same ominous figure who had unleashed chaos at her home.

Her home. The thought struck her like a physical blow. Her once sanctuary turned into a haunting memory tainted by gunfire. True, she had complete faith in Beau to handle the aftermath of the attack, but it was still her home—her domain—and the weight of that responsibility felt heavier now than ever. A flicker of doubt surged through her. Would she ever feel safe inside those walls again? And what exactly was this perilous situation they were entangled in? When would the suffocating anxiety finally dissipate, and they could breathe freely once more?

Suddenly, a phone vibrated, cutting through the tension in the air. Doc reached into his pocket and answered the call, his expression shifting into one of focused intensity as he spoke. "Doc," he said, his tone steady yet cautious.

Nettie, usually not one to pry, found herself leaning closer. Her curiosity piqued as she wondered what could warrant a phone call during such a critical protection detail. Yet, she held back the urge to ask, sensing the moment's gravity.

After a brief exchange, Doc ended the call and stepped closer to her, a gravity in his approach that sent shivers down her spine. "He's closing up loose ends," he disclosed quietly.

Nettie felt her blood turn to ice at those words as both men moved closer to her. Even she, amid the turmoil, understood the chilling implication behind his statement. She had to confront the unsettling truth that she was the target. The realization hit her like a cold wave, sweeping away any lingering thoughts about Casper and his brother's case, which now seemed distant and insignificant, fading away like the landscape in her rearview mirror. Yet, despite the distraction of the past, she could not shake the feeling that danger still hovered ominously in the shadows, ready to strike at any moment.

Why did she suddenly want Casper to join her security detail? Perhaps it was because he had an uncanny ability to appear just in time to rescue her from the shadows of uncertainty. Or maybe it was because she craved his comforting presence, his steady hands entwined with hers, providing solace amid the chaos. She regretted persuading Cassie and JD to care for her kittens while she was away. The absence of their soft purring and warm, small bodies nestled in her arms left a hollow ache in her heart.

"All clear," Pup announced, securing the leashes around the energetic bodies of the two labs, who dutifully followed his lead, their tails wagging as they eagerly anticipated their next adventure.

"Nemo?" Doc queried, his tone serious yet calm.

Nettie blinked, slowly grasping that he was addressing the man through the communication system she had witnessed them operate at the bustling airport. The muted response was inaudible to her, but she deciphered the moment of silence as an assurance of safety as her guards guided her toward the welcoming embrace of her home, ushering her inside with a protective vigilance.

Pup moved to her side, the warmth of his presence surprising. He gestured theatrically toward the two dogs by his side. "This is Daisy," he said with a proud smile, "and this handsome fellow is Bomber." Each dog turned their attentive gaze toward him, ears perked and tails wagging slightly as if they understood their names and were pleased to be acknowledged. Nettie couldn't help but wonder if she was imagining it—could dogs truly smile?

"Nice to meet both of you," she said, her cheeks warming with a dash of embarrassment for speaking to the dogs as if they were people. Yet, the thought of interrupting Pup's gentle bond with them kept her hands still by her sides. She promised herself that later, when the canines were off duty, she would take the time to give each a proper pet and scratch behind the ears.

As the day unfolded, Doc led her down a softly lit hallway toward the main suite. "This will be your sanctuary for the duration of your stay. All I ask is that you never lock the door. Close it as much as you like, but never lock us out." His words evoked a sense of unspoken trust, a promise of safety.

Nettie nodded, stepping into the suite with a gasp that escaped her lips unbidden. The room was a beautiful haven, featuring a spacious king-sized bed draped with crisp white linens that beckoned her for rest. An adjoining ensuite gleamed invitingly, boasting an empty closet that awaited her belongings and polished bathroom counters ready for her to arrange her toiletries. She turned back to Doc. "My bags?"

Cowboy appeared then, striding in with a reassuring grin as he handed her the small overnight case. The contrast between her bags and the magnificent suite was stark, and she felt self-conscious for a brief moment.

Doc frowned slightly, his brow furrowing as he glanced at the modest size of her duffel and laptop bag. "Is that all you brought?"

Nettie looked down at the small bag, belatedly realizing how inadequate it seemed for her stay. Of course, this was all she needed—she had planned to visit Cassie and JD overnight before returning home. But now, with her carefully laid plans unraveling like a loose thread, she felt the weight of uncertainty pressing upon her.

"Do they have a washing machine?" she inquired, a hint of hope in her voice. The prospect of washing her clothes daily and rotating between her two outfits felt manageable. It was a small price to pay for the comfort of simplicity.

"Yes," Doc replied with a nod, then turned and walked away, his figure casting a shadow as he guided Cowboy back to the brightly lit main area of the house. Nettie only caught a fragment of his words, "Tell Casper —" before they faded, leaving her momentarily alone in the quiet space.

With a sigh, she redirected her focus from the enticing allure of the large bed draped in soft linens. Work was to be done, and she was driven by an insatiable need for justice that always beckoned her. She set her laptop on the polished wooden table, alongside her notepad filled with scribbled thoughts and various files, ready to delve into the urgency of her tasks.

As her fingers danced across the keyboard, the familiar rhythm enveloped her. The idea of working remotely, tucked away in this serene environment, unexpectedly brought a sense of solace. She could now immerse herself in her work, channeling all her energy into the causes that fueled her passion until it would be safe to return to her previous life.

Despite dedicating herself fully to her work, her mind remained stubbornly anchored to thoughts of Casper and the two women who lingered like shadows in her memory. No matter how hard she tried to focus on the tasks at hand, the haunting image of losing him consumed her—only to confront the painful realization that there had never truly been a 'them,' and there likely never would be. It had all boiled down to a single, fleeting kiss, a momentary spark that held more weight in her imagination than in reality. She desperately needed to cling to that truth, to push aside the tantalizing fantasies that danced in her mind, insisting that a future they could never share was just an illusion.

A familiar voice sliced through the silence as she listened intently, causing her heart to race uncontrollably. It was unmistakable. He was here, stepping into her world again, sending a thrilling jolt through her.

CHAPTER TWENTY-FOUR

"DUDE, WHAT WAS that all about?" Cowboy inquired between bites of a hefty sandwich he had grabbed from the well-stocked kitchen, crumbs scattering onto the floor.

Casper exhaled deeply, his expression clouded with memories he wished could remain buried in the past. "Just some history I'd rather not revisit."

Doc leaned back slightly, his gaze measuring, making Casper shift in his seat and wince as he struck his wound. "Is she your daughter?" he asked, probing gently yet insistently.

With a heavy sigh, Casper leaned forward in the chair, elbows resting on his thighs. His fingers raked through his disheveled hair, revealing the strain etched into his features. "Christ, I don't know," he admitted. He settled back, arms draping over his thighs, locking eyes with Doc. "I guess she could be. The timeline fits."

"You know," Cowboy said, leaning back in his chair with a thoughtful expression, "this whole situation reminds me of when my ex popped back into my life unexpectedly." He laughed softly, shaking his head as if the memory was amusing and frustrating. "It wasn't pretty."

Curiosity sparked in Casper's eyes as he leaned forward. "How did that all turn out for you?" he asked, eager to hear more.

Cowboy's face broke into a wide grin, a mixture of nostalgia and pride dancing across his features. "Oh, let me tell you, it took a mountain of effort to win my girl back," he replied. "But in the end, I did manage to pull it off."

Casper's expression shifted slightly, a hint of confusion knitted between his brows. "But," he clarified, "I'm not trying to win a girl."

Cowboy erupted into laughter, a hearty sound that echoed through the room. "Ah, just keep telling yourself that," he teased, playfully patting Casper on the shoulder as he stood and strolled back to the kitchen, the clinking of his sandwich plate cutting through their conversation.

Casper glanced over at Doc and Pup with an earnest look. "I really am not," he insisted.

Doc shook his head, a smirk playing at the corners of his lips. "Thou doest protest too much," he quipped, clearly amused by the whole exchange.

Casper leaped from his chair, the scraping sound of the legs against the floor punctuating the room's silence. He made his way to the kitchen, the cool air offering a refreshing contrast to the tension that hung in the air. "Did you encounter any problems?" he inquired moments before pulling open the gleaming door of the refrigerator. The light inside flickered on, revealing an impressive array of food and drink. He reached for a bottle of crisp, cold water, his eyes scanning the well-stocked shelves, filled with enough provisions to last them for over a week. It never ceased to amaze him how Devon managed to prepare for any possible scenario that lay ahead.

Behind him, Doc stood casually against the doorjamb, his muscular arms crossed tightly over his broad chest, exuding a calm confidence. "No issues on my end. How about you?" he replied.

After taking a long, satisfying swig of the refreshing spring water, Casper shook his head, the bottle crinkling in his grip. "No problems, but I've got news that could alter the course of our mission."

"Why the hell didn't you lead with that?" Doc asked, his brow furrowed in annoyance.

With a dramatic roll of his eyes, Casper shot back, "Because you all were too busy poking around in my affairs first."

"Touché," Doc conceded, a smirk tugging at the corners of his mouth as he turned on his heel, striding toward the living area to gather the rest of the group.

Casper quickly followed.

As Doc, Pup, and Cowboy gathered around Casper in the living area, he leaned in, activating his microphone with a deliberate push. "Nemo?" he called.

"About time you showed your sorry face," came the reply, laden with easy camaraderie.

"You missed me that much, huh?" Casper shot back, a smirk tugging at the corners of his mouth as he glanced toward the dark silhouette of the trees just beyond their safe house, where Nemo was likely tucked away, blending into the shadows.

"Like a Southerner misses the mosquitoes," Nemo quipped, his tone dripping with playful sarcasm.

Casper's expression shifted as he surveyed the room, his gaze landing on Nettie—their eyes met briefly, and he felt a prickle of unease. How much had she overheard? He wasn't quite prepared to delve into the intricacies of his personal life with her. Why would he? Their shared moment—a kiss—had felt fleeting, a spell cast amid the chaos of their world.

Yet, the weight of the unsaid hung between them. He'd experienced plenty of intense connections without ever baring his soul, so why did it seem different this time? The atmosphere thickened with unspoken words as he wrestled with the unexpected impulse to explain himself.

"You may as well come out and join us," Casper called out, the sound echoing through the corridor as all heads turned toward Nettie, who stood hesitantly at the end.

"I—uh," she stammered, clearing her throat nervously. "I just wanted something to drink." Her eyes flickered between the group and the floor, but Casper could sense there was more to her hesitation. He could almost bet that her real intention was to eavesdrop, yet a part of him hoped she had ventured from the safety of her room, drawn by the sound of his voice.

"Well, grab something from the fridge and come hang out with us," he encouraged, a friendly smile on his face. His gaze shifted to Cowboy, anticipating the usual sarcastic comment or an inappropriate quip aimed at Nettie, and prepared to give him a sharp warning glare.

To his surprise, Cowboy raised both hands in mock surrender, a playful grin spreading across his face. Mischief danced in his eyes as he met Casper's gaze, silently promising to keep his tongue in check—for now.

Once Nettie settled in the floral armchair vacated by Pup, she reached down and stroked Daisy's fur. The dog lay protectively at her feet without Pup issuing a verbal command. "Her fur is so soft."

Pup beamed with pride, his chest puffing out at the compliment. "Thanks," he said, a broad grin stretching.

Casper rotated his neck, feeling the subtle crack of his joints. He knew he had to intervene quickly. If he allowed Pup to continue, the boy could launch into an endless monologue about dogs, his favorite topic. "Nettie," he said, shifting his attention to her, "how much did you overhear?"

Her eyes locked onto his, intense and inquisitive. "Not much," she replied, her tone revealing a layer of understanding that suggested she was aware of the complicated situation with his daughter.

That realization weighed heavily on him. He had a pressing issue to tackle, one that loomed more significant than the unresolved problems regarding family—an urgent matter that could transform his relationship with her yet again.

Casper leaned forward. "I won't beat around the bush," he declared, his eyes momentarily flickering away from the group to rest on Nettie sitting across from him. The tension in the room thickened as he delivered the shocking news. "David Baker is in the hospital."

Nettie's eyes widened in disbelief, and her hand flew to her mouth, stifling a gasp. "What's wrong?".

"Single car crash." A flicker of doubt crossed Casper's mind about the details of that accident, but he quickly pushed it aside. He needed to keep Nettie safe. The instinctive urge to shield her surged within him as he sensed someone was closing in on the edges of a case they were both entangled in. He felt a volatile anger brewing beneath the surface but couldn't afford to let it spill over now.

In an instant, Nettie shot up from her seat, the worry in her eyes transforming into determination. "I have to go see him and make sure he's okay," she insisted.

"Nettie—" Casper implored, standing and stepping forward to calm her.

"Was his wife and child with him?" she pressed on.

"Nettie—" Casper tried again, desperation creeping into his tone.

"Oh, poor Julie and Ashley," she murmured, her heartache evident.

Casper touched her arm gently, trying to ground her in the moment. "Nettie." He waited until she looked at him, her full attention now captured. "You aren't going anywhere but to work."

The air crackled with surprise as an exclamation of disbelief echoed from behind him, startled voices murmuring, "What the fuck?" along with the throaty command, "Bring it in, Nemo." The shift in the tension was palpable as the men around them transitioned from a state of protective custody to a vigilant protection detail, ready to shield Nettie and ready themselves for whatever lay ahead.

"What do you mean, 'I'm going back to work?'" Nettie asked, her brows furrowed in confusion, the sudden shift in her circumstances taking him by surprise. "I thought it wasn't safe, and that was why I was brought here?"

Casper stood with his arms crossed over his chest, his expression serious. "That's correct," he replied, his tone firm.

"You convinced me that someone was out to get me," Nettie pressed, her eyes narrowing as she scrutinized him.

"Someone is," Casper affirmed, his gaze steady and unwavering.

"Then why on earth am I leaving?" Nettie's voice was tinged with panic. "I thought I was working remotely to stay safe."

"DA King revoked that approval," Casper explained, his posture indicating that he was not about to bend on this issue. "He wants you in the office and the courtroom because you have cases to pick up from ADA Baker."

Nettie's eyes widened. "Does this include your brother's case?" she whispered.

Casper nodded slowly, the weight of the confirmation hanging heavy in the air between them. "It does."

She stepped away from him. "Then I can't be around you," she insisted. "I won't risk being discredited or disbarred. Those men can protect me."

Her gaze shifted to the others in the room. Desperation was evident in her eyes as she implored them for support. "Can't you?"

The men nodded in solemn agreement, their silence a tacit acknowledgment of the gravity of her situation. Yet, it was clear that this was Casper's operation, and he held the reins to her protection, whether she liked it or not.

"If everyone could find a seat, I'll go over the plan," Casper said as he surveyed the group. He watched patiently as they settled into their spots—Pup perched on the arm of Cowboy's chair, his small frame contrasting with Cowboy's rugged bulk. At the same time, Doc maneuvered himself into an oversized armchair that seemed almost overwhelmed by his broad shoulders and robust build. Although Casper towered over his companions, it was Doc's impressive physique that indeed commanded attention. He was built like a linebacker, all sinewy muscle and strength, without an ounce of excess weight.

Nemo stepped through the door with a quiet resolve, his rifle resting in his hand. He made his way to the stripped couch where Casper sat.

"She's right," Casper addressed the group. "I can't be part of her visible protection detail."

A wave of realization swept through the group, illuminating their expressions as smiles blossomed on their faces. They exchanged knowing glances, their eyes glinting with mutual comprehension of the deeper meaning behind Casper's words. The air grew electric with camaraderie, and each man silently acknowledged their shared understanding of their circumstances. Their bond deepened in recognition.

Nettie leaned forward, her brow furrowing in confusion. "So," she began slowly, "just these four?"

Casper's face broke into a wide grin, his eyes twinkling with mischief. "Oh, you'll still have the five of us," he replied confidently.

"But I thought you just said—" Nettie started, but Casper cut her off smoothly.

"I said visible protection," he clarified, leaning back on the sofa with ease. "No one will know I'm part of your protection detail. I'll be the one inside your home, keeping watch."

Nettie's body went rigid, the weight of his implication settling heavily on her. Time seemed to stand still as his words lingered in the air, and then, as if struck with sudden clarity, she sprang from her seat, her eyes wide with disbelief. "Oh hell no, you won't be!" she exclaimed, disbelief and indignation coloring her tone.

CHAPTER TWENTY-FIVE

"IT'S A LOGICAL conclusion," JD stated confidently in the bustling CI office on Gulf Island as he leaned back in his chair. The faint sounds of typing and murmured conversations served as a backdrop while Casper absorbed his words. Across the table, Cassie observed him thoughtfully. Sitting beside her was a newcomer named Daisy, who had just returned from her research expedition.

As Nettie returned to the office, flanked by Doc and Cowboy, Casper remained at the table with JD and Cassie. Daisy's demeanor was proud, and a hint of excitement in her tone chimed in. "I meticulously sifted through all their cases. This is the only instance where their paths intersect." Her words hung in the air, heavy with the weight of their implications.

Cassie's brow furrowed slightly as she added, "That's assuming you believe David's accident wasn't simply an accident. If it was just a mishap, you risk jeopardizing everything you've built by pursuing this line of inquiry." The tension in the room was palpable as

Casper weighed her caution against the unsettling gnaw in his gut.

Before Casper could gather his thoughts, JD interjected, "The only element that seems disconnected is the series of threatening notes. They surfaced before your brother was apprehended. And the first shooter claimed not to know the notes. Or at least that's what he insisted before he met his untimely end."

Casper felt a deep pang in his chest as though the weight of the investigation's implications was pressing down on him. "Then we're looking at two separate individuals involved in this," he concluded, struggling to make sense of the chaos.

Cassie raised an eyebrow, a mix of skepticism and concern illuminating her features. "Do you genuinely believe your brother could have orchestrated the entire scheme from inside a prison cell? I'm talking about the first shooter."

"It's a possibility." The words tasted bitter on his tongue. "He associates with a dangerous crowd, one I would choose to steer clear of at all costs." A sense of betrayal washed over him, twisting in his gut at the thought that his brother might be linked to the alarming string of incidents involving Nettie. He pondered what his brother's thoughts might be when Casper intervened to save her, time and again. But dwelling on that notion was a luxury he couldn't afford. He had to resolve this case swiftly so that Nettie could reclaim her life, free from the shadow of HIS agents infringing on her privacy or invading her home for her supposed protection.

Casper rose to his feet, the weight of determination settled on his shoulders. "You focus on the notes," he suggested despite the swirling chaos in his mind. "I believe we're dealing with two different individuals in this case. I'll handle the shooter angle." With that, he turned away from the cluttered table, only to pivot back, a grateful spark illuminating his eyes. "Thank you."

JD acknowledged him with a nod, his expression softening as he cast a fond gaze at his fiancée. "Anytime, my friend. We owe you more than you can possibly imagine."

A broad grin broke across Casper's face, momentarily dispelling the turmoil. "So, when's the big day? When are you two finally tying the knot?"

Cassie's face lit up, radiating joy. "Soon," she replied. "We're just waiting for Mom and Levi to come back."

Casper felt a swell of happiness for the couple. Their journey had been fraught with challenges, yet they had emerged stronger and more united than ever. The bond they shared was something that Casper deeply yearned for in his own life. Yet, it was like chasing shadows at dusk—ever elusive.

Nettie drifted into his thoughts like the gentle ripples of water, her image bringing forth a vivid tableau of a shared life full of laughter and dreams. For a fleeting moment, he envisioned them side by side—she, with her bright smile as an attorney navigating the legal landscape of Mississippi, and he, an agent in the bustling realm of Maryland, dedicated to his work. However, that romantic vision slipped away like sand through his fingers, leaving behind a stark reality. The constraints of their careers anchored them firmly in their respective states, making any notion of togetherness feel utterly impractical. The possibility of their paths crossing seemed limited to fleeting moments of passion, yet even that seemed uncertain and distant in the face of their hectic lives.

"Good luck, man," JD said, rising to his feet, the shadow of concern etched on his face. "You're going to need it."

Cassie cleared her throat softly, her gaze darting to JD. A spark of pleading flickered in her eyes.

Sensing the tension in the air, Casper asked curiously, "Was there anything else?"

"No," JD replied firmly, but the moment was lost as Cassie shook her head decisively.

"He should know what he's walking into," she insisted, her tone grave.

"What the hell are you talking about?" Casper snapped, anxiety creeping into his voice. The weight of uncertainty pressed down on him, and he grew increasingly concerned about his brother and the unsettling climate surrounding them.

"Well," Cassie began, "Nettie asked me to look into you because she suspects—no, she believed—you might be involved in the incidents. You know, trying to craft a narrative of her beloved hero to influence her during your brother's case."

Casper felt a wave of insecurity wash over him, draining away the confidence he had once carried. "What?" The revelation struck him harder than a punch to the gut, leaving him reeling. The thought that Nettie, someone he trusted deeply, could suspect him of being behind the troubling incidents was a bitter pill to swallow.

"Anyhow, I have information on Marie and her daughter, Kayla, if you want. I could only go so far without Levi, but Devon could do much with the information."

Casper's gaze flickered to her. Uncertainty was etched across his features. Part of him hesitated, fearing the truth that it might unravel. Yet, a deeper instinct stirred within him—the desire to embrace his responsibility if he was indeed the girl's father. The first thing he would do would be to confiscate that cursed phone from her possession, a device that seemed to fuel more trouble than connection.

As he braced for whatever news awaited him, he tentatively reached out, and Cassie placed a small, unassuming file in his palm. Its weight felt significant as if it harbored secrets that could alter everything.

"I'm trusting you not to disclose this conversation to Nettie," Cassie warned, her tone serious. "I believe you need to understand the full extent of your situation and what you're confronting from all angles."

Casper closed his eyes momentarily, gathering his thoughts, then opened them with a renewed sense of purpose. "Thanks. I'll keep it quiet." He meant it wholeheartedly. Now, he faced the formidable task of convincing Nettie that he was one of the good guys, battling against the doubts entwined around him like a thick fog.

As he sat in the driver's seat of his rugged Jeep, the afternoon sun glinting off the vehicle's glossy exterior, he found himself fixated on the worn folder resting on the passenger seat. The silence was abruptly shattered when his phone rang, causing him to jump slightly. With a quick motion, he accepted the call through the Bluetooth speaker embedded in the dashboard.

"Hey, man," he greeted, trying to shake off the lingering tension.

Jesse's voice came through the speaker. "How are things? How did the meeting go? Sorry I couldn't sit in, but we pulled an urgent government case that required pulling some guys off vacation."

"Did you need the men here?" Casper asked, his brow furrowing with worry. He was reluctant to reduce the security detail around Nettie until he could get a handle on his brother's erratic behavior and the looming threat that encircled her.

"No, we're good," Jesse replied, his tone more reassuring. "Only those who voluntarily returned are going. As expected, we have enough staffing. It's a kidnapping case involving a diplomat's child, so I had to turn away agents who were itching to help."

Casper felt relief and worry wash over him as he processed the situation's urgency, glancing back at the folder that seemed to hold the weight of his decisions.

"Can I ask you something personal?" Casper hesitated for a moment, searching for the right words. With his experience and understanding, Jesse seemed the perfect person to confide in about his predicament.

"Of course! What's on your mind?" Jesse replied.

Casper took a deep breath, gathering his thoughts. "How did you navigate the challenges of being a single father while embarking on your career with HIS? Did you ever experience any conflicts when leaving Reagan for extended periods with Mrs. Kessler?"

"It wasn't easy, I won't lie. I was fortunate to have Mrs. K. in my life long before Kate and I tied the knot. She was so much more than a housekeeper to us. Now that we're married, she still helps by looking after Reagan, but we've prioritized ensuring that one of us is always home with her. But what's happening? You seem a bit anxious."

With a mixture of dread and an unexpected surge of pride in his voice, Casper finally revealed his news. "Well, Jesse," he said slowly, his heart racing, "I might be about to become a father."

With the quiet on the other end of the line, Casper thought he'd lost Jesse before his boss said, "I told you not to sleep with the client."

Casper could feel a storm brewing inside him as he recognized where Jesse's mind had wandered. He took a deep breath, trying to push the anger down, but it bubbled beneath the surface. "No. No. It's not her," he insisted, the words tumbling out fervently. Deep down, he couldn't deny the flicker of desire he felt for Nettie, but the reality weighed heavily on him. "Kayla is sixteen."

"Are you certain she's yours?"

Casper shook his head slowly even though Jesse couldn't see it, the weight of uncertainty pressing down harder. "No. Cassie did some digging, but before I dive into this mess, I'd prefer to see if Devon can uncover some answers. I've already got too much on my plate." The chaos swirling around him was almost too much to bear. It felt like a tidal wave threatening to crash. He realized he desperately needed to find a way to regain his equilibrium, perhaps with a quiet meditation session to center himself again.

"Not a problem," Jesse replied, his tone steady. "Just send him whatever you have. He'll dig into it for you."

A wave of relief washed over Casper at Jesse's reassurance. Knowing a plan was in motion made the burden feel a little lighter. "Thanks," he said, as he began to feel a glimmer of hope amidst the turmoil.

"Okay, while we're working through that, how is the protective detail shaping up?" Jesse inquired.

Casper took a breath and began detailing the situation. He explained the unfortunate incident involving the other Assistant District Attorney, weaving in the new adjustments to their plans. "She's at the office now, trying to keep things normal. I've assigned Cowboy and Doc to watch over her during the day, and for the night, Nemo and Pup will take their shifts."

"Those are solid pairings. Did you consider having one of the women stay with her at home? I can send Rylee if you need reinforcements."

Casper's jaw tightened slightly. "I've got it all covered."

"Let me guess," Jesse said. "You're planning to crash there yourself."

Casper rubbed the back of his neck, his discomfort palpable. "Yeah, but don't worry about it. She thinks I'm one of the bad guys, and I've got a steady career waiting for me in Maryland, so nothing will happen," he hurriedly added, the words spilling out in one breath.

"Uh huh," Jesse replied, his tone serious. "Just ensure you keep it that way. I mean, not that she thinks you're one of the bad guys, but that nothing untoward happens."

"Sure thing," Casper said.

"Now," Jesse pressed, shifting the conversation back to business, "where are you with the case? Have you managed to get any leads yet?"

Casper took a deep breath, dread pooling in his stomach as he prepared to unveil the truth to his boss. "I do have a suspect," he admitted, his voice low and weighed down by the gravity of his revelation. "It's my brother."

CHAPTER TWENTY-SIX

SITTING OUTSIDE HIS childhood home's dim, familiar silhouette, Casper slid the Jeep into Park. He gazed at the darkened windows, each a reminder of years past, and contemplated how to broach the sensitive topic that weighed heavily on his heart—the conversation he desperately needed to have with his brother. The house loomed before him, silent and empty, amplifying his unease.

Realizing the gravity of his accusation—that his brother was involved in a plot to have ADA Nettie Broussard killed—he felt a heavy weight settle in his chest. When he uttered those words, he knew he would sever any semblance of familial love he shared with his brother and mother. She would rally around Aaron, unwavering in her support of his brother, regardless of how compelling the circumstantial evidence might seem. And therein lay the crux of his dilemma: they had no tangible proof, only a troubling coincidence that gnawed at his instincts.

What if he was mistaken? A part of him desperately wanted to be wrong, yet another part echoed a disquieting suspicion that his instincts were leading him to a sinister truth. His brother's sudden urgency for bail raised alarm bells in his mind. It was unlikely he would have secured that freedom with Nettie serving as the prosecutor, a fierce adversary known for her relentless pursuit of justice. It made him question the peculiar accident involving ADA Baker. Was it a coincidence, or was something darker at play? The uncertainty wrapped around him like a thick, suffocating fog as he delved deeper into a web of intrigue and mistrust.

He resolved to gather his belongings, fully aware that he would no longer be welcomed back home after their heated discussion. As he climbed out of the Jeep, he felt his foot catch on an unseen object beneath him, and he nearly twisted his ankle. Steadying himself, he crouched down to investigate and discovered a bullet glinting in the waning light—likely dropped in haste. A wave of unease washed over him. Was Aaron now taking justice into his own hands? He had previously outsourced his dirty work, hiring others for the first two shootings, but now the thought of Aaron personally eliminating the first shooter sent a chill down his spine.

He leaped back into his Jeep, leaving his belongings behind in a whirlwind of urgency. They were just material possessions, easily replaceable. Panic coursed through him. He had to reach Nettie. His instincts screamed that she was in peril, and every fiber of his being echoed with the fear of what might be happening to her.

Casper gripped the steering wheel of his vehicle tightly as he directed his Bluetooth phone to call Doc. A wave of anxiety washed over him—was Nettie still at work? Outside, the deputies conducted thorough checks, ensuring no one could sneak in a weapon. That meant Aaron was stuck without a way to launch his attack. But did he even know where the safe house was? It loomed in Casper's mind—where Nettie would be kept tonight and every night until Casper deemed it safe to let her go.

The phone crackled to life. "What's up?" Doc asked quietly, as though the moment's weight demanded silence.

"Where are you?" Casper replied, urgency creeping into his tone. He turned slightly too sharply, his Jeep tires protesting with a high-pitched squeal. He forced himself to ease up on the accelerator, reminding himself that reckless driving could lead to an accident. The men were with Nettie. She was safe for now, but the lingering threat gnawed at him.

"In court," Doc responded. "She's finishing up now. Then we'll head back to her office before we go to the safe house." His voice's mix of relief and worry mirrored Casper's tumultuous thoughts.

"Get her out of there as soon as you can," Casper insisted, sharp and urgent while he tapped his fingers on the steering wheel, impatiently watching the red light flicker.

"Problem?" Doc inquired.

Was there a problem? Absolutely. The weight of the situation pressed heavily on Casper's chest, a sense of dread curling in his stomach as he imagined what might be happening. His brother, consumed by desperation and fear of impending imprisonment for his crimes, was plotting to murder Nettie, believing that eliminating her would be his only escape from the clutches of the law.

"Yes. No. I can't shake this feeling."

"We're all too familiar with your instincts. We'll get her to the safe house as soon as she wraps up her paperwork after court," Doc replied, before abruptly ending the call.

As the sun dipped lower in the sky, casting long shadows across the pavement, Casper took a sharp U-turn, steering his vehicle back toward the safe house. He was eager to coordinate with the rest of the team, ensuring Pup and Nemo were fully prepared for their impending shift on the protection detail. The weight of the situation pressed heavily on him. Safeguarding their charge was paramount, and he intended to be ready when the time came.

****

Nettie felt a shock wash over her as she witnessed the abrupt shift in Doc's demeanor following the court proceedings. His urgent tone and swift movements left her no time to process what was happening. He hurried her to gather her files, practically ushering her away despite her boss's protests echoing behind them. With a determined gait, Doc dismissed the District Attorney with a wave, as if their words held no weight, before leading her toward the waiting SUV.

As they drove toward the safe house, Nettie's mind was a whirlwind of thoughts. She couldn't shake the nagging guilt that being at the center of this chaotic situation was causing so much trouble for the agents tasked with her protection. The thought that their lives were being upended because of her made her stomach churn.

Yet, there was a flicker of hope on the horizon. Earlier that day, she had spoken with David. Though he had been injured, he revealed he had lost control of the car just before crashing into the tree. The veiled mention of any other vehicles or obstacles remained unspoken, leaving her to question what lay beneath the surface of his words. They sped toward an uncertain refuge, the gravity of the situation heavy on her heart.

As they drew nearer to the house, her gaze fell on the unmistakable silhouette of the Jeep parked in the driveway. A jolt of unexpected warmth fluttered in her chest, a sensation she wished she could suppress. Casper had always held a certain allure for her, but she knew it was merely physical attraction—a spark that had ignited within her but never fully blazed to life. She had experienced similar feelings for other men in the past, yet she had managed to keep those impulses at bay, and she could do so again. Now that he was no longer her adversary, she felt a strange mix of desire and resolve, ready to maintain her composure in the face of her unpredictable emotions.

Disappointment washed over her as she wandered through the common areas of the house, her eyes scanning for any sign of Casper. The absence of his familiar presence left a pang in her chest. She assumed he must be out inspecting the yard and the sprawling woods beyond. With a heavy sigh, she made her way up the staircase to the bedroom that had been assigned to her.

As she pushed the door open, her breath caught in her throat. A strong pair of arms instantly seized her, pulled her into a warm embrace, and captured by a sudden, passionate kiss. At first, she instinctively struggled against the unexpected intrusion, but the moment she recognized Casper's scent and familiarity, her resolve melted away. Her lips began to respond to his urgency, and she felt herself surrendering to the moment.

The weight of her purse and briefcase slipped from her fingers as she wrapped her arms around him, drawing him closer. All rational thoughts of inhibitions faded into the background, so much for avoiding her growing desire. But, amidst the whirlwind of emotions, she told herself it was just a kiss—a moment she could contain. Just one kiss.

As Nettie stretched on her toes, she leaned closer to Casper, her heart racing in anticipation. Suddenly, he broke the kiss, pulling away just enough to lean his forehead against hers. The warmth of their skin and the rhythm of their heavy breaths filled the room, creating an intimate cocoon around them.

"I'm sorry," he murmured, the tone of regret lacing his voice like a bittersweet melody.

But Nettie didn't want to hear his apologies. They meant nothing in the whirlwind of emotions swirling inside her. All she craved was the taste of him, the connection they shared. With a determined spark in her eyes, she lifted her chin, bridging the gap between them once more. Their lips met again, igniting a flame of passion as she kissed him deeply. Their tongues intertwined in a sensual dance of desire that left them both breathless.

With his towering six-foot-two frame, Casper leaned down to meet Nettie, who stood a diminutive five-foot-one tall. He broke their passionate kiss and said, "Nettie, we need to stop, or we'll do something we both regret."

Nettie, fully aware of the truth in his words, decided to throw caution to the wind. Ignoring the warning, she kissed him once more, her resolve clear: she didn't care if their lovemaking led to feelings of regret. The heat of the moment consumed her.

When Casper finally broke the kiss, a wave of confusion washed over Nettie, and she braced herself for rejection. She had never experienced the sting of a man telling her no, and the thought left her unsettled. Despite her twenty-five years of life, her romantic encounters had been limited to just a handful of men, none of whom had Casper's maturity or presence. The age difference loomed large in her mind, casting a shadow of uncertainty.

But just when she thought he would pull away entirely, he surprised her most delightfully. With a gentle but firm grip, he lifted her effortlessly, cradling her against him as he carried her toward the grand King-sized bed that dominated the center of the room. As he lowered her onto the plush mattress, he did so with the utmost care, as if she were a delicate porcelain doll, ensuring she was perfectly situated and safe before stepping back to admire the moment.

"Are you absolutely certain, Nettie?" Casper inquired. He scanned her from head to toe, his gaze lingering on each curve and detail before locking onto her eyes. The intensity of his stare was palpable, brimming with an unmistakable desire that sent a shiver down her spine.

With a deep swallow that felt almost like a weight in her throat, Nettie nodded firmly, determination flickering in her eyes. After gathering her thoughts, she finally found her voice steady and clear. "Yes, I'm sure."

Casper swiftly shed his shirt, revealing a well-defined physique that delighted her heart. The muscles in his arms and chest were sculpted, hinting at the hours he must spend keeping himself in peak condition for his demanding job. With a casual grace, he settled onto the edge of the bed, methodically removing his boots and socks. A warm smile spread across his face as he glanced over his shoulder at her, inviting her into the moment.

After shedding the last remnants of his clothing, Casper eased himself onto the bed next to her, the tension in the air thickening with unspoken desire. "I don't think I've ever been more certain in my life," he murmured, his tone husky with longing as he captured her lips in a kiss that felt as if it could ignite the world around them.

Nettie threaded her fingers through his short hair, feeling the warmth of his skin and the solid strength of his shoulders beneath her touch. As her fingers grazed over his broad back, she noticed a rough scar that told tales of battles fought—stories she would need to explore later. But at this moment, all that mattered was the explosive chemistry that had simmered between them, a heat they had both stifled while locked in their roles as adversaries. Perhaps their fierce animosity fueled the flames now roaring to life, urging them to abandon all caution and embrace the passion that surged between them.

A wave of warmth enveloped them as their lips met softly, and Casper took his time undressing Nettie. He caressed the fabric of her blouse, gently pulling it down her shoulders. "God, you're beautiful," he murmured. He traced the outline of her figure with his eyes.

She entwined her fingers around his neck, drawing his lips tantalizingly close to hers. Just before sealing their connection again, she murmured, "Don't use the Lord's name in vain."

CHAPTER TWENTY-SEVEN

A PLAYFUL SMILE danced across his lips as their lips locked, an undeniable spark igniting between them like a jolt of electricity that surged through his body, radiating straight to his groin. He could feel the heat rising, the chemistry palpable and intoxicating. He realized he had to reign in the moment, slow the whirlwind of desire coursing through him, or risk turning a memorable encounter into a hasty, reckless coupling.

Breaking the kiss, Casper's gaze lingered on her as he examined her slender, athletic form. She maintained a petite and remarkably toned physique despite the long hours she clocked in at work—nearly seventy each week. He couldn't help but marvel at her dedication, though the thought of asking her how she achieved it slipped away, unspoken, into the air around them. What consumed him was an undeniable yearning, an intensity he had never felt for any other woman. It bewildered him and sent a current of electricity through his thoughts, leaving him both exhilarated and apprehensive.

"I've wanted you since the moment I discovered you on that dusty road, full of attitude and fire," he confessed, low and breathlessly as his fingers gently intertwined with a lock of her hair, feeling its softness beneath his touch.

Nettie let out a soft groan, a mix of embarrassment and amusement washing over her. "Please don't remind me of that night. It still makes my cheeks burn," she replied, a playful pout forming on her lips.

He let out a soft chuckle, the sound warm and inviting. "You were quite the prosecutor, wobbly and determined as you navigated the scene." He recalled how she had stood her ground, fiercely unyielding even in her unsteady state.

Nettie playfully swatted his chest, a spark of mischief in her eyes. "Oh, come on. Are we going to reminisce, or are we going to make love right now?"

That was the unspoken invitation he had been yearning for, igniting a fire that prompted him to draw closer. "I'm going to love every inch of your body. Starting here—" He leaned closer, his lips brushing softly against the delicate curve behind her earlobe, where her warm skin met the air. The intoxicating aroma of her perfume enveloped him, a heady mix that drew him in, igniting a fire of desire. Each gentle kiss was a whispered promise, mingling with the sweet, lingering scent that seemed to wrap around them like a silken veil.

As his lips journeyed slowly down the delicate curve of her neck, he could feel the electric stir of gooseflesh prickling her skin beneath his touch. It was a palpable sign that she, too, was caught in the same wave of heat and longing that surged through him, an unspoken connection that intensified with every gentle caress.

When his mouth closed over her taut, rosy nipple, her back arched off the soft bed. A low moan filled the air, overtaking the sharp, ragged breaths that had echoed moments before.

"I love your scent…your taste…and—" He abruptly silenced himself, the words fading on his lips. He had nearly let slip the word "you," but he knew deep down that it wasn't accurate, so why did it cling to the tip of his tongue at such an inopportune moment? He had never voiced such feelings to another woman, except Marie, when he'd been a teenager, so what was it about her that ignited this intense urge to confess? It was as if a magnetic pull compelled him to express sentiments he had always guarded, leaving him perplexed and vulnerable in her presence.

"Mmm," she murmured as her fingers gently wove through his hair.

A tumultuous conflict brewed within him as he was caught between the desire to savor each moment and the urge to forge ahead hastily. Ultimately, he decided to tread a middle path, embarking on an intimate journey that led him down her curves. With each soft kiss he planted along her stomach, he left a trail of warmth and tenderness, cherishing their intimate connection.

Nettie's bright and cheerful laughter bubbled up like music as he softly navigated his way down to her belly button. A spark of delight danced in her eyes as she playfully tried to shift his head away. "That tickles," she exclaimed, light and teasing. The warmth of the moment enveloped them.

Casper flashed a playful grin, his eyes sparkling with mischief. "Is that so?" he replied, amusement dancing on his lips. He took a mental note of her reaction, intrigued by the spark of interest it revealed. But for the moment, he pushed those thoughts aside. He had a mission to focus on as he continued his journey southward, the landscape unfolding before him with every step.

When he finally reached her core, he paused, captivated by the rich, heady, and utterly intoxicating fragrance that enveloped him. It seemed to wrap around him like a warm embrace, a perfect blend of sweetness and warmth that stirred something deep within. When they eventually parted, he knew that the aroma would linger in his memory, an indelible mark etched into his senses forever.

The thought of their impending separation cast a shadow over his spirits, a weight dimmed the warmth in his heart. Yet, he quickly found a way to shake off the gloom, focusing instead on the intoxicating allure of her body. Every curve and contour drew him in, igniting a fire within him that urged him to cherish every moment they had together.

The initial lick was so intoxicating that it nearly shattered his fragile grip on composure, sending sensations electrifying through his body. But, the sight of her arching her back and leaning her head back, moaning in pleasure, kept him tasting her—licking and sucking on her clit—until she cried for him to stop. Disregarding her pleas, he felt her delicate hands gripping his shoulders, desperately trying to draw him closer. Yet, with a determined resolve, he continued and inserted one finger into her wetness. A groan reverberated through his taut body, releasing some of the tension coiling at the base of his spine.

She was ready for him, her heat a welcoming feeling against his finger and tongue. Only, he needed to ensure she came before he entered her because—like an untried schoolboy—he wasn't sure he could control himself once inside her delicate heat.

"Casper," she moaned with longing as she pulled at his shoulders, trying to draw him closer into her embrace. Again, her fingers grasped him, a mix of desperation and desire playing across her features as she struggled to close the distance between them.

"Call me by my name," he commanded softly. His gaze traced the contours of her body, basking in the warmth of her allure. Each curve seemed to beckon him closer, feeding the flame of yearning within.

She paused, confusion flickering in her eyes as she searched his face for understanding.

"Call me Ash," he urged. The need for his actual name to escape her lips filled the air with a charged intensity that wrapped around them like a shroud.

With a playful smile dancing on her lips and her eyes sparkling with mischief, she gently murmured, "Ash. Ash McNabb, come here this instant and kiss me."

"How could he possibly resist such an overwhelming demand?" He slowly inched up her body, his lips almost brushing against hers, while his body arched gracefully over her, creating an electric tension that filled the air between them.

As Nettie reached down, her delicate fingers stretching out to make contact with him, he gently grasped her small hand, halting her movement. A wave of uncertainty washed over him. He doubted his ability to withstand the warmth of her touch in that fleeting moment. "No," he replied gently, as he observed the subtle furrow of her brow, a hint of concern clouding her features. "I'm already on the edge."

As she slowly retracted her hand, a playful smile danced on her lips, the warmth of her touch lingering between them. "Good," she murmured, her eyes sparkling seductively. "Because I'm right there with you."

With his forehead against hers, Casper slowly entered her, each inch pulling at the threads of his slowly fleeting control. "You feel so good," he said before taking her mouth in a deep, forceful kiss while he thrust into her fully.

Nettie gasped in his mouth, and he rejoiced within because he could tell that it was a gasp of pleasure not pain. He couldn't believe he was inside the little nymph that had captured his attention from the moment he met her drunk ass.

Moving slowly, he broke the kiss, capturing her gaze as the burning need within him grew to an oncoming crescendo. He knew he had to act fast, or he'd leave her wanting, and that had never happened before, and he wouldn't allow Nettie to be left in that state. So, he reached between them and massaged her clit, rubbing circles.

She closed her eyes and moaned, the sound traveling straight to the base of his spine, radiating heat to his balls.

"Come for me, baby," he said, watching the exquisite pleasure wash across her lovely face.

Before she responded, he felt her tighten around his cock and grab his shoulders in a death grip. He took her mouth and thrust his tongue inside, swallowing her moans of pleasure before he allowed himself to lose control and thrust into her until he came, spent inside her without a condom.

Casper froze, his ecstasy fleeting. No condom. He'd never been so reckless before. He knew he was clean, and he suspected she was also, but pregnancy could always happen. That wasn't something he wanted to handle now since he supposedly had a sixteen-year-old to deal with.

As a whirlwind of thoughts swirled in his mind, he gently rolled away from Nettie. A sense of calm washed over him as she nestled close, her body curling against his like a contented feline that had just awoken from the most blissful of naps. Her arms stretched luxuriously, the soft curve of her back arching gracefully, embodying the serene ease of a cat basking in the sun's warmth.

"That was...." She didn't finish her sentence but trailed off, kissing his collarbone.

He couldn't believe his cock twitched at her touch so fast after making love to her. And they had made love. Yeah, he'd like to fuck her fast and hard, but making love to her was something he'd remember for a lifetime, and he wouldn't allow negative thoughts and reality to slip in and ruin the moment.

"Just give me a minute," he said with a mischievous grin, his eyes glinting with playful energy. "We'll go again soon enough."

She chuckled and playfully smacked his chest with her delicate hand, the warmth of her touch lingering. "I might need a nap first," she replied, pretending to yawn as she leaned back, a teasing smile dancing on her lips.

Before Casper could push her on her back and cover her body with his, a knock sounded on the door. He groaned, and she froze as if suddenly remembering they weren't alone in the house.

"Casper. You left your phone out, and your brother is on the line. I told him you were occupied, but he was insistent in wanting to know—"

Casper didn't move a muscle, refusing to budge from Nettie's arms for the likes of his brother. A simmering determination coursed through him. He would confront his brother later, but his immediate priority was to keep Nettie safe. As long as she was by his side, a fierce sense of protection enveloped her, making her safer than she had ever known. He felt a primal urge to shield her from any threat, vowing silently that nothing would harm her while he was there.

"What?" Casper shouted.

"Uh," Doc replied, hesitantly. "You might want to come to the door, man."

A surge of anger bubbled within Casper, hot and fierce. It was infuriating that the men could deduce what he was up to. The mere fact that they were aware of his presence in her room spoke volumes about the intimate sounds he and Nettie had made. It felt like every whispered secret and stifled moan had traveled through the walls, revealing more than he ever intended.

"Just spit it out," he urged. Though she had wrapped herself in layers of fabric, concealing every inch of her body from prying eyes, he couldn't shake the feeling that something was amiss. He lingered beside her, unwilling to break the fragile bond that tethered them together. As he studied her, he felt a swirl of uncertainty. Was she nervous about the possibility of someone stumbling upon them, or was there an undercurrent of regret in her demeanor? He clung to the hope that her fear was rooted in the moment rather than the decisions that had brought them here.

"Just come to the door," Doc insisted.

With a frustrated curse, Casper bolted upright from the bed, the sudden rush of adrenaline propelling him into action. He hastily shoved his legs into his pants, the zipper dangling open, exposing a glimpse of his hurried state as he approached the door. Peering through the tiny crack he created, he demanded, "What?"

"Your brother wants to know if you've got—and I quote—'that bitch attorney' to change her mind."

The sharp intake of breath from the bed echoed in the tense silence, and his heart plummeted as he caught sight of Nettie's face, glistening with unshed tears. The painful realization struck him. She likely interpreted Doc's brutal words as a cruel tactic to sway her loyalties. He couldn't allow that. He wouldn't let her think this was about manipulating her feelings.

With a swift motion, he yanked the phone from Doc's grip and slammed the door shut behind him, blocking the outside world. "Where are you?" he barked.

"Home," came the curt reply.

"Stay the fuck there. I'm on my way." He ended the call abruptly, pivoting to face Nettie, whose tear-filled eyes mirrored a mix of confusion and hurt. The weight of the moment settled heavily in the air between them.

"Nettie—" he began.

"Get out!" she shouted. Her harsh words slicing through the room's silence. She pointed firmly toward the door, her eyes blazing with anger and hurt. "Just get out of here!"

"Nettie, I swear—" he pleaded, hoping to bridge the chasm that had suddenly opened between them.

Without hesitation, she hurled a soft pillow at him, the fabric flying, a physical manifestation of her frustration. "Get out!"

Realization washed over him like a cold wave. He understood he had lost the chance for more than fleeting moments together. With a heavy heart, he snatched up his clothes scattered around the room, each piece a reminder of their shared intimacy. He paused at the door, stealing one last glance at Nettie, her silhouette framed by the fading light, knowing that life as he knew it would never be the same without her by his side.

CHAPTER TWENTY-EIGHT

NETTIE COULDN'T SHAKE the disbelief as she reflected on her actions. How could she have been so foolish, letting herself be lured into a moment of passion by Casper, the very man whose brother she was prosecuting? The memory of their intimate encounter sent a shiver down her spine. It felt like a manipulative game he had crafted to win her over to his side. He hadn't explicitly voiced any demands, yet the unspoken words hung heavily between them, especially after their privacy was abruptly shattered.

The blush of mortification crept over her cheeks as she recalled the instant realization that others were just beyond the walls, blissfully unaware of her vulnerability. In that charged atmosphere, what was meant to be an intimate connection quickly turned into an embarrassing situation, leaving her to grapple with conflicting emotions.

With a reluctant sigh, Nettie tossed aside the covers, the soft fabric slipping away like memories she wished she could forget. She padded across the cool wooden floor to the bathroom, each step echoing in the stillness of the early morning. As she gathered her clothes, the faint scent of Casper lingered in her mind, igniting a whirlwind of emotions. She could almost feel the lingering warmth of his hands brushing against her skin, skillfully removing each piece of clothing with a tenderness that thrilled and terrified her.

A low groan escaped her lips. This was proving to be far more challenging than she had anticipated. The thought of his touch revived her vulnerability, leaving her heart racing. She knew that if he brushed against her again, she would crumble and fall into his embrace, succumbing to his magnetic pull over her.

As she stood before the mirror, apprehension washed over her. How would she face the other men after everything that had transpired? They had to be aware of Casper's irresistible charm and cunning ways by now. The familiar weight of judgment hung heavily in the air, and the mere idea of their knowing gazes made her stomach twist with anxiety.

Feeling the need for a more relaxed outfit, she unzipped her suitcase, revealing a jumble of clothes packed for her stay. Rummaging through the contents, she found a worn pair of well-fitted jeans and a soft, faded T-shirt. Comfort was her priority. If she faced any embarrassment today, she might as well do it feeling at ease.

Once dressed, she made her way to the window and peered outside, catching a glimpse of Casper's Jeep as it sped down the road. A wave of unsettling thoughts washed over her. So, he was on his way to meet his brother, no doubt discussing that he had crossed a line by sleeping with the prosecutor, potentially compromising her judgment in the case.

The realization simmered within her, igniting a spark of determination. Although the temptation lingered to play petty and consider slapping extra charges onto Aaron's case in retaliation, she dismissed the notion. She had his file in her possession and was resolved to handle the case with integrity. Her commitment to fighting for justice remained unwavering, and she would ensure that all the details were meticulously examined, no matter the personal stakes involved.

But before anything else, she felt an urgent need to understand where the men were in their investigation into who was pursuing her and when she might finally reclaim her ordinary life, free from the shadow of Casper. Hearing his name sent shivers down her spine, a painful reminder that she had been deluding herself. Against all odds, she had inexplicably fallen for the man who had once been her adversary. It wasn't merely his role as her savior that captivated her—he had rescued her not just once but multiple times, each act a testament to his undeniable strength. Nor was it solely about the intense sense of safety he provided by arranging security details to protect her long enough to see her next birthday. The complexity of their connection, a tangled web of emotions, left her both bewildered and achingly aware of the fragile line between love and enmity.

Summoning her courage, Nettie slid her feet into a pair of crisp white ankle socks, the fabric soft against her skin, and laced up an old yet sturdy pair of tennis shoes that had seen better days. With her heart racing, she approached the door, her fingers hesitating over the cool metal doorknob. This was it. She could do this. She would do this. Taking a deep breath, she turned the handle and stepped into the softly lit hallway, moving toward the inviting warmth of the living area.

As she entered, her gaze landed on Doc, who looked up from the couch with kind eyes and a gentle smile that instantly made her feel at ease. "Hey, Nettie," he greeted her, his voice untainted by judgment or secrets.

"Hi, Doc," she replied, sinking into the plush armchair that welcomed her like an old friend. Her eyes roamed, searching for Cowboy. She suspected he was outside, patrolling the grounds as he often did, ever vigilant and protective.

Nettie's thoughts drifted back to the pressing question in her mind. "Where are you with finding out who is after me? I want to resume my regular life." Her words hung in the air, heavy with urgency.

Doc leaned forward, placing his book aside deliberately, his brow furrowed in concentration. "Casper thinks he has it figured out. He is working with Coastal Investigation on that part. We're just security," he explained.

So, Casper believed he had the situation under control, but what were his true intentions? A fleeting vision of their time shared before their paths diverged crossed her mind—a reckless moment wrapped in desire. She straightened in her seat, fighting to maintain her composure and pride, unwilling to let uncertainty overshadow her resolve.

"I want to go see them," she insisted as she felt the weight of confinement pressing down on her. She knew she had little power over how and where they shielded her from danger.

Doc, the sturdy figure in front of her, shook his head slowly, a look of concern on his face. "Why don't you just call them?" he suggested, his tone a blend of kindness and firmness that made her frustration boil.

"No," she replied vehemently, her eyes flashing with determination. "I want to get out of this house. I need to escape these walls that feel like closing in on me."

Doc studied her intently, his gaze scanning her features for any hint of doubt or wavering resolve. "I understand," he said, glancing down momentarily as he rubbed the back of his neck with his broad palm. When he finally met her eyes again, he continued, "But only Casper has the authority to make that call. And right now, he's off the grid."

Nettie's brow furrowed in confusion. "What do you mean, off the grid?"

Doc sighed, the sound heavy with unspoken concerns. "He left his communications device here and turned off his phone. I can't reach him."

To regain control of the situation, Nettie thought quickly, her mind racing. "Well, in his absence, aren't you the man in charge?" she proposed, a spark of hope igniting her.

A smile spread across Doc's face as if he had just pieced together the puzzle of her thoughts. "I am," he acknowledged.

"Good. Then let's get moving before it gets much later," Nettie urged eagerly, her determination resurfacing. "Cassie and JD will be heading home to their son soon enough."

****

Casper turned his Jeep into the familiar driveway of his childhood home, the gravel crunching beneath the tires like the sound of memories long buried. Unlike the warm embrace of nostalgia that usually accompanied his visits, a cold wave of loneliness washed over him. He felt like a shadow in his mother's eyes, a constant reminder of an ex-husband she wished to forget. The thought stung. He had disappointed her again by failing to heed her command to call his father, a man he hadn't spoken to in years. The last time had been marred by his father's new wife, who had driven a wedge between them, insisting he sever ties with his old life.

As Casper exited the vehicle, he couldn't shake the feeling of impending doom, especially considering the difficult conversation he was about to have with his brother. If his instincts proved correct, he would find himself entangled in a web of betrayal, needing to gather evidence against the very blood that had shared his childhood. The thought of pursuing an attempted murder charge against his flesh and blood was a weight in his chest, one that threatened to unravel the already fragile threads of their family.

Initially, doubt crept into his mind, whispering that he might not rise to the challenge ahead. But then, like a gentle balm, thoughts of Nettie enveloped him. Dear sweet Nettie, her laughter is like a soft melody in his ears, her smile brightening even on the dullest days. He found his mind drifting back to the tender moments they had shared, each memory packed with unspoken words that lingered between them. Had he truly fallen in love with her? The very idea felt surreal, almost out of reach. Their interactions had been fleeting, charged with an undeniable tension, save for the crescendo of intimacy they had experienced that day, their bodies entwined in a fragile and profound dance.

He was resolute in his commitment to protect her, prepared to make any sacrifice necessary to ensure her safety and help her reclaim her everyday life, even if that meant she would have to do so without him by her side. Deep down, he wished she would consider following him to Maryland, where they could forge new memories together. However, he knew the gravity of her accomplishments—she had passed the bar exam in Mississippi, which brought her a sense of pride and professional stability. He couldn't bear to ask her to abandon that hard-earned success to retake the bar exam in Maryland, where his work as an agent for HIS would inevitably demand long, grueling hours and frequent absences. The uncertainty of his future weighed heavily on him, rendering any promises empty, and he couldn't risk asking her to walk away from her dreams for a path fraught with his professional challenges.

Aaron stood in the wide-open doorway, the golden light of the setting sun spilling around him, casting long shadows on the floor. He squinted against the brilliant glow, frustration etched across his face. "Hey man, what's so urgent? I've got guys waiting on me," he called out.

Casper ignored the tangled thoughts of his and Nettie's disheartening future, focusing instead on the pressing matter. "Let's go inside," he urged, stepping closer to the threshold, ready to confront whatever awaited him.

With a nonchalant shrug that suggested indifference, Aaron confidently strode into the house, followed closely behind by Casper. Just inside the entrance, Casper abruptly halted, his gaze landing on their mother, who stood with her arms crossed and a disapproving glare aimed squarely at him.

"So," she began, "you decided to grace us with your presence."

Casper inhaled deeply, feeling the tension coil in his chest. He exhaled slowly, counting his heartbeats to tame the rising tide of anger within him. "Sorry, Mom. I've been busy," he replied, his tone measured.

"Hmph," she scoffed, turning on her heel and heading to the kitchen—her footsteps echoed in the quiet house. "Supper will be ready soon. You'll stay and eat with us."

It wasn't a request. It was a command, implied in the firmness of her voice, and Casper understood all too well that leaving the house before the meal was served was not an option unless Aaron chose to throw him out instead. "Sure, Mom," he responded, knowing he had little choice if he wanted to keep the peace between him and his mother.

Aaron sank heavily into the worn cushion of the couch, its fabric frayed in places from years of use. "All right, sit down, and let's uncover what's so urgent," he said impatiently. "I'm hoping it has something to do with changing the mind of that bitch of a prosecutor."

Casper clenched his jaw, struggling to keep his temper in check at his brother's harsh words. This wasn't a time for personal vendettas. He was here to untangle a complex case, not ignite another conflict with Aaron or their mother, especially not after the fiery accusation of attempted murder he'd soon level against his brother. He settled into a well-worn armchair, its fabric a muted shade that had faded over the years, and forced a smile. "No, I haven't seen her," he replied, the words slipping from his lips like a well-rehearsed script.

"I thought you were protecting her," Aaron shot back, his gaze piercing as he scrutinized Casper's expression.

The accusation hung in the air, and Casper was surprised to learn how his brother had discovered this secret. The sheriff had assured him that this information would remain confidential.

Unsure how to initiate the delicate conversation, Casper leaned forward, resting his elbows on his thighs and casting a wary gaze toward his younger brother. "How are things?" he ventured, hoping to break the tension in the air like a thick fog.

Aaron's expression hardened as he narrowed his eyes, suspicion flickering across his features. "Is that why you demanded I wait like a petulant schoolboy?" His biting tone cut through the silence, darkening the atmosphere further.

Realizing his approach was flawed, Casper shifted his strategy. "How's sobriety?" he asked. He held onto the faint hope that his brother would embrace this topic, yet anxiety gnawed at him, and he feared the response.

"Sobriety, my ass. Who wants that?" Aaron's retort was sharp, full of defiance as he leaned back, arms crossed tightly over his chest.

Casper took a measured breath, leaning back in the chair to assess his brother. The bloodshot eyes glaring back at him spoke volumes. It was clear Aaron had veered far off the right path. "How about rehabilitation? Have you considered it?" His words came out softly as though they might coax Aaron into a more reflective state.

In an explosive reaction, Aaron surged to his feet, startling Casper. "Is that why you're here? To preach your holier-than-thou standards and assume I want to be like you? Because if so, you can see yourself out right this instant!" His voice was a torrent of anger and desperation, echoing off the walls of the cramped living room.

Slowly, Casper rose from his seat, towering over Aaron by a solid six inches, his heart pounding. "No. That's not why I'm here," he said, striving to maintain a calm facade despite the growing tension.

"Then spit it out!" Aaron snapped, impatience simmering just below the surface.

Feeling a desperate urgency, Casper decided to lay everything on the line. "Are you trying to have ADA Broussard killed?"

In that startling moment, their mother's horrified gasp from the doorway shattered the tense standoff. Both brothers turned to find her standing frozen, her eyes wide with shock and disbelief. "Get out!" she demanded, shaking with fear and fury. "Get out of here and don't come back."

CHAPTER TWENTY-NINE

CASPER'S GAZE DARTED between his mother, her mouth set in a firm line that spoke volumes of her disapproval, and his brother, whose sly grin hinted at mischief. His command to leave rang in his ears, but determination surged. He couldn't abandon his quest to gather evidence and protect Nettie, ensuring she could safely return to her everyday life.

Obediently, he pivoted and stalked away, the tires of his Jeep screeching in protest as he tore out of the driveway, anger boiling within him.

His mother had never been so furious with him, and to hear her say never to return home was a depth of disdain he had never witnessed before. She'd always favored Aaron over Casper, but this marked a strange and unsettling shift. It was as though her love had transformed into a harsher, more formidable force. Her disapproval was palpable, intensifying the tension in the air when he posed a question to his brother—one she found intolerable. The idea that she might entertain the notion of Aaron being involved in something so evil was unfathomable to her.

In the past, he would have been compelled to comfort her after Aaron found himself in trouble, enduring her lengthy tirades about the perceived injustices that befell Aaron, no matter the context or circumstances. However, this time, it felt different. He was relieved of the burden of navigating the storm of her emotions. Or was he? The looming question haunted him: Would he find his way back to her side once they took Aaron away in handcuffs?

The thought of inadequately gathering evidence to hold Aaron accountable gnawed at him, sitting like a heavy stone in his stomach. And Nettie—such a fragile spirit—was tangled in the relentless web of protective custody, condemned never to experience a life free from trepidation, forever glancing over her shoulder, waiting for the next threat to materialize in the dark.

He reached over and pressed the Bluetooth button on his dashboard, feeling anxious. "Call Devon," he instructed.

After a few rings, Devon's voice replaced the familiar tone. "I was about to call you," Devon said, an undertone of urgency lacing his words.

"What do you have?" Casper inquired, leaning forward in his seat, eager for insight.

Casper could hear the faint rustle of papers and the rapid clacking of keys as Devon typed away on his computer. "Well, I couldn't connect your brother to the shootings. Aside from the initial shooter—who was a complete loner—I couldn't link anyone else either."

"So," Casper replied, disappointment creeping into his tone, "you have nothing."

Devon quickly corrected him. "I didn't say that. I can tell you who's been sending her the notes. He left DNA on the last one. It was just a trace but enough to identify him."

Casper was taken aback—he hadn't realized that the sheriff had shared such sensitive evidence with the HIS. But then again, it was no surprise. Devon had a knack for extracting information from anyone when solving a case.

"You're not going to believe this," Devon began, "but it's her colleague, ADA Baker. I've already dispatched the sheriff to the hospital to speak with him and uncover the truth behind this chaos. My instincts scream jealousy. She was not just a favorite but a shoo-in to ascend to the DA's position when he stepped down next year." He paused to clear his throat, the tension palpable through the phone line. "But that's merely my intuition for now. We'll have a clearer picture once the sheriff gets back to me."

"Why didn't you send me there?" Casper asked, a hint of frustration creeping into his voice, feeling slighted by being overlooked for such an important task. He saw the turnoff for Gulf Island and decided to meet with JD and Cassie to discuss this development and how to trap his brother before he succeeds at his task.

"Because," Devon replied, his tone firm, "you need to prioritize Nettie's protection above all else. This situation pales in comparison to the severity of the shooting."

Though Casper nodded, agreeing with the rationale, a sense of disappointment lingered. He still wished he'd been the one contacted before the sheriff. But he brushed off those thoughts—after all, he would survive this oversight.

As he steered his Jeep into the white shell parking lot of Coastal Investigation, a sense of resolve washed over him. He thanked Devon for the vital news before ending the call. Leaping from the vehicle, he felt a powerful determination surging to unveil the truth and assist Nettie. The weight of his supposed betrayal loomed large. She would never forgive him for the intimate night they shared after his brother's cruel words. He knew he had some serious atoning to do, and yes, he would beg for her forgiveness because his need for her was that profound.

As he stepped into the softly lit office, two tiny kittens launched themselves at him, their playful energy palpable. Their razor-sharp claws clawed at his worn denim jeans, dragging them upward until he scooped each one into his arms and cradled them to his chest. "Hello, Callie and Madam," he said, grinning. "Have you missed your mistress?"

The kittens responded with a chorus of soft purrs and enthusiastic meows, their little faces radiating joy. He couldn't help but laugh, the sound bursting forth and momentarily lifting the heavy weight of anxiety that had settled in his chest over the mountain of problems awaiting resolution.

"Yes," Cassie said, a warm smile spreading across her face. "They've become quite the troublemakers at home, driving Cooper and Phoebe absolutely bonkers! We thought we'd bring them here today to tire them out before tonight's big reunion."

JD approached with a curious expression, extending his hand toward him. "Hey, what's brought you in so late?"

He glanced at the clock. It was indeed late in the day. The sun had dipped low in the sky, casting long shadows across the office. He knew JD and Cassie didn't adhere to the conventional banker's hours.

"Well, I talked with my brother," he replied, glancing at Cassie.

Her lips formed a perfect "O" of surprise while JD let out a chuckle, a hint of mischief dancing in his eyes. "I can only imagine how that conversation went," he said, gesturing for him to sit down. "I'm guessing he didn't admit to being a party to the shootings, did he?"

Casper settled into the sleek conference chair, the polished surface of the conference table gleaming under the bright overhead lights. With a playful grin, he placed each cat on the tabletop, watching their playful antics unfold. Callie, with her enthusiastic energy, pounced on Madam, and they both tumbled into a furball of joyous chaos, their soft purring punctuated by the occasional meow. For a fleeting moment, Casper felt a lightness in his heart, almost forgetting the gravity of the situation that had brought him there.

Suddenly, Cassie's laughter pulled him back to reality.

Casper let out a heavy sigh. "No. I mean, I didn't get an answer because my mom overheard and sent me packing."

"Ouch," JD remarked, sensing the weight of Casper's words. "What are you going to do?"

With a determined gaze, Casper replied, "I need to solve this mess and get Biloxi in my rearview mirror as quickly as possible." His tone was resolute, masking the undercurrents of anxiety that bubbled just beneath the surface.

After Casper shared the insights he had gathered from Devon, there was a consensus that JD would promptly contact the sheriff to extract any pertinent information from ADA Baker regarding their ongoing investigation. Although Casper had a strong inclination to tackle this task personally, with Cassie's guidance, he recognized the necessity of concentrating on unraveling the core aspects of the case, leaving the more routine matters to her and JD.

"Have you uncovered any evidence linking my brother to the shooters?" Casper asked, anxiety in his tone.

JD shook his head, his expression grim. "No," he replied. "The first shooter was a ghost—he left behind no clues, not even a trace of where the money might have come from. As for the second shooter, we have a grainy still from the security camera. He was caught with a stolen license plate and a mask obscuring his face completely. So, unfortunately, we have nothing solid to go on from that angle either."

"It's going to have to be confession, then," Casper said, determination radiating from him. "I'll find a way to speak with my brother and worm it out of him, somehow." A chill of doubt crept into his thoughts for the first time in his life. He wasn't confident he'd succeed at this daunting task. His brother could outtalk Casper any day of the week and twice on Sunday, a master of words woven with charm. Yet, he had to muster the courage to try—a gamble to catch Aaron in a lie or perhaps uncover a thread that could tie him to the mysterious incidents gnawing at Casper's mind.

As the sound of car tires crunching on the shell parking lot reached her ears, Cassie glided to the front window, her eyes sparkling with recognition. "It's Doc, Cowboy, and Nettie," she announced, turning back to see Casper's face contort in frustration, a curse slipping past his lips.

Without hesitation, she made her way to the door, her heart fluttering with excitement as she swung it open to welcome the trio inside. Throwing her arms around Nettie, she exclaimed with warmth, "It's good to see you, my friend."

****

Nettie pulled back slightly, her eyes darting anxiously around the room, each glance revealing her unease. "I saw Casper's Jeep out front," she exclaimed.

Cassie scrutinized her, an eyebrow raised as she turned away to locate Casper. "He's—Well, he was here just a moment ago. JD, where's Casper?"

JD shrugged nonchalantly, rising from his seat with two tiny kittens in his arms. He gently handed the furry companions to Nettie, a playful grin spreading across his face. "I bet you missed these little gals."

Nettie felt her heart swell at the sight of the adorable kittens—her little angels who filled her days with joy and warmth. Though she constantly reminded herself that she was merely fostering them, deep down, she knew she couldn't bear to part with these precious creatures. "Yes," she replied softly, gathering them close and pressing tender kisses on their tiny heads. "Hello, little ones. Have you been treated well?"

JD wrapped his arm around Cassie, pulling her closer. He then turned to Doc and Cowboy, his tone shifting to a more serious note. "Does Casper know you left the safehouse with Nettie in tow?"

Doc's discomfort was palpable as he shifted his feet awkwardly, his gaze dropping to the scuffed floor before finally replying. "We tried to contact him," he said hesitantly, "but Nettie was adamant about seeing you both immediately."

Nettie was grateful he had chosen not to delve deeper into the unsettling events at the house. That conversation would have to wait for a more private moment with Cassie, away from prying eyes and ears. "Yeah, I have questions," she replied, her expression serious.

"All right, let's head to the back. We can hash it out at the conference table," JD suggested, keeping a watchful eye on Nettie as she continued her search for Casper amidst the clutter of the office.

Once they settled around the sturdy wooden table, Nettie cradled Madam in her arms and placed Callie on the surface, where the tiny kitten immediately began to meow insistently, her little cries filling the air with urgency. Cassie reached out to scoop up the fluffy ball of energy, cradling her gently against her chest.

"Just don't get too cozy with that one, Cassie," JD warned, a playful glint in his eye. "We're not bringing home another cat, especially not a whirlwind like that mischievous kitten. We still have Bella to wrangle through her teenage phase."

Nettie's laughter rang out, lightening the mood in the room as they navigated the day's tangled emotions.

As tires crunching against the gravel of the shell parking lot echoed through the air, JD leaned back in his chair and quipped with a bemused tone, "What is this today? Grand Central Station?"

Cowboy, stationed like a sentinel at the entrance, turned to peer outside. "It's Aaron," he announced.

Before Nettie could process this information, Cowboy stepped out into the dusk, and Doc, sensing the urgency, grasped Nettie's arm gently yet firmly, urging her up from her seat. "Where can I stash her?" he asked JD and Cassie, his expression a mix of concern and determination.

JD gestured down the dimly lit hallway toward the back office. Doc didn't hesitate. With a swift motion, he took the tiny kitten from Nettie's arms, placed it in JD's care, and guided her down the narrow corridor, his grip reassuring but insistently protective.

Nettie felt a whirlwind of thoughts as doubt nagged at her. Did they truly think Aaron posed a threat? While she didn't want to be a burden, the notion of harm directed toward her was chilling. "Is he the shooter?" she managed to ask Doc, her voice trembling slightly as he silenced her with a finger pressed to his lips, his other hand instinctively reaching for the gun holstered at his side.

Goosebumps crawled up her arms as the moment's gravity hit her, amplified by the tension radiating from the men. If Aaron was indeed the shooter, how would Casper handle such a gut-wrenching revelation? Despite her efforts to convince herself otherwise about her feelings for Casper, the thought of him grappling with this tragedy sent fresh waves of worry crashing over her.

CHAPTER THIRTY

CASPER OBSERVED INTENTLY as Cowboy thoroughly patted down his brother, ensuring he concealed no weapons beneath his clothing. The tension in the air was palpable, and Casper refused to allow his men to confront this threat without his support. Steeling himself, he slowly emerged from his hidden vantage point, his movements deliberate and cautious.

"Dammit, Ash, you scared the shit out of me!" Aaron exclaimed when he saw Casper materializing beside him. "No wonder they call you Casper. You just show up like a ghost in the night."

Cowboy's hearty laugh echoed in the stillness around them. "This is nothing," he said, amused by the sudden appearance.

"What brings you here?" Casper asked his brother, his brow furrowed with concern.

"We need to finish that conversation," Aaron replied, urgency threading through his words. The weight of unspoken matters hung heavily between them, and Casper sensed that whatever lay ahead would require all their attention.

"He's clean," Cowboy announced, as he gave Casper a subtle nod, signaling that his brother was unarmed and posed no immediate threat.

"Talk," Casper commanded, his tone unwavering. He stood firm at the entrance of the CI building. He had no intention of letting Aaron enter, where Nettie was most likely concealed, vulnerable to any potential danger lurking. The weight of her safety pressed heavily on his chest.

"I swear to you, I had nothing to do with anyone trying to hurt that prosecutor," Aaron pleaded, his eyes wide with earnestness, reflecting a depth of emotion that Casper couldn't easily dismiss.

Casper studied his brother intently, searching for signs of deception but finding only an intense sincerity that struck him. Then, like a jolt of lightning illuminating a stormy sky, the realization hit him with painful clarity. "Mother," he murmured, the word escaping his lips like a haunted whisper.

Aaron nodded slowly, a shadow of worry crossing his features. "I don't know for sure, but I wouldn't doubt it," he replied.

Casper turned to Cowboy, a determined look clouding his features. "We're going to visit our mother. Take care of Nettie while I'm gone."

Casper pivoted on his heel, his younger brother Aaron trailing closely behind him. "Do I have to be part of this?" Aaron's tone was hesitant, tinged with a hint of reluctance.

"Absolutely," Casper responded, nodding decisively as he approached his Jeep. "Remember, I'm no longer welcome there. You're going to help us get in the door."

With a resigned sigh, Aaron shuffled to the other side of the Jeep, the white shells crunching beneath his sneakers. He climbed in and buckled his seatbelt, the click echoing in the moment's stillness, just as Casper slammed the door shut and turned the ignition.

In an instant, the engine roared to life, and Casper released the brakes, spinning out of the shell parking lot with a rush. The vehicle lurched forward as the weight of their mission loomed in the air.

****

Nettie listened intently as the distant sound of a vehicle's engine faded away, a cloud of uncertainty settling over her. Had Cowboy chased Aaron off just when she thought she could reclaim her life? The thought was disheartening, and she turned her gaze toward Doc, searching for reassurance in his eyes. "Can we come out now?" she asked.

The cramped quarters around her didn't feel particularly confining. There was more than enough space for comfort. But Doc's enormity beside her genuinely made the situation feel tenuous. He filled the room with his physical presence and an overwhelming sense of duty, his body shielding her like a fortress against whatever dangers lurked outside.

Doc shook his head, his eyes ever alert for any lurking threat that might threaten Nettie.

A sense of unease tightened in the air, and with a resigned sigh, Nettie remained rooted in her spot behind the imposing figure of the giant, her heart heavy with worry. Thoughts of what might be happening beyond this cramped, secure space tugged at her insatiably. She yearned to know, to understand the unknown that lay just out of reach.

Suddenly, the front door of the office building swung shut with a dull thud, and Cowboy's voice rang out, steady and reassuring. "All clear."

At last, Doc turned toward her, the tension in his shoulders easing as he slid his weapon back into its holster. A warm smile broke across his face, offering hope amid the uncertainty. "Let's go back out there, shall we?" he said.

As they settled around the table, the gravelly crunch of tires echoed from the parking lot, drawing Cowboy's attention to the window. "Looks like you have a female client," he remarked, his tone a mix of intrigue and anticipation.

Cassie turned to him, a warm smile spreading across her face. "It's probably Daisy coming back," she replied reassuringly, her eyes sparkling with understanding. "She must be curious about all the vehicles here," she added.

"How old is she?" Cowboy asked, his gaze fixed intently outside the window.

"About twenty-five," Cassie replied. "Why do you ask?"

Cowboy finally turned to face her, his expression serious. "Because the woman entering is distinctly middle-aged."

JD muttered a curse under his breath, frustration evident in his posture, while Cassie gave him a disapproving look. "I can't believe we're getting a new client now," JD lamented, his eyes narrowing with determination as he met Cassie's gaze. "You can take this crew—including the rambunctious kittens—to the house, and I'll handle the client myself."

Cassie leaned closer, a warm smile blossoming, and pressed a grateful kiss on JD's cheek. "Thank you, truly."

Nettie couldn't contain her excitement at the turn of events. Finally, she would have the chance to speak with Cassie privately, away from JD's inquisitive ears. It was the perfect opportunity to unload her heart and seek her desperately needed wisdom.

As the group rose from the table, Nettie and Cassie hurriedly scooped up the tiny, squirming kittens in their arms. Just as they turned toward the door, it swung open, revealing a newcomer. With a courteous tip of his hat, Cowboy offered a polite greeting, "Ma'am."

The visitor stood just inside the threshold, her wide, apprehensive eyes sweeping the room. She saw the men, each visibly armed, and a flicker of alarm crossed her features.

Nettie could sense the woman's unease. She likely feared she had stumbled into a law enforcement office rather than a private investigation agency.

Stepping forward, JD gave a reassuring nod to the woman. "They're just leaving, so I'm free to discuss your case with you," he said, his tone steady.

The woman barely acknowledged him, her focus shifting as she continued deeper into the room, her steps hesitant. "I'm looking for my sons," she stated.

Nettie felt an unsettling prickle race down her spine, a warning echoing in her mind. Something about the woman set her on edge, and an instinct pulled at her gut.

"Let this group exit first, and then we'll sit down and discuss your sons," JD suggested, his demeanor calm yet commanding. He leaned down to place a soft kiss on Cassie's cheek. "Go now," he urged gently. "I've got this."

The group began to move toward the door, but suddenly, the woman's eyes widened in recognition. "Aren't you that ADA who is so good?" she asked.

A swell of unexpected warmth washed over Nettie at the woman's words. Though she had never indulged in vanity, she felt pride in being noticed for her work. "I am," she replied, flashing a genuine smile.

"Good." The woman's expression shifted dramatically, her eyes narrowing with determination. She reached for her purse, and Nettie felt an electric tension filling the air—Doc and Cowboy stiffened, their bodies instinctively preparing for a confrontation. The woman must have sensed the charged atmosphere, as she quickly added, "I'm just getting something for an autograph."

As she rummaged through her purse, the mood in the room thickened. When she finally revealed a weapon, pointing it directly at Nettie, the world tilted perilously on its axis. In an instant, Doc surged forward, positioning himself protectively in front of her, his hand deftly drawing his firearm. Simultaneously, Cowboy aimed his weapon at the woman, the weight of the situation pressing heavily upon them. In her peripheral vision, Nettie saw JD mirroring their actions while Cassie, cradling a mewling kitten in her arms, stepped confidently into the fray.

With a softness in her voice that contrasted starkly with the threat at hand, Cassie addressed the woman. "I'm not sure what you intend, ma'am, but trust me when I say that you stand no chance against this group of protective agents surrounding Nettie."

The gun in the woman's grip trembled slightly, her resolve faltering as she hissed, "She wants to put my son away forever, and I can't allow that."

Nettie's heart raced as she observed Cassie and JD's unspoken communication. Their eyes locked in a shared understanding. Cassie took another cautious step forward, and continued, "You must be Ash and Aaron's mother."

The woman glanced quickly and anxiously at Cassie, her expression betraying her unease, before shifting her gaze to where Nettie peered cautiously from around Doc's broad frame. "I am," the woman finally uttered.

Nettie's gut twisted with uncertainty. She couldn't shake the belief that neither Cassie nor any men should sacrifice themselves to protect her. She didn't trust that this woman would risk her life after attempting to take hers.

"Mrs. McNabb," Nettie spoke, her tone firm as she stepped out from behind Doc's imposing figure, only to feel him instinctively shift sideways, his sturdy bulk once again forming a protective barrier around her.

"Let me by," she insisted, jabbing a finger into Doc's back, feeling the warmth of his body contrasted sharply against the tension in the air.

"Not going to happen," he replied. "You can talk to her from there if you want, but I won't allow her an open shot at you. She has to go through me first." The strength in his words offered her comfort, yet fear still coiled tightly in her chest.

As if oblivious to the danger, Cassie took another step forward, determination etched across her features. Nettie's heart raced in response, pounding wildly against her ribs. "Cassie," she whispered urgently, desperation lacing her voice, but Cassie pressed on, undaunted.

"Did you orchestrate the two shootings at ADA Broussard?" Cassie questioned, her eyes nearly slitting with suspicion and resolve.

Nettie couldn't wrap her mind around the idea that this woman, even as the mother of Casper and Aaron, could be the mastermind behind such chaos. Doubt flickered in her thoughts, for she knew all too well that criminals had a knack for surprising her in the most unsettling ways.

"She did," came Casper's voice, slicing through the tense air from the shadowy recesses of the back of the building.

Nettie jumped, startled by his sudden appearance. She hadn't heard him come back at all. With wide eyes, Nettie turned to glimpse Casper's mischievous wink before he redirected his gaze toward his mother, an intense expression sending a shiver down her spine.

Nettie's heart plummeted into an icy pit in her stomach when she noticed he wasn't brandishing a weapon. Instead, he stood there with his arms raised high in surrender. The chilling thought raced through her mind

—could a mother truly aim a gun at her child? Fear tight in her chest, she desperately wished that wasn't the case.

"Where is Aaron?" she asked, each word amplified with anxiety.

Casper's expression hardened as he replied, "He's tucked away safe, spilling everything he knows to the police about your little escapades." He took a bold step forward, and Nettie felt panic rising within her. She wanted to scream at him to halt, to arm himself before approaching a woman who could easily wield a gun against three others without flinching. The tension in the room was palpable, and every instinct screamed that this confrontation was perilous.

Mrs. McNabb's voice rose to a piercing screech, filled with anger and betrayal. "How could you do this to me?" she spat. "You were supposed to protect Aaron and help him avoid trouble, not pile more chaos onto our already overflowing plates."

From her vantage point, Nettie saw Casper inching away, almost slipping out of her vision as he positioned himself slightly ahead of Doc. "I tried," he responded. "But your constant interference threw everything off balance."

"You jeopardized everything when you chose to side with her," Mrs. McNabb retorted, fury flowing in her voice.

"I see both sides of this, Mom," Casper countered, a hint of desperation creeping into his tone.

"Don't call me that!" she snapped. "I'm no longer your mother. You've ruined everything that Aaron and I shared."

Casper stepped entirely out of Nettie's view. "You were the one who stifled him. You pushed him into actions he should never have taken—like drinking excessively and gambling away the family savings," he said.

"Guys," Casper said. Nettie's heart raced as she watched Doc methodically replace his sidearm, the smooth motion perplexing her. A glance to the side revealed JD mirroring Doc's actions, his expression unreadable. She couldn't catch a glimpse of Cowboy, but she could only imagine he had followed suit, tucking his weapon away.

A wave of fear surged within Nettie, intensifying as she considered the possible consequences for Casper and Doc. Would Mrs. McNabb shoot one of them to get to her? A sense of dread gnawed at her. Why were they allowing her this opportunity? The urge to seize Doc's firearm and protect everyone overwhelmed her, yet she knew he would never permit her to remove it from the safety of its holster. He wouldn't allow her to make a move without his vigilant presence blocking her from Mrs. McNabb's view.

"Mom," Casper continued, calmly, "whether you like it or not, you're my mother. You can salvage this situation by simply putting your gun away. Look around —my men are showing you their trust by holstering their weapons first."

Nettie stood resolute, a fierce determination burning in her chest. She couldn't bear the thought of a man putting himself in harm's way for her sake. Though she wrestled with the notion that it was illogical, her heart ached at the prospect of anyone getting hurt—or worse, losing their life—because of her. In a moment of clarity, she decided to take matters into her own hands.

She kicked Doc sharply behind the knees with a swift and unexpected move. As he buckled forward in surprise, she grabbed his weapon and deftly sidestepped, her heart racing as the tension in the air crackled.

Then, like a sudden storm breaking, the chilling sound of screaming pierced through the chaos, sending shivers down her spine before flying bullets filled the office.

CHAPTER THIRTY-ONE

NETTIE STOOD FROZEN among the agents, her heart pounding as she watched Mrs. McNabb collapse to the floor, a dark crimson stream pooling beneath her. With an anxious gaze darting around the chaotic scene, Nettie spotted Cassie crouched low to the ground, clutching the screaming kitten she had refused to let go. In the swirl of panic, Nettie realized with a jolt that she had dropped her kitten when she had kicked Doc's knees, the weight of her oversight crashing down in this frantic moment.

With the unfired gun pointing at Mrs. McNabb, shaking in Nettie's hands, Doc gently leaned over, his voice soothing as he said, "Easy, Nettie." With careful movements, he extended his hand toward the gun, delicately prying it from her trembling grasp. As he did, tears cascaded down Nettie's cheeks, glistening like fragile pearls against her flushed skin.

"Get her out of here," Casper gasped, the strain of pain thick in his voice.

Nettie felt her stomach clench as she hurried to Casper's side, where he was gradually sinking to the floor, a mysterious wound marring his body, sending an icy grip of fear through her.

Doc reached out and grasped Nettie's arm, but she swiftly pulled away, a determined glint in her eyes. "As of this moment, I no longer want your protection," she declared, conveying a resolute belief in her ability to navigate the world alone.

Nearby, Cowboy knelt beside Casper, his skilled hands searching for injuries as he sighed heavily upon contacting Casper's chest. "Thank God you were wise enough to wear a vest," he said, relief washing over his rugged features as he rose to his feet, pushing back his weathered cowboy hat. "He's going to be fine—just a bruise and some discomfort, but he'll pull through."

Nettie's frustration bubbled over as she knelt by Casper, slapping him lightly on the shoulder. "How could you be so reckless?" she exclaimed. "You could have been killed!"

Casper managed a faint smile, though the pain flickered in his eyes like a candle in a breeze. "Better me than you," he replied softly.

Nettie couldn't suppress a retort, her heart aching at the sight of him. "That's debatable," she said, a mix of irritation and affection surging within her, her instinct urging her to lean down and embrace him, to hold him close and shield him from whatever danger lay ahead.

After Nettie forcefully pushed him away, Doc instinctively reverted to his calling—he doctored. Nettie's gaze fell upon him as he knelt beside Mrs. McNabb, his hands pressed firmly over her wound, crimson blood seeping through the spaces between his large fingers like a slow, tragic river. Doc glanced over at Casper, who let out a heavy sigh, a sound saturated with worry and resignation.

"Aaron's in the backyard. You'd better bring him inside," Casper urged.

Nettie felt a swell of sympathy for Casper, who lay there, his expression a mix of confusion and grief. It was clear that he was about to be torn away from his mother, a woman who had shot him without remorse.

JD stepped closer. "I called 911, and help is on its way."

Cowboy vanished into the shadowy recesses of the room and shortly reappeared, ushering in Aaron, who hurriedly made his way to his mother's side. "Mom," he implored, pleading for her to respond to him.

With a tremulous hand, Mrs. McNabb reached up and clasped her son's arm. "I'm so sorry, son. All I ever wanted was for things to be better for you," she murmured.

Aaron scanned the area, his heart racing, and spotted Casper sprawled on the ground, meticulously extracting a bullet from his vest. "Did you—Did you shoot Ash?"

Mrs. McNabb's reply was barely above a whisper, fraught with tension. "He was trying to ruin everything," she uttered, as crimson blood seeped from the corner of her mouth.

Nettie longed to turn away from the private scene, but her feet felt rooted to the spot. The chaos had unfurled around her rapidly that her heart raced frantically, pounding against her chest as if trying to flee from the turmoil.

She felt an overwhelming sense of relief wash over her as she realized that Casper had emerged from the tragedy without any physical injuries. However, her heart ached with uncertainty regarding his emotional state. His mother had explicitly told him not to call her that, and in a moment of conflict, she had shot him, attempting to sever the bond they shared. The weight of these events left her pondering how he truly felt, caught between his physical safety and the emotional scars that lingered.

Oh, how she longed to pull him into her arms and whisper soothing words, assuring him that everything would turn out fine. But deep down, she grappled with the uncertainty of her promise. Could she really guarantee him that solace? The weight of guilt settled heavily on her shoulders, a reminder that she had been nothing more than a pawn in a game that revolved around his brother's defense in a criminal case. The sting of that memory made her draw back, her heart tightening as she stood up from the floor, her eyes scanning the cluttered room for the kitten she had accidentally dropped in her moment of distress.

As if sensing her turmoil, JD gracefully approached her, extending his hand with the wayward kitten cradled within, its tiny body trembling softly. "She's okay," he said, offering a flicker of reassurance in the tense atmosphere.

JD moved toward the door with a purposeful stride, swinging it open to allow in the emergency personnel, their urgency punctuated by the shrieking sirens heralding their arrival. Cassie remained nearby, her composure firm as she stood protectively next to Nettie, who held the other kitten nestled in her arms. "Are you all right?" she asked, concern etching her features before she answered the question herself. "Of course you aren't. Come with me. Let's find some privacy in an office before the police arrive."

Taking one last lingering glance at Casper, whose wide eyes were filled with an intensity that made her heart flutter with confusion, she followed Callie to the back office. The door closed softly behind them as they sought refuge from outside chaos.

Once settled in the cozy office, with Cassie seated confidently behind the desk and the playful kittens frolicking atop it, Nettie sank into a plush armchair, feeling comfort and sorrow. "I've been so foolish, Cassie," she confessed. "I thought he cared for me." Hot tears streamed down her cheeks, contradicting her inner resolve not to cry over him, as the weight of her unfulfilled hopes enveloped her like a heavy fog.

"You fell for him, didn't you?" Cassie asked, her fingers gently stroking the soft fur of the tuxedo kitten, its shiny coat reflecting the bright office lights.

Had she truly fallen for him? Was that the cause of this heart-wrenching pain coursing through her? She had desired him physically, but she cherished their playful banter and deep conversations the most. The thought of being without him tugged painfully at her heart, yet she was a licensed attorney in Mississippi, and he had a bustling career up North.

Finally, she nodded, a soft glow of acceptance settling over her features. "I believe I did," she murmured, her gaze distant as if lost in thought.

"What are you going to do about it?" Cassie inquired. She gently lifted the tiny kitten, cradling the delicate creature against her chest. The kitten purred softly, oblivious to the gravity of the conversation.

Even with her experience as a prosecutor, confronting the situation left Nettie feeling cornered. Ultimately, she could find only one response, a bittersweet simplicity that resonated deep within her. "There's nothing I can do," she replied, her voice thick with resignation.

"Hmm," Cassie mused, her brow furrowing in contemplation. "Does that mean you're going to let him go?" she asked, an edge of disbelief in her tone.

Nettie reached out and lovingly picked up the remaining kitten, cradling her gently. She pressed a soft kiss to the top of the feline's forehead, feeling the warmth of its tiny body. "Yes and no," she finally articulated. "Yes, he's free to return to Maryland, but no, because he left me these babies behind. They will forever remind me of him." She gazed into the kitten's innocent eyes, a mixture of sorrow and affection swirling within her.

After a moment of contemplative silence, Cassie finally broke the stillness. "You know, we've been looking for an attorney to join our team. Someone who can navigate the complexities of our cases and ensure we stay on the right side of the law." A light laugh, almost melodic, escaped her as she added, "I'm just tired of bailing JD out of jail."

The mention of JD's habitual run-ins with the law sent Nettie a shiver of relief. She was grateful to be far removed from the tumultuous backrooms of the Gulf

Island court system, where JD's escapades likely led him to face the judge again.

"If you're contemplating leaving the prosecutor's office and all those unscrupulous people you're forced to confront," Cassie continued, a glimmer of opportunity shining in her eyes, "you would be more than welcome to join us here." She rose with the kitten in her arms. "Now, let me check in on the status in the other room. You stay here, take a breath, and think things over."

Nettie opened her mouth, ready to protest and ask Cassie to wait for her, but a sense of wisdom silenced her. Perhaps Cassie was right. She did need a moment of solitude to gather her thoughts. Could she leave her position in the prosecutor's office to become part of an investigative firm? Would stepping away mean sacrificing her fight for justice? Yet, Cassie had reassured her that they worked on cases relevant to the courts, so maybe she could still contribute to the vital cause of ensuring justice was served, helping the innocent find the evidence they needed.

The weight of the decision weighed heavily on her mind. She loved her job and cherished the camaraderie with Joann, but deep down, she sensed she already knew the answer to her quandary.

A sudden rustling at the door drew her attention, and when it swung open again, she said, "Cassie, I'll take it."

But before she could elaborate, a surprising voice sliced through the atmosphere. "Take what?" It was Casper, standing behind her with a puzzled expression.

Nettie's heart clenched painfully in her chest as her eyes widened at the sight before her. The man she had loved with every fiber of her being stood just a few feet away, the fabric of his shirt marred by a dark hole near his heart, a chilling reminder of how narrowly he had escaped death. Relief washed over her like a tidal wave but quickly ebbed, leaving a gnawing dread behind. With the immediate danger passed, she couldn't shake the unsettling thought that he might vanish from her life for good. Doubts spiraled in her mind, whispering that he would never return home to her. If he did, she resolved silently, she would seek him out, come what may.

"Hi," she managed to say, instinctively squeezing the tiny kitten in her arms tighter, causing it to squirm uncomfortably and let out a distressed yelp.

"Nettie," Casper said as he stepped forward, closing the door behind him with a soft click that echoed in the space.

Her breath hitched, a mixture of fear and longing crashing over her. He had locked them away together, and with that action, a question loomed heavy in the air— did he still intend to use her to bolster his brother's case before he slipped away for good? A bitter taste surged in her mouth. It felt like a slow betrayal. "Don't waste your time," she said sharply, her tone edged with steely resolve. "You can turn around and walk out now. I'm not going to prosecute your brother's case."

Frustration bled into Casper's posture as he raked his fingers through his tousled hair, a gesture she had recognized. "Christ, Nettie, do you really think that's what I'm about? That was my sole intention in sleeping with you?"

"Don't use the Lord's name in vain," she shot back. The truth hung unspoken between them, a heavy weight: she couldn't admit how foolish she'd been to let his charm ensnare her, leading her into a night of passion.

"Sorry," Casper said. "I need to talk to you. About us."

Nettie sank heavily into the plush armchair she had just vacated. "There is no us," she replied softly. You live up North, and I'm rooted down here in the South."

He stepped closer, his expression turning serious as he searched her eyes. "What if I told you that I loved you? Would that change anything?"

Nettie's heart fluttered at the weight of his confession, only to plummet like a stone in her chest. "How? We're still separated by miles and miles of distance," she murmured, her mind racing. How he phrased it—a question rather than a declaration—left her uncertain. Did he truly love her, or was he caught up in the moment? She couldn't ignore the part of her that hoped it might matter.

"I've been offered a job in town," he continued, "and I might move back home. Would that change things for you?"

Nettie's body went taut at his words, a surge of hope and anxiety coursing through her veins. Yes, it could mean everything—if only it were real. "Is this some kind of game you're playing?" she asked, skepticism creeping into her tone as she searched his face for the truth.

Without responding to her doubt, he closed the distance between them, carefully lifting the tiny kitten she held and setting it gently on the desk. His piercing gaze locked onto hers, intense and unwavering. "No game. I love you, Annette Broussard."

At his heartfelt admission, Nettie's breath hitched, caught between disbelief and joy. Yet one crucial question lingered in her mind. "Did you sleep with me just to help your brother's case?" The words spilled out, urgent and demanding, as she steeled herself for the answer, needing the truth before she dared to share her feelings with anyone—except Cassie.

Casper shook his head slightly, a playful spark in his gaze. "No. I slept with you because I wanted you, and I couldn't bear another moment in your presence without having you entirely for myself."

Nettie arched an eyebrow, intrigue still lighting her features. "And what about your brother's situation?" she asked, curiosity overriding her earlier hesitations.

Casper shrugged casually yet resolutely as he slipped his arm around her waist, drawing her closer. "He's on his own," he replied matter-of-factly.

Nestled in his embrace, she relaxed, resting her head against the steady rhythm of his heartbeat. A soft sigh escaped her lips as she melted into the warmth of his chest. "Is this real?" she murmured, uncertainty threading through her voice.

With a gentle, caressing touch, Casper lifted her chin with his thumb, his eyes searching hers earnestly. "It is. Now, tell me you love me, Nettie," he urged.

She narrowed her eyes, a flicker of defiance igniting within them. "Who says I do?" she challenged playfully, though a smile danced on her lips.

He chuckled softly, the sound soothing and teasing all at once. "I know you do," he replied confidently.

Sighing, she relented, her heart pounding in the warmth of their moment. "Yes, I love you. Now, are you satisfied?" she asked, playful exasperation mingling with affection.

"Not yet," he whispered, his breath a tantalizing caress as he brushed his lips softly against hers, igniting a spark that sent shivers down her spine.

EPILOGUE

CASPER APPROACHED MARIE in the bustling casino hotel, the sound of slot machines and distant laughter creating an almost surreal backdrop to their tense meeting. She sat at a small table, her fingers nervously tracing the rim of a glass, and her daughter, Kayla, was nowhere in sight. "Thank you for meeting me," he said, "without Kayla."

Marie shrugged, her expression indifferent, as if to say his presence was of little consequence. "It's no skin off my hide," she replied, a hint of cool detachment in her tone.

Internally, Casper sighed, the words forming a knot of frustration in his throat. He leaned forward slightly, the weight of his questions heavy on him. "Tell me the truth. Is Kayla my daughter?"

Marie met his gaze squarely, her eyes sharp as a blade. "Yes, she is." The finality of her response hung in the air, thick and suffocating.

"Why didn't you tell me before now?" His heart ached at the realization of time lost—years of potential memories slipping through his fingers. "Why did you marry someone else and not me since I was her father?"

A pained expression flickered across Marie's face before she shifted uncomfortably in her chair, her posture closing off. "You didn't make enough to support us," she said quietly, her eyes drifting away as though the truth was too heavy to bear directly. "So I found someone who did."

The grief settled in Casper's gut like a stone, weighing him down as the reality of his loss began to sink in.

The thought of calling her a "money-grubbing bitch" flitted through Casper's mind, but he swiftly pushed it aside, knowing that succumbing to negativity wouldn't resolve anything. He sighed, his brows furrowed in confusion. "What exactly do you expect of me now?"

Marie's lips pursed for a moment, and then she offered a beaming smile that didn't quite reach her eyes. "I want you to take her off my hands."

Casper blinked, momentarily taken aback by her unexpected request. He imagined how Nettie would react to the idea of him suddenly becoming a father figure to a teenage girl, especially just as their relationship was beginning to blossom. Yet, he understood that his budding romance could not overshadow his responsibilities as a father. The only problem was that he didn't know what it meant to be a father, aside from the occasional disciplinary action, like confiscating a phone. "Okay," he managed to say.

Marie seemed momentarily shocked by his agreement and shot to her feet with newfound energy.

"Great! I'm packed and ready to catch the next flight to California."

"California?" he asked, curiosity mingling with concern.

"Of course! That's where all the wealthy live. I'm so tired of struggling and living like a pauper," she replied. "I deserve better after everything I've dealt with in life."

Casper felt the weight of frustration pressing down on him. He longed to argue and demand answers from the woman before him, but he quickly dismissed the thought. It was crucial that Kayla remained shielded from the harsher truths surrounding her mother's abandonment, and he couldn't bear the idea of adding to her pain. "Where is she?" he asked impatiently.

"She'll be down in a moment," Marie replied, her tone matter-of-fact as she adjusted the bag slung over her shoulder. "She can't enter the casino, so you'll have to meet her in the hotel lobby." Without glancing back, she strode toward the door, leaving Casper sitting there, filled with anticipation and dread.

He muttered to himself as he stood up, "Now what?" His heart raced as he made his way to the hotel lobby, where Kayla was likely waiting to receive the most devastating news of her young life.

As he rounded the corner, the bustling atmosphere of the lobby enveloped him. He spotted Kayla a few feet away, her face lit up with excitement as she spoke animatedly into her phone camera, capturing every moment for her followers. The sight of her drew a sharp sigh from his lips. What on earth was he going to do about this? He couldn't shake off the unsettling thought that his daughter—his daughter—was a budding influencer, pouring her energy into online fame. At her age, such aspirations felt both foreign and misguided to him. Yet, he resolved to tackle those concerns later after they dealt with the monumental issues at hand.

As Kayla spotted him striding toward her, she quickly told her followers that she would return shortly. Her brow furrowed as she slipped her phone into the back pocket of her worn jeans. "Where's Mom?"

"She's gone to California," he replied, the words tumbling out before he could soften their impact. "She left you in my care."

Kayla narrowed her eyes, suspicion flickering like a candle flame caught in a draft. "For how long?" she pressed.

He met her gaze, honesty in his eyes. "She didn't say."

An unsettling silence enveloped them as they both processed the gravity of the situation. Finally, Kayla broke the stillness. "So, you're my real father?"

Casper swallowed hard, nodding slowly. "I am."

A hint of defiance emerged as she crossed her arms. "Do I have to call you Dad?" she asked, rolling her eyes dramatically as if the mere thought was absurd.

"No," Casper replied, although a small part of him yearned for the day she might feel comfortable bestowing that title upon him.

Kayla grabbed her bag with a slight shrug, the movement casual yet tinged with an unspoken resilience. "Okay, let's go," she stated, her tone indifferent, but Casper could sense the turmoil beneath the surface.

He was taken aback by how effortlessly she seemed to accept the news, which pierced his heart with an ache for whatever struggles she had faced in her young life. How could someone so resilient carry the weight of being abandoned by her mother without flinching? It dawned on him that this might not be the first time she had experienced such heartache.

For a fleeting moment, anger flared within him, and he felt an impulse to confront Marie and demand an explanation for how she had treated their daughter. But he quelled the emotion, reminding himself that his priority now lay in creating a secure and loving environment for them.

"Where do you live?" she asked, her eyes sparkling with curiosity. "Is it on the beach?" A hopeful tone danced in her voice at the thought of life by the ocean.

"I'm afraid to burst your bubble," he replied gently, a hint of amusement playing at the corners of his mouth, "but I actually live in Maryland."

Kayla paused, her expression shifting to surprise. "But it's cold up there," she remarked, a frown creasing her forehead as she imagined the chilly winters.

"Don't worry," he reassured her. "I'm moving here soon. I accepted a position with Coastal Investigation and am excited to find us a home in this area." Initially, he had thought about moving in with Nettie, but having Kayla in his life had changed everything. His focus now was on providing her with a loving, stable environment. He realized he would need guidance in this new chapter, and he knew JD, who had navigated the challenges of unexpected fatherhood after temporarily losing his son years ago, could lend valuable advice.

"Can I help pick out the place?" she asked eagerly, her youthful enthusiasm shining through. Then, a sudden thought struck her. "Wait, do you have a wife? Someone who will want me to call them 'Mom?'"

Casper shook his head slowly, his expression thoughtful. "No, I don't have a wife, but I have someone very special. I hope one day to ask her to be my wife."

"Will I like her?"

"I think you will, but I want you to get to know her and decide for yourself," he replied, feeling optimistic about their future together.

"When do I get to meet her?" Kayla inquired, her curiosity evident in how her eyes sparkled with anticipation.

Casper smiled softly, though a gnawing worry crept into his mind. Had he overstepped by inviting her to come home with him? He hadn't anticipated this sudden shift in their relationship. "She's waiting in the Jeep," he replied, hoping his tone conveyed reassurance.

"You have a Jeep?" Kayla's face lit up, excitement bubbling in her voice. "I love them!"

With a chuckle, Casper guided her through the sleek, automatic hotel doors. Crisp air greeted them as they stepped outside, and he led her to his Jeep parked in the bustling drop-off and pickup zone. Just as they approached, Nettie emerged from the vehicle, her warm smile in stark contrast to the hint of tension he noticed in her posture when he saw Kayla alone.

"Hi, I'm Nettie," she said, extending her hand toward Kayla with a genuine smile. "It's really nice to meet you."

Kayla took Nettie's hand but fell silent, the lively teenager Casper had engaged with moments before fading into someone more reserved. He sensed the ebbs and flows of emotions ahead, fully aware that navigating this new chapter would come with its own challenges.

As Kayla settled herself into the back seat of the Jeep, the soft leather creaked under her weight. Nettie leaned in closer to Casper, lowering her voice conspiratorially. "I saw Marie leave alone," she remarked, her eyes sparkling with curiosity.

Casper nodded thoughtfully, a furrow of concern etching his brow. "I'll fill you in on everything later. Right now, I need to find a safe place for Kayla and me to stay," he replied, determination lacing his tone.

Nettie's bright smile spread across her face, and her excitement was palpable. "I can't believe we both accepted positions with CI! It's going to be amazing working with you," she exclaimed, her enthusiasm infectious.

Leaning down, Casper gently kissed the tip of her nose, an affectionate gesture that made Nettie giggle. "You too," he murmured, his eyes warm with appreciation.

A groan came from the back seat, pulling Casper's attention away. He chuckled softly, amusement dancing in his gaze, and moved to the driver's side. Once inside, he started the engine, the comforting roar filling the vehicle as he shifted into gear. Glancing back at Nettie and the groaning Kayla, he asked with a playful tone, "Is anyone hungry?"

"I am," Nettie asserted.

"I only eat a vegan diet," Kayla declared, her tone tinged with a conviction that left no room for debate.

Casper let out a resigned sigh, feeling the weight of the conversation settle in. This was the beginning of many such discussions to come. "Of course you do."

ABOUT THE AUTHOR

SHEILA KELL writes about romantic men who leave women's hearts pounding with a happily ever after built on memorable, adrenaline-pumping stories. She is a four-time winner of the Readers' Favorite Book Award for romantic and contemporary suspense.

As a Southern girl who has left behind her days with the United States Air Force and as a University Vice President, she can usually be found in Florida with her family and cats. When she isn't writing, you can find Sheila with her nose in a good book, trying to leash train her cats, or wishing she had a genie to do her bidding.

Ways to connect

https://www.sheilakellbooks.com

https://www.facebook.com/sheilakellbooks

https://www.goodreads.com/sheilakellbooks

https://www.bookbub.com/authors/sheila-kell

Sheila loves to hear directly from readers. Feel free to email her at sheila@sheilakell.com.

Don't miss out on new releases, exclusive excerpts, and giveaways! Join her newsletter: https://www.SheilaKell.com/subscribe

Join her Facebook Reader Group:

https://www.facebook.com/groups/sheilakellbooks

www.ingramcontent.com/pod-product-compliance
Lightning Source LLC
Chambersburg PA
CBHW011132190726
48289CB00012B/3003